MY MANZ AND ' EM

By J.M. Benjamin

Cover design by Anna K. Stone of www.cre8tivdesigns.com
Cover photograph(s) J.M. Benjamin
Interior Design by J.M. Benjamin
Edited by J.M. Benjamin

For more info, contact the author, or order a copy of this book, send correspondence and payment to:
Real Edutainment Publishing, L.L.C.
P.O. Box 868
Plainfield New Jersey 07063
www.realedutainmentpublishing.com

e-mail or visit J.M. Benjamin at:
jmbenjamin.author@yahoo.com
www.myspace.com/jmbenjamin_author
www.allaboutjmbenjamin.com

For book signings and speaking engagements contact publicist at: lolitaporter@realeduainmentpublishing.com

ISBN: 978-0-9791990-0-4
Real Edutainment Publishing L.L.C. 0600288518

First Paperback Edition

J.M. Benjamin

Dedication

I dedicate this book to myself. For staying
focused when I could have easily given up. I am
living proof that you can do anything you put
your mind to.

-J.M. Benjamin

Acknowledgements

All praises due to The Most High. Nothing or no one except He can be credited to keeping me focused and safe throughout my recent journey in life. In Him I trust, for He knows best. Allah is Akbar!

Again, I want to thank Ms. Nancey Flowers of Flowers In Bloom Publishing for believing and continuing to believe in me and my work. No one could have done a better job with my freshman novel, *Down in the Dirty,* than you. I will forever be indebted to you for the love. Friends 4 Life! To Chandra Sparks Taylor and Tiffany M. Davis for the quality editing you provided *Down in the Dirty*. Thank You.

To my publicist and friend, Ms. Lolita Porter, mere words can't express my appreciation. Without your dedication and work ethic on my behalf, a lot would not have gotten done and opportunities would have been missed. I know I'm not the easiest to work with so, I thank you for your patience and anything over looked please don't charge it to my heart.

To my graphic designer, editor, and most importantly, friend, Ms. Anna K. Stone of cre8tivdesigns, a jack of all trades. Your unconditional love and assistance in my plight is priceless, and your encouraging words got me through some situations. It was a pleasure to have worked with you and I look forward to whatever the future holds. My best to you and all the students at Southside Academy High School in B-More.

To my partner (Real Edutainment Publishing) and childhood friend, Kevin R. White aka "Money Kev". Dawg, you saw my vision and felt my plight, and now Real Edutainment Publishing is a reality! Together, me, you, and Pete are going to take this company to another level and build a home for upcoming great authors. This is how we do from "The New". Love is love, my best to you and your family. Tammy let my dawg do his job now! (smile)

To my children, Yaseena, Jamillah, and Jameel, the three of you are my world. I only want the best for you, but you must also want the best for yourselves and each other. I may not be there when you want me to be, but I'm always here whenever you need me. I love you.

My mother, Rev. Jean Marie Word, aside from God and myself, there is no other that believes in and loves me more than you do. You've always stressed the importance of getting me intact and helping myself first before I can help others. Hopefully my actions have out weigh my words. I am proud to have made you proud. My father, Jimmie M. Benjamin, Sr. I continue to refresh our blood-line. It's not how you start, but how you finish! I love you both.

To my big bro, As Salaamu Alaikum, All I can say is, "We provin' em wrong ain't we!"
Our whole lives we've struggled as the under dogs from the bottom, trying to make our way to the top, "together", only to be knocked down. That's because we were going about things the wrong way. Now, we have learned a new way, a better way, and once again, we are making our way to the top, "together". This time Pete and Squirm can't be and won't be knocked down. "We went from negative to positive and it's all good!' I love you.

My big sister Kima, you have come along way and I want you to know that I am proud of you, keep doing what you're doing, and to my little sister's, Sham, Eish, and Khadee, I love the women you have become. I look forward to the day we all bond and come together as a family and as siblings. I love you.

My grandfather, Rev. Fred Spann, to have you still here to see me and Pete live our lives as men is a blessing within itself. For as long as I can remember you have always shown us what it consists of to be a real man. May God continue to smile upon you and keep you in his care until He calls on you to rejoin our beloved Bonkey (R.I.P. grandmother- Mattie Evelyn Spann Apr. 23rd 1936- Aug 2nd 2006), We love you Bonk! To my other mother, Christine Lucas Spann (R.I.P. Aug 19, 1953-Dec 2, 2006). My cousin Shaniqua "Peanut" Spann, you need to know that I appreciate all that you have done. Had it not been for you, My Manz And 'Em and Treacherous & Teflon manuscripts would probably still be collecting dust in the closet waiting to be typed, I owe you lil cuz and I got you. I love you. And to the entire Spann family, I love you all.

To my favorite aunt, Elsie "Aunt Lennie" Banks, the love I have for you is beyond the meaning of the word. Our family reunion was an unforgettable time. You are indeed the mother of our family. My best to you and Uncle Joe. And my cousins, the Banks sister's, Jackie, Niecy, Lynn, Cindy, and Vergie, thanks for all the love and support from day one, love ya'll. My cousin's Lynn 2 and Bunny, thanks for everything, much love.

To my childhood friend, Yolanda, 2006 was a rough year for everyone (R.I.P. John Davis), but overall we weathered the storm. You continue to show me what it consist of to be a true friend, giving all, expecting nothing, but deserve everything! Without your friendship I would not know the official meaning of the word. I love you for you and all you stand for. To the rest of my friends, Heather, Eisha, Elyssia, Kejo, Monique, Asha, and Teisha, thanks for your ongoing support in all of my endeavors. Any man would be lucky to have women like you.

To the Ross family, the unconditional love that you have shown me will never be forgotten. You will always be my extended family. My best and genuine love to you all.

J.M. Benjamin

Much love to my Muslim brother and friend, Al-Saadiq
Banks, the lovely Crystal Lacey Winslow, the infamous
Kalico Jones, K'Wan, Isadore Johnson, Shannon Holmes,
DeShawn Taylor, Richard Jeanty, Ty Goode, Endy, Deja
King, Kashamba Williams, Miasha, Dana Rondel, Janine A.
Morris, J.T. Keitt, Seth Ferranti, Wahida Clark, my comrade
and friend Randy Kearse (I Love "Changin' Your Game
Plan"), Gioya Mc Rae, Iesha, Fi Fi Cureton, Kurin, T.N.Baker,
Danielle Santiago, and any other author that showed me
genuine love and support since I've been in this game. I can
honestly say that all of you are not only quality authors, but
quality individuals also. Keep Grindin'!

To Dexter George and Jesel Forde of Source Of knowledge
book store (N.J.) for the continuous and major love, Kwame,
Karen, and Kevon of A&B (N.Y.), Ranisha of Naribu books
(N.J.), Nik of House Of Africa (N.J.), Keys of Urban
Knowledge (N.J.), Tonya and Stephanie of Urban Knowledge
(MD), Karibu books (M.D.) James Muhammad and Dee of
Dynasty books (N.C.), my man Tru of Tru books (CT),
Cornelius of Urban Word (P.A.), Ms Carla Canty of 89.9
QUTE F.M.(CT), Wendy Williams of The Wendy Williams
Experience (WBLS), Mr. Guy Black of WBLS, Omar Long of
Tru Music (Rutgers N.J.), Big Tyme & Shell of Streetz 96.5
FM (N.J.) Troy Whitehurst of 98 FM(N.C.) Bernice Paglia of
The Courier News (N.J.), OOSA On Line Book Club, Sugar
and Spice Book Club, Coast 2 Coast Book Club, Ayesha
Gallion of Newark Writers blogspot, along with all the
Waldens, Borders, and Barnes and Nobles in various states
that showed me love. Yvette Hayward of The African
American Literary Awards, pleasure, it was an honor to have
been nominated and won such a prestigious award.

Special thanks to a few black owned businesses in my
hometown; Butch of Nu-Cuts barber shop (Park Ave), Kim
Ross of Heads Together beauty salon (West 7th Street), Alnisa
of Alnisa's Creation (Front Street), Trenay of Hairs How We

Do (Watchung Ave), Khadeejah of Kharox Productions and Matricuts beauty salon(East Front Street), Brother Al of Bro Al's barber shop(West 3rd Street) and Bro Al's Steak and Take (Grant Ave), Krush of Darryl's barbershop (Watchung ave). The love is greatly appreciated. You showed that black entrepreneur's of Plainfield do come together and support. I will continue to support you the way you support me, much continued success to all of you!

Ms. Yvette Hayward of The African American Literary Awards, (winning the award for "Best Street Fiction" of the year was an honor) and Kevin Weeks of G-Unit records, thanks for the love, real brothers do real things!

To all the brother's and sister's on lock down, whether County, State, or the Feds, hold ya head's. I'mma keep showin' that it can be done in hopes that all of you become motivated. The book Changin' Your Game Plan by Randy Kearse is a must read for each and everyone one of you who are behind the wall. I contributed my journey and success story to this book as a means of inspiration. There really is such a thing as success after incarceration. To my cousin Azmar "Azzie" Calhoun, As Salaamu Alaikum, stay strong and stay focused, you'll be home before you know it. To my brother in faith and in heart, Jamad Mumin, As Salaamu Alaikum, may Allah continue to watch over you and grant you leniency. My comrades, Vincent Jackson, Shawn Hartwell, Keith "Twin" Wooten, Andre "Ali Hall Storm "Kasim" Weeks, Karim, Prince Wint, Larry "L" Cave, Kenny Atkins, Ry-Ry, Soogei, "Chuck –A-Luck" Brent, and Gerard "Chuku" Graham, you brother's have all impacted my life in some way or another and for that, I got eternal love and wish you nothing but the best. Never will I forget you brothers. To my literary brother's behind the wall, Rock Hansen, Deon "Dee" Smith, J. "Skinny" Reddish, Peter Shue, Assante Khari, Gary "Boo" Wiggins, and the rest of the brother's who continue to bust their pens. I told you once I got in I was gonna make my

J.M. Benjamin

presence felt. It's not easy and that ain't playin' fair, but stay
hungry, it's doable!

To my hood, "The New Projects", who would've ever
thought! I went from pumpin' crack and smack to pumpin'
paperbacks. Gotta new product! How many authors can say
they got their hood and their Manz And 'Em as their book
cover? Huh? We've come along way. Bullet proof love to the
legends of "The New", Antwan "Chet" Johnson, Rodney
"Doma" and Brian (Poodah R.I.P.) Dudley, Marcellus "Buie"
Richardson, Raheem "Rah" Tucker, Terrance "Cordez" and
Demetrius "Meato" Smith, Troy "Tizz' Butler, Lawrence
"Wajdee" Cobb, William "Krush" Royal, Andre "Turk"
Hughes, Ryan and John "Pookie" Godley, Prince Chambers,
Rossie "Rock" and Caron "Lump" Morgan, we all have to go
through something to get to something, I hope you all continue
to make it through. And for the new generation, let what you
watched us go through be an eye opener and learning
experience of what not to do. Love is love to the entire Hood!

Last but not least, once again, to the home front, Plfd stand up!
Everyone in the town from the East End to the West End, In
and Outside the hood, the way you embraced my "Down In
The Dirty" was crazy, the love is definitely appreciated. Your
support has been a motivation to keep grindin'. I will continue
to prove that it's never too late to turn a negative into a
positive and there's more to Plainfield then what goes on in
the streets. Let's stop adding to the destruction of the town and
add to the construction of the town. This one is for you!

To all who have supported me, whether we've met or not,
thank you. Without you there would be no J.M. Benjamin.
Keep my voice alive and I will continue to keep you
entertained!

-J.M. Benjamin

MY MANZ AND ' EM

J.M. Benjamin

PROLOGUE

1996...

"Yo, with this shit right here we about to come up baby!" An amped Malik shouted to Phil.
"Yeah no doubt dawg, But yo, you wild though kid," Phil added shaking his head as he chuckled.
"What? Why you say that?" Malik looked puzzled.

"Nah, I'm just sayin'," he paused. "I thought we was just gonna rob that nigga from Connecticut when he came out here with this shit. I ain't know you was gonna knock 'em off," Phil solemnly said. Malik continued to look at Phil awkwardly. He wondered what could have possibly brought on Phil's comments. They had pulled too many capers together in the past for his partner to have any

1

problems with his methods of getting the job done. He and Phil had always been in agreement when it came down to putting in work and that was one of the main reasons why he was Malik's right hand manz. From day one their plan had always been the same-get what they had to get by any means, so Malik was thrown by Phil's sudden concern.

"Man, fuck that nigga!" Malik barked. "He knew the risk he was taking comin' out here dolo like that. No hammer? No vest? No back up? No nothing? Who the fuck he thought he was? I wasn't feelin' the nigga anyway. That nigga thought he was the biggest thing since Nino Brown. And on some real shit, that nigga wasn't feelin' us either. You might not have caught it but I did," Malik spit. His tone became more aggressive. "You don't remember? He use to always say that lil slick shit about he don't know why he fuck with us Jersey niggas every time we copped from him. That shit use to have me tight on the low. Mu'fucka got what he deserved. Sleep and get slept on, you know how it goes. And he was right, he shouldn't have been fucking with us Jersey niggas. He got what his hands called for," mocked Malik in an un-remorseful tone. Phil just sat there and listened. He knew that everything Malik was saying was gospel according to how they rolled. Just as he had known what Malik's next words would be. After all, that was his manz. They knew each other all too well. "But yo. Why the fuck you buggin' off that shit anyway? What's wrong with you?" questioned Malik.

"Aint nobody buggin' dawg, I'm good, I just thought—."

"Nigga, the only thing you need to be thinking about is how we gonna move this shit so we can get this paper." Malik finished Phil's thought. "We got three birds of raw and two pounds of smoke right here and you thinking about that bitch ass nigga. Come on baby boy, get ya shit together. Niggas gonna be on our dicks when they see how we went from makin' peanuts to peanut butter. Shit, I'm tryn'na have me a mu'fuckin' Ack coupe for the summer nigga, nah mean?" Malik regained his composure at the thought of spending some of the proceeds he intended to make off of the drugs in front of him.

"Yeah I feel you kid, and you right, fuck that nigga," Phil spouted in agreement.

"That's what the fuck I'm talkin' about," shouted Malik. "That's my manz I know," he exclaimed giving Phil a pound handshake. "Now let's take care of this shit so we can hit the block."

"No doubt," agreed Phil. "But yo, before we start cookin' some of this shit up I gotta take a shit. That muthafuckin' Domino's runnin' right thru me," Phil held his stomach as he got up off the love seat.

"Aight, hurry up though so we can take care of this. I know money comin'. I wanna cook at least a half and bag up all of them trees. You know how

3

that smoke money be comin'," Malik yelled back to Phil.

As Phil reached the bathroom, he took a quick glance back over his shoulder and saw Malik heading for the two backpacks. He went into the bathroom and closed the door. Malik took one of the three kilos of coke and a pound of marijuana, and headed towards the kitchen. After placing everything on the kitchen table, Malik grabbed two plates out of the cabinet over the sink. Just as he closed the cabinet door shut and was about to turn around-"Boom!" The sudden sound startled Malik. Instinctively Malik reached for his weapon. Fortunately for him, he came up empty handed.

"Freeze motherfucker!"

"Don't move, don't you fucking move!"

"Put your hands in the air! Let me see your fucking hands now!"

Several voices filled the room, making demands. Caught off guard and in a state of confusion, Malik dropped the plates trying to comply with the orders being given. His only concern was that he did not become another statistic. He heard so many stories on the news and had read in the newspapers about situations like this. At that moment, all he could think about was what happened to a kid he knew named Ralphie "D". Images of how Ralphie D's life was innocently taken over a mistake, continued to invade his mind. Malik thought it would be just his luck that some trigger happy cop would put about three dozen holes in him, thinking that the glare from his jewels was a weapon. There was no doubt in his mind that the judicial system would somehow deem it a justifiable death. There was no way he was going out like that. Malik took extra precautions in his movements, making sure to move nice and slow. He felt the tip of a gun poking him in his back as a white hand began patting him down- most likely in search of a burner. Malik normally carried hardware, but not when he was about to go out and hustle. The Second Street housing project, where Malik hustled, was too hot to stand out there with heat on you- unless you were trying to go straight to jail. Besides, Malik knew once he was in his hood, if anything ever erupted, a burner was easily accessible. There were enough guns stashed throughout the projects to handle any situation.

"I don't have any weapons on me yo," Malik spoke calmly.

"Shut the fuck up!" The officer yelled. All in one motion, he yoked Malik up and slammed him to the floor. The move the cop put on him happened so fast that it caught Malik off guard and knocked the wind out of him. Malik gasped for air, unable to breathe, as the officer put his knee in his back and began cuffing him up. Malik tried to regain his breath, lifting his head and opening his eyes. When he looked up he saw two plain clothes officers escorting Phil out the door. It didn't dawn on Malik at the time that something was out of place. His mind was more focused on who could have tipped the police off to them, and about what. He and Phil had done so much together. It could have been anything from drugs to murder. In the streets, they were considered to be two rough dudes, and they both respected and played the game in every aspect- whether it was about making it or taking it. It was all a part of the game to them. Although Pete, Cheddar, and Doub, was his manz and 'em, Phil was his right hand manz-his partner in crime. They were like left and right. If they existed in the old days they would have been compared to Butch Cassidy and the Sundance Kid. Frick and Frack were what their other manz called them because they were so close. He knew that he and Phil were definitely going down for the drugs that they had in the two bedroom apartment they shared. He also knew that there had to be more to this raid than that, or else the police would not have been there. Even though they were getting a little paper, they were far from being major players in the game. Knowing that there were a lot of bigger fish to fry in the game where they were from, he wondered what would make the police want to run down on them like this. Malik knew how the cops operated in the town of Plainfield. Everybody did. It always went down the same way, when they raided a spot. They generally waited to run down on dealers around the first of the month, because they knew the hustlers in town increased their product. They were so predictable. There was no doubt in Malik's mind that he and Phil had been set up. Eventually, he would find out and when he did, Malik vowed to himself to make whoever was guilty pay drastically for their dishonor. If he couldn't, he was sure his manz would. Malik wasn't concerned about the drugs they found in the house, because he had never been locked up for anything drug related. With a good attorney defending him, he knew that he could get a decent deal if he pleaded out. But anything dealing with guns or violence was a different story; that was all he had on his criminal jacket. He needed to know what else he was up against no matter what it was.

Malik thought the judicial system to be all political, and when it came to politics it was all about money. Money talked and bullshit walked. He learned that by seeing some of the biggest gangsters and hustlers walk free or get a slap on the wrist for some of the worse crimes ever committed. He knew there was no way that his manz and them would sit back and let the judge throw the book at him, as long as they were out there getting money.

"Officer, what I do? What I'm being arrested for?" He asked, now regaining his breath.
The white officer just smiled. It was always like this with these street punks, so-called gangsters, he thought. They terrorized the city and flooded the community with drugs, and when the heat comes down on them they act innocent, as if they have always been law abiding citizens. It never ceased to amaze the officer. Throughout all of his years in law enforcement, it never failed. In almost every situation there was always one kid out of the bunch

7

that could not handle the consequences and repercussions of his actions. This made the detective's job that much easier, he thought as he recalled his past seventeen years of experience with street criminals. He could not help but to think about the old police saying about the real tough ones they came across through out the years. *You have to slap them once to get them to talk and ten times to get them to shut up.* He knew he didn't have to answer the kid he had lying on the floor cuffed up. It always humored him when he saw their facial expression once he told them what they were being charged with and how they came about being charged.

"My guess would be robbery and murder in the first degree," the officer belted with a straight face. "What?" Malik asked in disbelief. He thought that to be impossible. There was no way they had anything on him for any bodies. He was always extra careful when he put in work, he thought. There had been eight bodies in five years and not once was he ever questioned or a suspect in any of them. *That* was based on the way he covered his tracks. Even the one he just committed was perfectly planned just as the other five, if not better. So, Malik couldn't understand how that could possibly be.

"Yeah aight," Malik laughed aloud in his most convincing tone. "I ain't kill *nobody*!" he spat looking up at the officer. This was the part the detective enjoyed the most. If he had a dollar for

8

every time he saw the look he knew he was about to
see, he'd be a rich man.

"Oh yeah? Is that so?" the detective mocked.
"Well that's funny, because that's not what your
boy told us." The pale faced detective delivered on
cue as if he were reciting lines for the leading role
of an upcoming movie. Hearing what the officer
just said, no one would have known that Malik was
a light-skinned brother. What little color he
possessed in his complexion faded. He turned pale
white nearly resembling the officer. He still tried to
maintain his best poker face as if he were trying to
bluff with a pair of Deuces, not knowing that his
opponent was sitting across from him holding a pair
of Aces.

"Whatever," Malik shot hoping his voice didn't
crack. "Do what the fuck you gon' do," he added
with attitude.

"If you say so," the detective spoke through his
chuckle. By now, it was all over town that Phil had
worn a wire to set Malik up on the Connecticut
murder-robbery, even before Malik had gotten any
information or confirmation on what was going on.
Someone saw the cops taking the device off of Phil
just before he got into the back of the police car, un-
cuffed. It wasn't until Malik had gotten transferred
to the county, interrogated for hours with photos of
the dead Connecticut kid being shoved in his face
did he get word that Phil was being held in
protective custody. When he called Pete and the rest
of his manz and them, he was filled in on the word

on the streets. Malik knew that in the streets things may be stretched by the time it got to you, but the root of the story was always official. It was always that way. It was easier and quicker to find out something in jail and in the streets than it was for the police to solve a crime. That's how so many unsolved crimes got solved, because of guys like Phil in the game. They acted like gangsters, thugs, and major hustlers who respect the codes, rules, and laws of the streets. But, they were really rats, snitches, and dudes of no integrity who cooperated with the police. Giving them information they would never figure out or learn in their Criminal Justice class. Without niggas that do crimes but couldn't do the time, the police would be out of jobs Malik thought. He couldn't believe that his man, Phil, had crossed over and flipped on him. Not gangster Phil that vowed to hold court in the streets if they ever tried to take him down. Not Phil who lived by the gun and would die by the gun. Not the same Phil that always talked about how he would ride or die for his niggas, like he was from Cali. Above all, not his manz Phil who was like a brother to him.

After sitting in the county for six months, Malik's lawyer was able to find out his situation through filing a motion. From what Malik was told, Phil was pulled over for a traffic violation and when they ran his name it came up that he had outstanding traffic tickets and was driving on the revoked list. The fact that he had no license, the officer smelled marijuana, *and* saw a blunt lying in the ashtray was enough to put Phil in a compromising situation. All of which gave the officer probable cause to search Phil's vehicle. Upon searching, the officer found what was right under the passenger seat of the car. Phil had twenty-five clips of crack, making him a third strike loser. Being a three-time felon, he knew he had to come up with something good if he ever wanted to see daylight on the streets again. Phil started singing like Alicia Keys and agreed to wear a wire after telling the police he knew about a murder.

Pete, Doub, and Cheddar were supposed to have paid the attorney's fee of 35 grand. But after paying only $21,000 of what the lawyer charged for representation, they began to give excuses about how hot the block had been. They told Malik how rough it was out there, and to just chill because he was their man and they had his back. Malik was far from being a dummy though, and the last thing he wanted to do was to jerk the one person that was fighting for him. He knew that his lawyer, along with the judge, and the prosecutor, held his fate in their hands, and without paying what he owed to his lawyer he knew that his chances of getting a good deal were slim. So, he turned to the only person that he knew he could always depend on no matter what, mom dukes. It was almost impossible for his mother to have $14,000. She was a woman who worked two jobs, supported two little girls, and lived pay check to pay check. Asking for fourteen grand was like asking for a million dollars, but she was all he had. Despite all the others he ran with in the hood, went all out for, remained loyal to, and lent money to without any intentions of ever seeing it back, when it was all said and done, the only one that was standing there with open arms was moms. Malik's mother took out a loan on her home and as promised came through for him, and he never doubted her. The final outcome of his case resulted in Malik pleading out to a 20 year sentence with a mandatory minimum of 10 years. He would have to serve at least ten years before he was eligible for parole. All the cooperation Phil provided had gone down the drain. By the time Malik's lawyer got through with them, the conduct of the search and arrest, the wiretap and no gun, the judge ruled that it was entrapment, and the drugs were inadmissible because the warrant was only for Malik and not to search the apartment. Rather than going to trial, Malik's lawyer advised him to cop out to manslaughter, which is exactly what he did. The day of his sentencing, the only people in the courtroom were the judge, the bailiff, the stenographer, Malik, his lawyer, his girlfriend, his two little sisters, and his mother. None of his so-called manz had even attempted to show face for support. They had no idea how much time he was facing or what he had gotten, and probably didn't care he thought. That's how he wanted it. Between his mom and his girl, Malik figured that he would be all right. But outside of his mother, he felt that he really couldn't count on his girl being there in the long run. She was from the streets and had a habit. Not a drug habit, but a heavy shopping habit. One that Malik supported, and like any addiction, it's a must that it be supported by any means. With Malik being away, unable to take care of her the way she felt she should be taken care of, it was just a matter of time before she crossed him up too. When it happened, he wouldn't be mad at her because he respected the game. He knew the only sure thing he had in his corner was his mom. He listened to his mother as she cried and promised him that some how some way she would come up with the money that he needed to pay his attorney, did something to Malik. As much as he had done for people in the streets, no strings attached, he couldn't believe that it had come down to this. That day, Malik also made some promises to himself. One, he would pay his mother back, with interest, or died trying. Two, he would never put anything or anybody else before his family, ever again. And three, because of the disloyalty they had all displayed, he would never depend on or deal with his manz and 'em again as long as he lived.

CHAPTER ONE

2006...

"Yo what's taking Kwa so long?" Asked Bashir "You know how he his. The only thing he on time about is prayer, other than that his butt is slow," said Malik.

"You right about that akhi," joined Muhammad as they filled the yard of Northern State prison with laughter.

Just then, Kwawe came running to the weight pile with his radio in hand.

"As Salaamu Alaikum. Yo, what took you so long akh? You know we get this money everyday, same time. You jerkin' rec brother," said Bash.

"Wa Laikum As Salaam, my bad akh, the brother had me tied up waitin' on this tape to finish dubbin'."

"Who?"

"You know the brother Sadi. He sent the Salaams too."

"Alhamdullaalahi. We thought you was running from this chest work-out."

"Come on brotha, you know me better than that. Chest my thing baby," said Kwawe flexing, making his pecs jump from under his shirt.

"Yo akh, what you got?" asked Malik.

"I got that old X joint, *It's Dark and Hell is Hot*. I had it before but my other one popped so, I had the brother bring me in a new one cause that piece is a classic."

"Word, that brother X be spittin'. You could've borrowed mine though, I got a copy of that."

"Nah akh, you know I like to have my own music."

"Yeah, no doubt, I feel you. Pop that in."

"I am, but aren't you supposed to be starting the work out off?"

"Yeah."

"Well get on that bench and stop stallin'?" said Kwawe to Malik.

Both Bashir and Muhammad laughed. They knew what Kwawe was leading up to when he asked Malik the question because they played like that all the time when it came to their workout. They always accused one another of neglecting their exercise routine as a form of motivation.

"You're real funny akh, just try to follow my lead though. We gonna get money today," Malik answered back.

Malik had known Kwawe for nearly nine and a half years now and considered him to be a very close friend. Not only was he his friend he was also his brother in faith. They all were. Malik was the

15

last one to embrace the fold of Islam declaring his belief a year after he had come to prison. When he first entered the prison system Kwawe was Malik's cellmate. He had been the one who had piqued Malik's interest about the Islamic religion. Hearing his birth name, when Malik introduced himself, Kwawe mistook him for a Muslim. Because of it, he greeted him with a greeting that was foreign. Malik gave him a puzzled look. Kwawe instantly caught it and apologized. Even though Malik wasn't really interested, in making small talk, he asked Kwawe what he had said to him and what language had he spoken. Kwawe explained that he had said "As-Salaamu Alaikum", which was Arabic and meant peace be unto you.

Coming from 10 B tier in Union County Jail, Malik thought that he was a pretty nice size. He gained 13 pounds from eating honey bun and banana sandwiches, working out on the universal weight machine and push-ups with the deck of cards twice a day. Nevertheless, his 170 pound frame was nothing compared to Kwawe's 230 plus lbs size. To Malik, it looked as if Kwawe had been down for twenty years or more and had worked out everyday of them. It wasn't until later that he had found out that Kwawe had almost 12 ½ years in with eighteen more to go on his sentence. He was eight years Malik's senior at the age of twenty-nine, catching his murder and attempted murder at the young age of twenty-two. Although he was still young, he looked much older with his Sunni Muslim beard that he kept neatly trimmed at all times. When he felt comfortable with Malik, Kwawe shared with him how he came about catching his case.

He was unexpectedly coming back from Atlanta one night after hustling down there for almost a month. When he got home, walked into the house, and went to the bedroom, he found his then girlfriend straddled on top of the next man in *his* bed. It just so happened that he had his gun on him and out of reflex he pulled out and started shooting, hitting his girl four times in the head, and the dude twice after he'd pushed her up off of him and attempted to dive out the bedroom window naked. Kwawe had emptied the remaining shots he had left in his sixteen shot glock. Amazingly, the girl survived, but the dude wasn't so lucky. He told Malik how all his mans knew about his wifey messing around on him, but nobody told him. For that, he cut them all off. Because, finding out on his own, cost him twenty-five years of his life in prison. So, he decided to do it on his own.

Throughout the months of the two of them being cellmates, he shared with Malik how he came into the prison wilding out, gambling, fighting officers, selling drugs, and all the other negative things that were available to you in jail. He told him how he basically turned his first two years behind the wall into a nightmare. He went to the box for stabbing another inmate up over a gambling debt. At the time, he had a bundle of dope and five fifty dollar jail house bags of weed in his pocket when the rovers ran down on him. That caused him to get two years in the box. There was an old head Muslim brother who had been in the hole for three years for constantly refusing to take his kuffi off in an un-permitted area. He took a liking to Kwawe, seeing in him what he couldn't see in himself at the time. He would talk to Kwawe whenever they were allowed outside recreation, and sent him reading material about Al-Islam. The first book he had ever given to him was the book of Tauhid, dealing with the Oneness of God. It was after reading that book that Kwawe wanted to declare his belief in Islam and become Muslim. He took on the attribute of Abdul Kwawe. After being in the box for six months, brother Umar and another brother named Shabazz witnessed him declare his faith in Islam in the administrative-segregation recreation yard over five years ago and he was on the straight path ever since.

Malik used to watch as Kwawe made his prayers five times a day and he respected how loyal and dedicated he was to his belief. When they became real close associates, Kwawe told him how he always kept Malik in his prayers. Whenever Malik was stressed, he would give him something to read from out of the Qu'ran, or other religious material about Islam. Kwawe took a liking to Malik and saw in him what the old head Muslim brother Umar saw in him when he was young and wild. He explained to Malik how his name was an Attribute of God, which meant Master and how Malik should have

Abdul in front of his name. This would mean that he was the servant of the Master. The more he spoke the more Malik listened with interest. Malik became so interested that he began attending Muslim services on Fridays. At first it was because Kwawe had invited him, but after a few times of going he got into what the Imam was saying and enjoyed it when he broke down the Qu'ran in English after reciting it in Arabic. He felt drawn to the Muslim community and was digging what they stood for. They always talked about brotherhood, family, being humble, respect, and things to that affect. That's what Malik felt that he was about. He was still hurt behind the fact that his main man had crossed him and got him all cased up, and his other mans and them had abandoned him. Yet, he didn't allow that to affect his judgment of other cat's character. He was intelligent enough to know that there were good dudes and snake dudes from all parts of the world. You just had to be able to recognize who was who. In his case, he let his love and respect for the streets blind him to who the dudes he ran with really were. After a year of reading, listening, and attending Muslim service, Malik felt that he was ready.

As DMX's raspy voice came over the radio. Malik laid on the bench and wrapped his hands around the weight bar.

"Dawg, that's my manz and' em."

"Abdul Malik, you gonna lift the weight up or what?" Bashir asks as he stood behind Malik spotting him.

"Chill akh, let me hear this," Malik answered knowing that DMX was about to end his conversation and the song was about to begin. DMX continued, *"Dawg! That's my mans and them, so if you fuckin' with me, then you fuckin with..."* The beat came in and Malik took the 225lbs out of the rack and began his warm up set. He did a count of twenty reps, put the weight back in the rack and jumped off of the bench. "Next!" Malik barked, amped from DMX words.

"Calm down brother," Kwawe says as he laid down on the bench to start his set. Malik ignored Kwawe comment and turns his attention to Muhammad.

"Yo akh, I told you, X is hot. I'm feelin him. That's how you suppose to get down."

"Malik I don't know how you get caught up in all that rap stuff brother. You're getting to old for that."

"Too old? Akh you buggin, I'll never get too old for Hip- Hop. Hip- Hop is a part of our culture. They rap about how we came up, and what our people goin' through. Brother's like DMX rap about how we was livin' out there, and it's real."

"Yeah, I know and we wasn't livin' right that's why we in here Akhi. I ain't talking about Hip-Hop anyway because Hip-Hop is a style, I'm talking about Rap music. Some of them brother's that make

them songs take the Hip-Hop out of the music. They
glorify violence, drugs, womanizing, and all the
other negative things that kids grow up believing.
Why you think the prisons are so over crowded?
Muhammad didn't wait for Malik to respond. "I'll
tell you why, because our younger brothers and
sisters are growing up believing what they see on
television and in movies, and hear in Rap music.
You gotta ride or die with your niggas, you gotta
have ice and platinum, a Bentley, pop Cristal in the
club, be a thug or a gangsta, smoking blunts and
bustin guns if you wanna be somebody or get props
in the hood. Muhammad mocked. "It's crazy out
there right now akh because our kids ain't got the
proper guidance, especially the little brothers out
there with no real role models. While our women
are out there working two and three jobs or for the
one that ain't out there living right chasin' brother's
like us for that fast money, we are in spots like this.
Our little brother's, nephews, sons, and cousin's are
out there idolizing the cats in the streets with the hot
whips, official gear, big shines, heavy pockets, and
all the chicks. Now they got these gangs akhi. Look
how the system is changing. It's flooded with
babies killing babies. It doesn't make any sense.
Them brothers out there we used to call lames and
suckas are the brothers that are really the dudes
doing their thing. We the lames and the suckas
cause we in here when we should be out there
handling our business." Malik didn't say anything
he just listened. He knew that Muhammad was

right. Muhammad always got deep with it no matter
what the topic was. Out of the four of them he had
the most time in and he was also the most
knowledgeable between them of their belief. He
made it his business to share his wisdom with
others. He had been down for eighteen years and
would never see the streets again. He wanted to
give back by enlightening brothers about the evils
of the world, so they would be prepared when they
returned to the street. In his day, Muhammad had
been charged with everything you could think of in
the game. He was considered to be a street legend,
one of the best that ever done it in the game. None
of that meant anything to him anymore. All that he
had gained in the streets caused him to lose the most
important things in life to him. Now his freedom
and the ones who loved him the most were all that
mattered to Muhammad now.

"You right akh, but the brother make good
music," said Malik. "And I ain't too old to be
listening to Rap either; I'm only 31. That's still
young, plus Allah blessed me to still look like I'm
21," he said stroking his baby goatee beard.

"More like 41,"said Kwawe coming off of the
weight bench. Bashir almost tripped over a weight
and fell from laughing at what Kwawe said about
Malik.

Malik turned on Bashir. "I know you're not
laughin' Bash. You look the oldest out of all of us."
"My beard makes me look like that, but don't get it

twisted, I'm in good shape and I can out last any young cat up in this piece."

Bashir was what you called a young old head. He was only 32 but always talked like he was 52. He was down four years less than Muhammad for an organized drug ring that he says he wasn't a part of. His criminal record as an adult was squeaky clean. But as a juvenile, it was over a mile long. Regardless to whether the system says that your record as a youth offender is sealed once you've turned 18, he was viewed as a menace. When he went to trial they threw the book at him and sentenced him to the maximum of twenty-five years. They were both from Middlesex County. That was the county where the judges were famous for handing out football numbers when they sentenced you. You were almost guaranteed to get double digits if you committed a crime in their township. In both Kwawe and Bashir's eyes they were short timers compared to other brother's that would never touch the streets again. But nobody's time was as short as Malik's. His first board was coming up in two months and he was anxious to find out the outcome.

"Yo, I don't know why you feeling what DMX saying anyway. Ain't you in here cause of *ya manz and 'em*?" Bashir spoke, quoting a line from DMX's intro. Instantly he hit a sore spot with Malik.

"Akh, you know what I'm in here for," Malik replied in a calm manner. He did not want to get into it with his Muslim brother nor did he want to let Bashir know that got under his skin.

Ever since Malik became Muslim he had never been disrespectful, hostile, or violent towards anyone in the jail, neither staff nor inmate, especially not another Muslim. He wasn't going to start now. He had restrained from that type of behavior and practiced and instilled humility within himself. He intended to take that out into the world with him when his time came to step back out there. He didn't think that he would make his first parole board, but he knew that eventually he would be released. When that time came he would be prepared and ready.

"Yo let's get this work out in!" Kwawe yelled trying to keep the peace. He knew what Bashir said to Malik bothered him. "Prayer will be in a minute and I'm trying to make it on time. Kwawe's intentions worked. All at once the three of them directed their attention to him. Bashir was the first to speak.

"Yeah, you gonna make it on time, but that's all you gonna make on time, with your slow behind."

"Word akh," said Malik. "You're a slow brother."

"Slow ain't the word," joined Muhammad. "You like a turtle."

"That's right. Allah tells us through the Prophet Muhammad peace and blessings be upon him to have sabr," Kwawe replied.

24

"Yeah patience," Malik translated in English.
"Not slowness," he added as they all shared a laugh.
The day had come to an end and the jail had been
locked down for the night.
Malik and Kwawe offered their Eisha prayer and
began eating their octopus and brown rice meal that
Kwawe had prepared for them.

"Shukran for the meal akh," Malik thanked
Kwawe in Arabic for their evening dinner.

"Afwan," Kwawe replied as they ate in silence.
After they were done Malik broke the silence.

"Kwa, I'm getting short akh. Them people
should be here to see me in a minute."

"Yeah, I know and I been keeping you in my
prayers. Inshaa Allah you make your first board."

"Inshaa Allah," repeated Malik. "And if I do
you know I'm gonna show love with flicks and all
of that when I get situated, and bless you, Bash, and
Muhammad with some dough and food packages
once I find me a job and make a few dollars. Being
in this spot taught me a lot about doin' time. I know
that if you don't have anybody on the outside
showin' you love, it can be rough. That's why I
thank Allah for ummi," Malik expressed using
Arabic in reference to his mother. "Cause she held
me down all around the board from food packages
to visits and then some. You know akh, I ain't got
to tell you. You know."

"Yeah, your Ummi is a good lady. May Allah
reward her for her efforts, but you ain't gotta
promise me nothing akhi. You know I'm aight up in

25

here, I don't need anything. If you wanna do something for me, when you get out find a Masjid and pray to Allah for allowing you to return back to the dunyah." Kwawe's face was intense now.

"Absolutely akh, that's mandatory, and I'mma still send flicks, haraam, halaal ones with me at the Eid celebration, maybe even over in Mecca at the Ka'abah, Inshaa Allah," replied Malik bringing a smile to Kwawe's face.

"I feel you akh that would be a beautiful thing, I just don't want you going out there thinking that you owe me or anybody else anything, because the only person that you owe is yourself. Stay out there once you get back out there. I've seen it over and over, while they're in here they wear their kuffi's, carry their Qu'ran, attend Jumah and Tahleem services, quote Hadiths and all of that. Then, as soon as they hit the front door the kuffi and Qu'ran goes into the trash and they ready to get back on the scene. You know what I'm talking about akh. I don't want that to happen to you. This is a beautiful religion, and way of life akhi," Kwawe said passionately. "Now is the time for you to strengthen your faith and your worship. Take that up out of here with you when you leave, Inshaa Allah. Don't leave it at the front door akhi," Kwawe expressed with sincerity.

"That's my word I'm not going to do that akhi. I'm never going to forget how Islam changed my life for the better and taught me how to be a real man. If it wasn't for Islam I probably would've gone crazy and wanted to kill something when I found out that my shortie was creepin' with one of my so-called manz. Me and that cat had been through thick and thin, shared the same bed, split Big Macs and all of that. Then he crabs me like that! Back in the day I would've held that grudge until I dealt with that cat on some street shit." He nodded. "But I know better now. And I know that Allah made me find that out while I was in here, so I wouldn't go home and try to be with that sister."

Malik remembered when he first found out about his man and his then girlfriend as if it were yesterday. One of the other inmates from his town saw him on a visit with Dawn and had approached him two years ago when they got back on the compound after visits were over. At first, Malik took offense when the kid stepped to him inquiring about his lady. Although they were both from Plainfield, he didn't deal with the kid like that when they were in the streets. Even though they had crossed paths many times at parties and Greek Festivals, and other events hustlers find themselves. The fact of the matter was that Malik was from the projects and the kid was from 3rd street. This was an area that had been his hood's rival for as long he could remember. It wasn't until years later that Malik had realized how coming to jail gave you a different outlook on certain individuals, and made you deal with people that you normally wouldn't out in the streets. He learned that some of the individuals you said you didn't like just because

they were from another block or another hood were
no different than you. Everyone was just trying to
overcome a struggle the best way they knew how.
Malik could tell that the kid Byron was a little
uneasy with stepping to him. He beat around the
bush when Malik told him that Dawn was his girl
and wanted to know why he was inquiring. Instead
of answering him, Byron went on to ask Malik was
he friends with Cheddar and them. His patience
wearing thin, Malik replied by saying "yeah." Even
though he knew things had changed between he and
his manz over the years. Byron went on to tell
Malik how his girlfriend just told him on his visit
that word around town was that Dawn was messing
with his man Cheddar. She had driven up to see him
in Cheddar's 500SL. He told Malik how his own
girl told him practically everybody in the town
knew about it. But, she didn't want Byron to be the
one to say something and for him to stay out of it.
Byron viewed Malik as a good dude and felt that he
deserved to know, and if the shoe were on the other
foot he would want someone to put him on too.
Malik told him how he appreciated him letting him
know that. He played it off as if what he was just
told didn't faze him in front of Byron, but on the
inside he was heated. Malik didn't want to call
Dawn on the phone and confront her about the
accusations that were made, because he wanted to
see her facial expression when he dropped it on her.
He knew that there had to be some truth to what
Byron told him. He had nothing to gain by

fabricating something like that, let alone put himself out there by telling Malik. Byron knew from being in the streets and even in jail that there were certain things you didn't play around with, and one of those things was mentioning another man's wifey. Malik waited until the next visiting day came around to question Dawn about the situation. Instead of her trying to deny it, she began to break down in tears. She tried to explain how it just happened and one thing lead to another, but Malik didn't stay to hear the rest of the explanation she had probably rehearsed a million times. According to the rules of the game, both she and his so-called man Cheddar were in violation. When he got home he would have handled the situation on some street shit, but being in prison and practicing Islam had prepared him for any and everything that could be used to throw him off his square. He took it on the chin, got up and left Dawn sitting there in the visitation room, went back to his housing unit, and immediately filled out a visitor removal sheet. That was the last time Malik saw or heard from Dawn. He and Byron had become good friends shortly thereafter, for the genuineness he had displayed towards Malik.

"Yeah, you've come a long way akh. You gotta realize you not the same brother that came in here over nine years ago. You've grown and you've changed for the better. All that nonsense and garbage that you once harbored inside of you is all behind you now. You know what you gotta do when you get back out there, and you know what you can't do or you know where you'll wind back up. Either way the choice is yours," Kwawe told him. Malik knew he was right and knew exactly what he had to do when he got out.

"Yeah I know akh, I know," Malik replied.

CHAPTER TWO

After answering all of their questions, then having him to wait out in the hall way, the board of parole had the officer escort Malik back into the interview room. Malik had a seat as the man in front of him slid the green sheet to him, stood up, and shook Malik's hand.

"Good luck to you Mr. Jones. I hope I never have to see you in front of me like this again." The chubby white man spoke, knowing that he did not mean a word he spoke to Malik. He believed that he would in fact see Malik again. It was almost guaranteed he thought. With Malik being a young black male, limited job skills and qualifications, minimum education, a felony conviction on his jacket, and not to mention a twenty-year back number he had on parole he was bound to return. Stereotyping Malik, he figured someone like him usually needed to come back two to three more times before they actually learned their lesson. Recidivism was what kept the prisons operating. Prison was a revolving door for many. In some way

31

the Caucasian man was sympathetic towards Malik
with the deck being stacked against him the way
that it was.

"Thank you sir," Malik responded. "And you
won't." He said with confidence, making it clear
that he had no desire to return. At the same time, he
knew that the thoughts that clouded the back of his
mind made it a possibility to have prison become
his place of residence again. The officer just smiled,
because like the other hearings he sat in on, Malik
made the same claim as they all had. It never
failed; they always returned. Being a black man
himself, he wished the best for Malik and hoped
that he would be one of the few brothers that never
returned, not for his sake, but for their people's. In
the officer's opinion, he believed that prisons
stopped the race's reproductive power and because
of the shortage of good, strong, African American
men, our women were turning to other races and
each other for companionship and support.

"Good luck my brother," he said to Malik as he
escorted him out.

"Thank you brother, I appreciate that."

Malik tried keeping his composure as he walked
back to the main compound, out of respect for all
the brothers that had to remain in the belly of the
beast, but he couldn't help but to crack a slight
smile when he saw Kwawe, Muhammad, and
Bashir all huddled up, apparently waiting for him.
In three weeks, he would officially be a free man-
physically. Free from being told when to eat, when

to sleep, when to use the bathroom, when to use the phone, and when to do things that he enjoyed doing. It had been a long and rough ten years, especially in the beginning when he was much younger and wilder, but he survived through it all. Despite abandonment from those who he once respected, trusted, and had love for in the streets- people he thought were his friends and had his back the way that he had theirs.

He knew that all praises were due to Allah for giving him the strength to endure and maintain what he had, and also for blessing his mother to be able to do the same and hold him down at the same time. He couldn't wait to call her and share with her the good news he just received, just as he couldn't wait to get out and show her how much he appreciated her being there for him. By the time he reached Kwawe and the rest of them, Malik was able to wipe the grin off of his face and regain his composure.

"What happened akh?" Kwawe was the first to ask. Malik answered with a straight face.

"You know them people play a lot of games Kwa." Instantly, they all began trying to hide their disappointment, not wanting to make Malik feel any worse than they thought he already had. They knew how bad he wanted to make his first board, and they were all hoping that he had as well.

"What they say?" Bashir asked.

"You know, the regular, blah, blah, blah. Have you learned your lesson? And what are your plans when you get out if you're granted community release." Malik spoke sensuously, trying not to laugh.

"Those people are crazy!" Muhammad started. "They'll give a child molester or a rapist parole back to back, but they wanna keep us locked down for life. The system doesn't make any sense." At hearing what Muhammad said, Malik knew it was time to put an end to the charade and let his brothers know the real deal. He knew how Muhammad got when he got on a roll. He'd go on and on all night about the injustices of the judicial system.

"Allah is Akbar," said Malik with a smile on his face, no longer able to hold it in. Realizing that Malik had been fronting, Kwawe playfully punched him in the chest.

"Stop playin akh, you outta here ain't you?"

"Three weeks from now akh!" He told them.

"All praises due to Allah!" yelled Muhammad.

"I knew you was frontin'," said Bashir punching Malik just as Kwawe had.

For the next four hours they all walked the big yard together and discussed Malik's good news and what they felt they should tell him before his time came to get back out into society. Each one of them gave him words of wisdom of their own and wished him the best. In return, Malik vowed not to forget about them when he got out and promised them that he'd stay in touch. It was these three individuals who played a major role in his growth process both

34

as a man and as a Muslim. They were a part of his family now, which was the most important thing to him. How could he forget them?

"You have a collect call from Malik *from a correctional facility, this call may be monitored or recorded do not use three way or call waiting or your call will be terminated. To accept this call press one now."*

"I can't stand this recording," Malik said under his breath to himself. In a few weeks he knew that his mother would never have to listen to it again.

"Hey hon!" his mother's voice cheerfully boomed over the receiver.

"What's up ma? How are you doing?"

"I'm blessed. I was wondering when you were going to call. I knew it was about that time though."

"Yeah I know. I was gonna call you over the weekend but I decided to wait until now. What's up with Jackie and Mandy, how are they doing?"

"Chile don't get me to lying. Your sisters are out here driving me crazy, runnin' those dang streets with their fast tails like they don't have no home training. I want to kill them sometime. They done got so grown now, startin' to smell themselves," his mother complained. It upset Malik to hear about his sisters being in the streets. He figured they would have learned something by seeing what he had gone through. The last thing he wanted to see was his little sisters falling victim to the many horrors of street life. He knew how guys who ran the streets preyed on young naïve girls who were fascinated by the lifestyle that hustlers lead. He himself had been guilty of the very same thing. Many times he used his status in the streets to capture a young girl's attention, and once he got it he took advantage of their innocence. If his sisters were to be subjected to what he had put someone else's sister, mother, aunt, or female cousin through, Malik knew that it would tear him up inside with guilt. Time had flown by so fast, and he couldn't believe how quick they had grown. It seemed like they were babies just yesterday. Now both Jackie and Mandy were teenagers, the age of being both promiscuous and rebellious. Malik was tired of hearing his mom complain about the same thing over and over for the past year and a half. He waited for the day to come home and put an end to it all so his mom could sleep in peace at night. He could only imagine how Jackie and Mandy's hanging out in the streets had been taking a toll on their mother daily. He also knew that he was the cause of some of his mother's sleepless nights as well. He could still remember the tears in her eyes the day he was sentenced to the mandatory 10 years. It killed him inside to know that he was the cause of her pain and tears. With a release date now, his time was rapidly approaching, and the time was finally coming for his sister's street days to be over.

"Don't worry ma, when I come home I'll put a leash on them, I promise."

"No, it's too late for that. I don't even want you getting involved in that mess. Then before you know it you been done got yourself all caught up in something by doing something to one of them boys out there. You know how your temper is and you know how you get Malik," his mother said, knowing Malik all too well. She wanted to believe that he was a totally changed man, but she was not one hundred percent convinced that he changed. Some of the things had been a part of him for so long.

"Come on ma. I told you I'm not on it like that anymore. That's what the old me would've been thinking when you first told me about it. Rather than me reacting to things now, I learned how to communicate and resolve matters differently. Know what I'm sayin ma?"

"Yeah I hear you, but don't forget I raised your butt and you been a confrontational little devil since the day you were born, so going to jail aint gonna make you change that, it probably made it worse."

"Ma you crazy," said Malik as he laughed. Even though he had worked on his attitude, his anger, and his behavior, throughout his incarceration, he knew that when it came to his beliefs, there was just one thing that he wasn't willing to change, and that was his belief about disrespect. All his life Malik had been taught not to ever let anyone disrespect him. If they did you do what you had to do to never let it happen again. That same irrational belief was what had gotten him in trouble time after time out in the streets and when he first came to prison.

He had attended several Anger Management, and Men's Issues programs with professional people who specialized in helping individuals with problems that they couldn't understand where they had extended from in their lives. It was in those programs that Malik realized his problem, which was how he perceived things in life, causing him to react opposed to rationalizing the situation allowing him to better deal with whatever the situation was and use better options. Learning that kept Malik out of many problems while doing time, but at the same time he knew that one of his options as a means of survival was to resort to a much more physical resolution and bring harm to those who he felt disrespected him, so in a way his mom was right. There were some things he just wasn't willing to let go.

"I ain't crazy, you know I'm telling the truth, but I love you anyway. You know you my baby. I just want to see you come home and get your life in order and be happy. I don't want you out there in them streets like you use to be. I couldn't take it anymore Malik. I can't see myself visiting you at any more jails either after this is over," she said. "Speaking of you coming home, have you heard anything yet?" she asked. "It's been three months since they came to the house and checked it out. The lady sounded like she approved, but I don't know, you know how those people are."

"Yeah I know ma. They came to see me today."

You could hear the excitement in Malik's mother's voice as she questioned him.

"What did they say?"

"They said I'll be coming home in three weeks," announced Malik calmly.

But Ms. Jones was not so calm.

"Thank you Jesus, Hallelujah!" she screamed, "My baby coming home!"

Malik smiled as he listened to his mother's praises. He had already anticipated her reaction to the good news, so he was not in the least bit surprised by her praises. Since he had accepted Islam as his belief, they often had religious debates. Even though they didn't share the same belief, Ms. Jones respected her son's belief. She was just happy that he had gotten closer to God, no matter what religion lead him there. Malik stood there holding the phone as his mother continued to carry on. Her praises turning into tears of joy. He waited until she had calmed down before he spoke. This was not only his time; it was hers as well. She had been there with him every step of the way and earned as well as deserved the right to be as happy as she was at that moment.

"Ma!"

"Excuse me baby, but I had to let that out. I've waited for this day for ten years, and the Lord done answered my prayers," cried Ms. Jones.

Her words went straight to his heart as he felt the love. Had it not been for him being in the presence of a bunch of men, he himself would have also cried with his mom, but now was not the time or the place for him to become emotional. Maybe at a later date when it settled in and he was in a more comfortable surrounding he thought.

"I know, I know ma," he answered. "Me too but a couple of weeks from now it'll be all over and we can put this behind us. Ma listen, I know don't have to tell you this but I don't want anybody to know that I'm coming home, alright?"

"You right, you don't have to tell me that. Who I'm gonna tell? Not none of them boys that ain't did nothing for you the whole time you been in there, that's for sure. And not that heifer that left you when you needed her the most either."

"Ma you crazy," said Malik as he laughed. "And she didn't leave me ma, I'm the one that broke it off."

"Um hm. If you that's what you want me to believe."

Malik laughed again. Over the years he really got to know his mother, and he learned how alike they were. He had inherited his ability to keep it real from his mother, because like her, he always told it like it was and didn't bite his tongue for anything or anybody. She had trooped the whole ten years with him. He knew she understood how he felt as far as no one deserving to know when he was being released. He just had to make sure.

"I'm not even talking about people like Dawn and Pete and them. I know you wouldn't do that. I'm talking about people at your church or something like that. You know how much church people gossip," he said, knowing that his mother wouldn't let him get away with his comment.

"Hey, don't be talking about my church folk. I don't say anything about your Moslem brothers," his mother responded back jokingly.

"It's not Moslem ma, it's Muslim, and besides we don't gossip like that anyway, but I'm just playing, you know what I'm saying. I don't even want you telling Jackie and Mandy, especially with them being out there in the streets. You tell them and it'll be all over the town before I even get home. I'm not even telling dudes in here from the town because they might blow it up. The only people that know are a few of my Muslim brothers that I've been friends with for a long time."

"Don't worry, ain't nothing going to be blown up or put out there or how ever you put it 'cause I ain't gonna tell a soul, you hear me?"

"Yeah I hear you, but what you doing trying to talk all hip?" Malik said to her smiling.

"What? I was repeating what you said, but when I'm driving up there to see you I hear them in those rap songs on that radio station. You know, I like that Wendy Williams, she a mouthy something, but she tell it like it is."
Malik couldn't help but laugh.

"Ma, what are you doing listening to Wendy?"

"Whatever. Last time I checked, I was grown."
Malik laughed for a second time.

You have two minutes left remaining on this call, the voice operator interrupted.

"Ma, this phone is about to cut off, so I'll talk to you some other time, okay?"

"Alright baby, I'll talk to you later, I love you."

"I love y --click."

"Psst," Malik uttered annoyed at the disconnection before he could finish his last words. Patience was a virtue he thought, as he hung up the phone. In just a few short weeks all of the stressful conditions that he endured in prison would all be behind him. The thought of freedom instantly eased his annoyance.

CHAPTER THREE

"**JONES!** You wanna leave or you wanna stay?" the officer shouted.

"Yo akh, go ahead, I'll take care of all of this stuff. You know I'll make sure the brothers get what you want them to get," Kwawe told Malik.

"I know that akh. Make sure you give the brothers the salaams for me, and tell Muhammad and Bashir I'mma get at them too when I get situated."

"No doubt. You got everything? All of our info and stuff?"

"Come on akh, I know that by heart. I got it all up here," said Malik pointing to his head."

"My bad," replied Kwawe as they embraced.

"Jones! I'm not going to tell you no more, move your ass if you wanna get out of here this morning. Don't think we won't hold your ass until 11:59 P.M." the officer shouted at Malik. Malik shot the officer a look that could kill, but didn't say anything because he knew he was right. They would do it too, if you pissed them off. He didn't want to go through the bullshit, not when he knew that his mother would be out front waiting for him to be released. She had waited for his release long enough. There was no way he was going to make her wait 16 more hours. Instead of feeding into the officer, he picked up his shoebox that held the only belongings that meant anything to him. The rest he left for the brothers who had to remain.

"As Salaamu Alaikum Abdul Kwawe."

"Wa Laikum Asalaam Abdul Maalik," Kwawe greeted back in return. He was pleased to see his brother in faith and friend departing. It would be quite awhile before he himself would get to experience the feeling. So until then, he shared it with Malik, wishing him all the best.

Malik stepped out of the front door of the prison with the $827.30 he had saved up from working in the facility kitchen along with a box that contained letters and pictures his mother sent him over the years. Through photo's he saw his mother age and his sisters mature. Malik also had in his possession, his Qu'ran and favorite black nylon kuffi. A smiled spread across his face at first sight. There she was, standing there waiting for him with open arms and tears in her eyes. Malik embraced his mother, giving her a big hug, sweeping her off of her feet, holding her in mid-air. This was a very emotional time for both of them. Neither of them said a word for a moment. As the tears began to roll down Malik's face, he thought of how delicate and fragile his mother felt in his arms. He had waited ten years for this day to come. The day when he would be able to hug his mother as a free man, and now that day had finally come. He was now tipping the scales at 205 pounds solid and strong as a bull. He couldn't believe how light his mother felt to him when he lifted her up. Not realizing his own strength and careful not to hurt her, Malik put her down.

"Boy look at you, you are huge! With your big self! You got that big in three wecks? What were you doing eating six times a day?" His mother said happy to see him.

"Something like that."

"You look good though baby, and I'm glad you out, I missed you," she said wiping her face.

"Yeah, it's good to be out; I missed you too ma," Malik replied as he helped wipe a few of the tears from her face with his hand.

"I can't believe it, my baby is free!" Ms. Jones wailed.

Malik smiled at her. He hadn't felt this good in a long time. He was happy to be out and see how pleased his mother was.

"Yeah ma, I'm free, so let's get up out of here before they change their mind."

"Hmm! Over my dead body!" she replied as they walked towards her car. Malik stared at his mother as she drove. Over the years he had seen her every weekend during visitation, but seeing her today was like seeing her for the first time in a long time.

He couldn't put his finger on it but something about her was different. He didn't know if it was that she seemed much smaller to him because he had grown so much, or the fact that her hair color had changed from the jet black that he remembered as a child to a full head of gray. Maybe it was how peaceful she looked now that he was sitting across from her in the car as opposed to sitting across from her in the gymnasium during visiting time. He couldn't remember a time when she looked more at peace when she came to see him. He could only remember expressions of pain, hurt, and worry that she often tried to camouflage. Seeing her now made him realize that all of those times he thought that it was something out in the world that had her feeling like that -that something was him.

"Malik, why are you looking at me like that boy?"

"I'm just looking. I can't look at my mother?" She smiled.

"Boy you're something else."

"But you love me though."

"You know I do. Now where am I taking you before we go to the house? You know I been up all night making your favorite meal?"

"Stop playing. You made turkey spaghetti with the garlic bread?"

"Yes, I made turkey spaghetti with the garlic bread," she repeated, mocking Malik.
Malik's mouth watered at the sound of his favorite dish. A dish that only his mom could make the way

he liked. He tried to make the meal in prison with the turkey sausage his mother used to send him in his food packages. It just wasn't the same cooking with stingers and hot pots.

"Ah man, yeah we gotta hurry up and get home," said Malik. "You don't know how long I've been waiting to eat some of that."

"Well it'll be there when we get there, now where we are going?"

"I gotta go downtown Elizabeth to report to parole first, then I'm good. That's it. We can go home after that."

"Okay, Elizabeth it is then."

As Malik sat there waiting for his name to be called, he saw familiar faces that he hadn't seen in years, even before he had gone to prison. Then there were others that were unfamiliar, that looked at him as if they had recognized him and knew who he was. He had never been on parole before. He had only heard stories about it from other inmates that caught violations for new charges or dirty urines. He didn't expect it to be like this. You sat around in a lobby full of convicted felons and waited until your name was called like you were at a busy fast food restaurant. He thought that it would be an in and out process. He knew the fact that he was out would be all over town even before he made it home, and that is not what he wanted. But, their wasn't anything that he could do about it, because

47

the streets were always watching and sound traveled.

The young white woman stuck her head out of the doorway and yelled.

"Malik Jones?" Malik heard his name called and knew that if anyone who thought that they had known him but doubted whether it was really him or not- their suspicion had been confirmed. After the woman blurted out his government like he had just won the Lottery, "Right here," he answered.

"Come with me."

After an hour and fifteen minutes of listening and being explained the formalities and conditions of his parole by the female officer, Malik was relieved to be getting out of the parole office. He could tell by her demeanor that Ms. Jensen was a real piece of work, but he didn't think that he would have any problems with her. A lot of things that she spoke about and said she didn't tolerate didn't apply or pertain to him anyway. He didn't drink and he definitely didn't use drugs. To show good faith, he gave her $100 of the money that he had earned in prison to go towards his $5,000 fine. She was both surprised and impressed by the gesture. Not many had come home and started making payments on their fines their first day out. Malik caught the pleasing expression on her face and knew why. After all, that *was* what it was all about anyway, Malik thought. It was all about money and politics. Over crowd the jails then release some of them so that they can pay their criminal fines and fees, and then take the money and build more jails so that they can make more money by housing more inmates, getting at least $35,000 a year for each inmate.

Malik stood there waiting anxiously for the elevator so that he could be on his way. Being in the heavily crowded room with the other parolees made him feel like he was still confined and he needed some fresh air. When the elevator opened, Malik stepped forward but someone getting off ran right into him. When the two of them made eye contact, he recognized who it was he had just bumped into.

"Pardon me," said the kid, not realizing who Malik was, even after looking up and seeing his face.

"No problem akh."

It wasn't until he had heard the familiar deep voice that it had registered to him. Just before the elevator closed Malik heard his name.

"Malik?" The kid asked, unsure.

"What up Pete?"

"Oh shit! Nah, not my mu'fuckin' manz!" Pete blurted out as he threw his arms around him and hugged Malik.

"What's the deal my dude."

Malik refused to return the embrace, but Pete hadn't noticed. Malik had prepared himself for situations like this in hopes that he would be able to keep his cool. He knew that whenever someone like Pete or one of his other so-called manz saw him again they would act as if it was all love. The scenario that he was presented with at that moment had played in his head so many times and he often wondered how he would really handle it. And now, here it was he was maintaining his composure like a trooper.

"Nothing much," Malik replied.

"Damn kid, you looking good, I didn't even recognize your ass. When you come home, today?"

"Yeah," replied Malik, remaining cool on the outside despite how he felt inside. Here it was, it had been ten years since Pete and the rest of his so-called manz left him for dead, and now Pete was standing before him as if there was no tension between them.

"Damn nigga, it's been a long time. It's good to see you."

"You too," Malik dryly replied.

"Yo, where you stayin'? I know you need some shit just comin' home we'll come scoop you and take you shoppin' and shit." Malik's first instinct was to haul off and punch Pete in the mouth for even coming at him like that. He couldn't believe Pete's cockiness like he was some sort of shot caller Back in the day Pete would've never tried to play big shot in front of him and stunt like Malik needed him, because he knew that Malik would have checked him- maybe even smacked the taste out of his mouth. On top of that he couldn't believe that Pete had offered to show his fake ass love as if he had been showing it all these years. *Where were you ten years ago when I really needed you*, Malik wanted to say, but instead he maintained his emotions.

"I'm staying at my moms, but I'm good, I don't need anything."

"Come on kid, this me, Pete. Big as you is I know you can't fit none of your old shit, plus that shit out dated anyway, so I'mma come and get you later and set you out. You home now nigga so that ain't about nothing," Pete said firmly as if he wasn't going to take no for an answer. This nigga had grown a lot of balls over the years Malik thought to himself. It was funny to him how money changed people. Malik thought back to when he was in jail, how all he use to hear some of the other dudes from the town talk about how Cheddar, Pete, and Doub were doing their thing in the game. Everyone had assumed that they were still his manz, and envied him because they knew he would be able to go home and get set up lovely when he touched. Unlike some of them who had to go back out there and start all over from scratch.

Malik was pretty much in the same predicament, because the same dudes he thought were his manz and 'em that were out there getting money, were the same niggas that were shitting on him while he was on lock down.

As he stood in front of Pete, a quote from Kwawe popped into his head, "Keep your friends close and your enemies closer." As that came to his mind, against his better judgment, Malik decided to take Pete up on his offer. If he wanted to show Malik

51

some fake love because of his guilty conscious then Malik intended to take full advantage of the situation and let him.

"If that's what you wanna do," Malik answered nonchalantly. "You remember where my mother lives?" Malik asked believing that Pete really had.

"No doubt, how could I forget. I know where ma stay," Pete replied as if he had just visited Malik's mother yesterday.

"How you gonna ask me something like that dawg," Pete asked. And what you mean if that's what we wanna do?" Malik didn't even answer him. He couldn't take it anymore.

"Yo, let me get up outta here, my moms outside waitin for me." When Malik heard Pete refer to his mother as "ma" it almost made him physically lash out at him. How could Pete call his mother ma and say he still knew where she lived, yet he, Cheddar nor Doub had been over to see or check on her once since Malik had been locked up. Not to check on her and the kids or to give her some money for him, Malik wanted to know. If he stood in front of Pete any longer and let him talk, he may eventually have said something that Malik would let catch his vein, causing him to act other than himself towards Pete.

"Alright, tell her I said hi."

"Yeah," Malik replied nonchalantly knowing he never would.

"Yo, again, it's good seeing you my dude, welcome home."

"Good to be home."

CHAPTER FOUR

JUST the way he remembered, Malik thought, as he stepped into the two bedroom apartment he once lived in as a child. At first, he thought that it had gotten smaller, but then realized that it was just that he had gotten bigger. He wasn't complaining though, because after living at his last residence for the past ten years, living in a cardboard box out on the street was an improvement. At least you had your freedom. He recognized every piece of furniture in the house as he stared at the printed light green pullout couch in the living room that he use to sleep on when his manz spent the night, before the streets had separated them. Malik reminisced on how they would stay up late watching Hot Trax, trying to see the naked white girls on channel 72 U-station on the black and white television, which was now replaced by a colored one. He also thought about the times that very same pull-out became the place where he laid his head once his two sisters had taken his old room, when he got knocked off board while hustling and couldn't pay his rent, or when him and his girl had beef and she kicked him out. Even though he was paying the bills, only her name was on the lease.

As he looked, he noticed some old pictures of himself that he hadn't seen since he had taken them. Flicks that went as far back as "88" when a high top fade was the hair-cut to have, and everybody was hustling to get a phat chain like a flat or a Gucci link from off of Canal St. and leather Gucci, Polo, MCM jackets from Dapper Dan's or 125 Mart. Who could forget the velour sweat suits, Malik thought, as he picked up one of the picture frames with him and his four manz in the flick on 42nd street. "The Deuce," they called it remembered Malik, before all the Mickey Mouse tourist attractions. Damn those were the days, he continued down memory lane. But those were all things of the past now. Malik made a mental reminder to himself to question his moms about having the picture up with him and the dudes that had betrayed him. Just seeing Phil in the photo with his arm around him left a bad taste in Malik's mouth despite how far he had come and how much he had grown. His mother even had pictures out of him that really took him back when he was still a little shortie back in elementary and Junior H.S., with his Cocoa-Cola sweat shirt on and his Cazal glasses. Now realizing how country he really looked, Malik smiled thinking back to how fly he thought he was. He wished that he could turn back the hands of time and go back to that era when his biggest worry was losing a snapping battle at lunch time in the cafeteria, or getting loaded up with homework for school breaks. He knew that he could never get those days back, because too much had

happened in his life, and he was now a man with a
criminal record- a black man at that. The more he
thought about how he became a convicted felon, the
more it angered him. This was something that he
had worked on getting over during his years in
prison. Nevertheless, this would haunt him for the
rest of his life, no matter how much he had grown.
Hearing his name being yelled snapped Malik out of
his thought. Not really recognizing the familiar
voices that sounded different over the prison phones
all these years. When he turned in the direction in
which they were coming from, he lit up at the sight
of his two little sisters who stood before him
looking all grown up. Just as he was able to fully
turn his body, both Jackie and Mandy bum-rushed
him and embraced him.

"I can't believe you're here!" Jackie was the first
to scream through her cries.

"Oh my god! Welcome home. We missed you so
much!" Mandy followed, running and flying into
their brother's embrace. You could tell that she too
was crying. Malik held them both in his arms
choked up himself at the reunion. They continued to
babble through their sobs, he kissed them both on
the top of their heads. It felt like an eternity since
the last time he had saw his little sisters. He had
missed out on so much being away.

"I missed yall too," was all he said.

Ms. Jones just stood there and watched the
reunion. Many nights she prayed to The Lord to
bring her family back together. Today her prayers

were answered. If she were to drop dead at that very moment, she would have died a happy woman she thought. In the absence of their fathers, she had done the best that she could to make sure that they would grow up to become something in life- have a better life than her and their fathers.

Malik and Mandy had the same dad, who Janet Brown married at the young age of 19 when Malik was 2 years old. At that time, Melvin Jones was one of Plainfield's biggest hustlers from out of the Second Street housing projects. Although Janet wasn't from the streets of Plainfield or any street for that matter, she was fascinated with the lifestyle that all the other girls in her school that dealt with hustlers, talked about. She doubted that she would ever have the opportunity to experience any of the glamorous stories that she had heard from her friends, like being taken on shopping sprees, getting her hair, nails and toes done every week, and being taken to nice restaurants and on trips and vacations, staying in fancy hotels. At the age of 15, or any other age, she knew that she didn't have luck like that.

One day while on her way home from school, after leaving Ferraro's pizza place with some of her friends, one of the most handsome guys she had ever seen blocked her path.

"Excuse me, can I get through," she said. Melvin looked at her and smiled.

"Of course you can, if you will do me one favor."

Janet gave him a puzzled look.

"I don't even know you," Janet replied.

"I know, and that's the favor I want to ask of you."

Now Janet was even more confused, because no one had ever talked to her the way that Melvin had. It wasn't that she wasn't pretty or anything, because she was beautiful. She had long, black, naturally silky hair, a butter pecan complexion, and a petite figure -thanks to the Cherokee Indian blood on her mother's side of the family. It was just that her shyness and quietness kept guys from talking to her, not to mention the fact that the whole school knew that she was a virgin, and wasn't putting out like some of the other girls in the school. But the stranger that refused to move out of her way until she did a favor for him seemed different.

"My favor is that you let me get to know you, and let me make you my wife," Melvin said in a bold manner. Janet smiled, but said nothing. Instead, she stepped off the curb and went around him. She walked right passed him shaking her head as her girlfriends followed. Melvin stood there admiring her as she put distance between them. He knew that there was something special about her, and he intended to pursue her until he found out. As they walked, one of her friends told her how crazy she had been for turning Melvin down. She thought any girl would have loved to be in her shoes at the time, because Melvin had it going on. Janet pretended to act like who he was and what he was about, didn't concern her, but the inside she regretted not introducing herself to him. The next day after school, Janet saw him again, only this time he was leaning up against a brand new looking Cadillac. All the girls in school were curious to know who he was waiting for, and was envious when they saw that it was Janet. At first, she contemplated whether she should act like she didn't see him, and keep walking, but the thought immediately went out the window when her girlfriends egged her on to approach him, and as shy as she was she did.

"What are you doing here?" she asked.

"Waiting for my future wife."

Janet smiled the way she did the day Melvin had made that comment about her becoming his wife.

"Why do you keep saying that?"

"Because it's true."

"How do you know that?"

"Because I'm gonna make it happen."

Janet didn't respond.

"Listen, I know that as beautiful as you are, dudes are stepping to you left and right, but if you give me a chance, I'll prove to you that I'm the one for you, just let me take you to get something to eat and we can talk," Melvin proposed.

The moment she agreed, and from that day forward Melvin picked Janet up from school, and introduced her to all the extravagant things in life that she had only heard stories about. He also let it be known that she was his girl and he was her man. In her junior year, she decided to give her virginity to Melvin because she loved him. Besides, he had been more than patient throughout the year and a half of their relationship. If she wasn't so naïve and knew what really went on with Melvin in the streets, she would have never allowed him to be in her life, let alone touch her. Not only did Melvin take her virginity, he took away her childhood as well, because Janet got pregnant. When she missed her period, she became worried, and instead of turning to her parents, she turned to Melvin. He expressed how happy he would be if she was carrying his first born. He told her how they'd get married, filling her young mind with dreams and false hopes. It wasn't until she was five months, and barely showing, that she had to come clean with her mother. She was caught vomiting in the bathroom one morning. She hadn't been to the doctor or anything, and her parents had been working so hard and so much that they hadn't noticed the changes. Both of her parents were outraged as well as shocked. Her mother, because Janet hadn't trusted her enough to come to her and confide in her, and her father because his little girl was no longer pure and innocent as he had thought. When her father found out the type of guy she had been dealing with, he demanded her to abort the child if she wanted to continue living under his roof, giving her an ultimatum. In an act of rebellion, Janet chose to leave, and moved in with Melvin, which was the biggest decision of her life that she would later on regret.

Melvin talked Janet into dropping out of school, while she was pregnant. He convinced her that she could go back later if she wanted to, after the baby was born. The day she gave birth, Melvin was nowhere to be found. This would have been a warning sign to any other woman; but when he finally showed up, he gave Janet some weak excuse and she bought it. They named their son Malik Melvin Jones, the opposite of Melvin's name, which was Melvin Malik Jones.

For the first year of little Malik's presence in the world, Melvin, Janet, and the baby had a family to be envied. When the second year came around things began to get shaky, and Melvin began staying out later and later. Sometimes even for the entire evening. He would always claim that he was out taking care of business. On her 19th birthday, Janet sat in the home in tears with Malik in her arms, waiting for Melvin to come home and take her out to celebrate her birthday. Melvin didn't show up until 4 A.M. the next day with roses in hand. Janet and Melvin had never had a fight or a heated argument their entire time as a couple. But that day Janet was so furious that she lashed out and charged at him in a blind rage. Melvin caught her by the wrists, as he weaved her kicks. He was trying to tell her to calm down but she didn't hear him through the screaming and yelling that she was doing. If it weren't for little Malik's cries, she would have continued cursing Melvin until she lost her voice. She snatched away from Melvin and went to her son. She picked him up and put him over her shoulder. When she turned around, Melvin was kneeling on one knee with a black velvet jewelry box in his hands opened, exposing the biggest diamond Janet ever saw. She was speechless.

"I'm sorry that I missed your birthday baby, but it wasn't my fault. You know I'd never do that intentionally, you're my heart and I love you. I just got back in town from Atlanta. I was picking up your gift and the traffic delayed me longer than I expected. Can you forgive me and do the honors of becoming Mrs. Melvin Malik Jones?"
New tears began to ball up in Janet's eyes, replacing the old ones. She had waited three years since the day Melvin had told her she would be his wife, and now that day had finally come.

"Yes, I will," she said as she laid Malik down, let Melvin put the ring on her finger and kissed him, forgetting about all the pain he had ever caused. Two weeks later they got married and honeymooned in Vegas. Nothing could've been better. Melvin was making more money, and moved them out of their one bedroom apartment into a home of their own. Janet enrolled in night school and got her diploma. While Melvin's mom's babysat Malik, she went to school for hair and nails. She still had no contact or communication with her own parents. When Malik was 7 ½, Janet found out that she was pregnant again, which was the turning point of her and Melvin's marriage. She expected

Melvin to be happy about the news, so when he suggested that she get an abortion, she was devastated. Lately, he had gone back to his old ways of staying out late, and being gone for days. She thought that the news of having another child would keep him closer to home. He had opened up a beauty salon for her when she graduated cosmetology school as a present. Over the years, it had become a popular spot for women to get their hair and nails done. It was notorious for being a haven for gossip. Ever so often, she would hear Melvin's name mentioned by some local or out-of-town female that didn't know who she was, only to be quieted by some other girl who did. She never confronted Melvin, not one time. She told Melvin that she refused to get an abortion, and that's when he dropped the bomb.

"Look, I'm stressed out right now and the last thing I need is to bring another kid into this world. I should've told you this a long time ago, but I ain't know how to because I didn't want to scare you away."
Janet's heart began to speed up, the first thing that popped into her mind was that Melvin had some life threatening contagious disease, and had given it to her.

"What? What is it?" Janet demanded to know.

"The reason why I'm always goin' to Atlanta so much is," Melvin paused and took a deep breath. "Because my wife and kids live down there."

As the words came out of Melvin's mouth, they shot straight into Janet's heart as if they were bullets, causing her stomach to knot up. She had cried many nights over the pain that Melvin had caused her. That night she refused to shed any tears. Instead she got up from the bed, started to dress, and began packing her and little Malik's bags. When Melvin realized what she was doing, he tried to grab her arm in an attempt to stop her. She pulled away from him, shooting him a look that could kill. He quickly backed off. At the time, she had no idea what she was doing or where she was going. She just knew that she had to get away from Melvin. When she was done, she snatched her son up, and carried him and the suitcases with their belongings out the door. Melvin spoke as she walked out, but his words went unheard. As she drove, her final destination was a mystery to her. She had a quarter tank of gas, and $43 dollars to her name. On top of that she was traveling with a child and one on the way. She was an only child. She had no siblings in which she could to turn to for any type of support and no real friends either. For the past nine years, her life had solely revolved around Melvin and her son. And now, she had no one she could call on. No one except the ones she had turned her back on years ago, choosing Melvin over them.

When the porch light came on, she saw her daughter standing there with suitcase in hand and a little boy at her side. Mrs. Brown immediately opened the door. It had been a long time since she

63

had seen or heard from her only child, and when she opened the door, rather than ask the obvious, she said nothing. She just embraced Janet with open arms, as Malik stood there watching.

In the beginning, her father was stubborn about accepting Janet's return, but that stubbornness soon melted away. After a few days with his only grandson, Malik became the son he never had but always wanted. After little Amanda Jones was born, a few months later her divorce to Melvin was finalized, and a heavy weight was lifted from her shoulders. He had no problem with agreeing to the divorce, which didn't surprise Janet. But he took the one thing from her that she enjoyed doing. He agreed to pay child support and alimony, but took the shop out of spite. Janet refused to let him break her spirits, and vowed to herself that she would never spend a dime of his blood money for her own benefit, and would only use whatever he sent for the kids only as a last resort.

It had been a little over a year, since she and Melvin's separation, and Janet began to established her own independence in the work field as a secretary at a well known corporation. She also managed to re-establish herself socially. It was then Janet met her soon to be third child's father, Jamar. She was skeptical at first; he had a lot of the same qualities as Melvin. But he was different. Jamar was good to her and her two children. She remembered how she was a little embarrassed about telling him that she had children, being so young. But Melvin put her at ease when he told her that she and her children were a package deal he'd love to invest in. Although she liked everything about Jamar, she knew that it would be a mistake to get involved with another man from the streets. She was living proof of the saying "good girls like bad boys". No sooner than Melvin moved her, Malik, and Amanda into a house, along came little Jacqueline Amira Lewis. Both Malik and Amanda were happy to have a new little sister, and they loved Jamar, as if he was their own father. But Janet was the happiest. She finally had the life she always wanted- beautiful children, a beautiful home, a career, a loving companion, and a relationship with her parents. She couldn't ask for anything more.

Just when she thought her life was as perfect as perfect could get, she was awakened by a phone call in the middle of the night. Jamar had been killed in a drug related robbery. Janet felt as if her whole world had fallen apart, and she couldn't go on living. On top of that, Jamar's family wanted her and the kids to move out of the house. It was in his mother's name, and she didn't know anything about Janet. They thought that she was one of his tricks living off of him for free with a bunch of rug rats to feed. She didn't even know that the youngest of the three was in fact her own grandchild. Janet didn't bother to volunteer that piece of information, because she didn't think that it would change anything. Instead, she took the

$25,000 that Jamar told her would always be in the safe in case of an emergency and moved out of the house. From that day on, she knew that she would never deal with another man from the streets again. Malik was 13, Amanda was five, and little Jackie was about to turn one, when Jamar was killed. Jackie was too young to be affected, and Amanda was at the age where it really didn't matter. Malik was a different story.

When they moved into the West Second street housing projects, it began to show. The first time Janet really had suspicion that Malik was involved in things he had no business being in, was when she got a call from the police station telling her to come pick him up. He had been arrested for possession of narcotics. When they got home, Malik told her that the package of drugs was found by his foot because one of the other boys dropped it and he didn't know until the police officer accused him of being the owner. Although Janet had been involved with two men from the streets, still she wasn't from the streets, so she believed Malik's story the first time, opening a door for more stories to come. She did not want to believe that what her son had been exposed to early on in his life by his father and her youngest daughter's father had impacted the decisions and choices he was making as a young man. As time went on, it was evident that it in fact had.

There were times when Janet cleaned Malik's room and stumbled across a new pair of

sneakers or an outfit that she knew she hadn't
bought for him. When she confronted Malik about it
he would credit one of his friend's parents, claiming
they had bought it for him, or a friend let him
borrow them. One particular day, while Janet was
getting ready to go to the laundry mat, she went to
Malik's room to change the linen on his bed. When
she lifted his mattress to strip the bed, she didn't
want to believe her eyes. But Janet knew that she
had perfectly good vision and her eyes were not
deceiving her. Lying there as clear as day was a zip
lock bag with packs of what she knew had to be
drugs. Considering the rubber-banned knot of
money, and the black semi-automatic 25 beside it,
Janet knew that her son was hustling, and for
sometime now. Janet was furious. Tears began to
form in her eyes, as disappointment and anger
flooded her heart. She snatched everything up that
laid on the mattress and took it to her room. Tears
burned her eyes as she waited for Malik to come
home to confront him. She had enough. This time
she had something solid and refused to accept any
of his excuses. When Malik finally arrived home,
Janet tore right into him. Never in a million years
would she have thought Malik would have said
what he had that day.

"Ma, all I'm trynna do is make enough money to
take care of you and the family the way Jamar use
to. I just wanted to be the man you needed me to be,
not a coward like my dad was." A sharp pain
stabbed at Janet's heart at the sound of her son's

words. She was no longer in a state of rage. She had calmed. Instead of continuing her reprimand and putting her foot down, Janet blamed herself for allowing her children to be subjected to the negative things that surrounded their lives. By dealing with men from the streets, and having to raise her family in an environment that was flooded with drugs and breeded violence, Janet could only imagine what Malik indulged outside of her household. Hearing her son's words was a reality check for Janet. She listened as Malik told her how he was saving up his money to move them out of the ghetto and back into a place like Jamar provided. He was only a young boy, yet he was depriving himself of his youth, as he tried to be a man. If she had only been strong enough back then to tell Malik that what he was doing didn't make him a man. She thought, If Jamar was still around maybe Malik's life would've turned out differently. Nevertheless, she loved him and she knew that no matter what she said, he would continue to do whatever it was he was doing—with or without her consent. As far as Janet was concerned he was already too far gone. She could see it in his eyes. There was an unmistaken look that she had seen in both Melvin and Jamar's eyes. So, against her better judgment she chose to accept her son's behavior, a decision that she would later regret.

As Malik hugged his two little sisters, he noticed his mother standing afar staring at them. He could tell that she was crying, and he knew that it was because she was happy.

"Ma, come here," he called out, and his mother walked over towards them.

Malik opened his arms wider and his mother joined the embrace. To Malik, it didn't get any better than that. He was home now, a free man, and he was back with the three most important people in his life.

"I love ya'll," he said.

"We love you too," they all replied.

CHAPTER FIVE

PQTQ was glad to be leaving his parole officer. He
was growing tired of playing the role like he had
just gotten off of work. He reported in like he
always did, every other Tuesday. He always had to
laugh at how easy it was to beat the parole system.
Here it was, he was still hustling, partying, drinking
and smoking weed, all the things that had landed
him a one to three in the first place. They had no
clue. He thought he had it all figured out. He had
never worked an honest job a day in his life. He
didn't have any intention of doing so, not as long as
he had connections that supplied him with pay stubs
to support his story he told to his P.O. Whenever he
went to parole, he would always take a bottle of
clean urine with him in a little bottle that sat in stash
spot in his underwear. In six months he would be
off of parole though, and it would all be over. No
more reporting. No more piss tests. No more jails.
In six months he would officially be a free man and
wouldn't have to answer to anyone. As he got into
his SUV and unlocked his glove compartment to

pull out his jewels, his thoughts went back to Malik, whom he ran into earlier. It had been a long time since he had seen Malik, and it was good to see him. A lot of time had passed and people changed. He knew that he, Cheddar, and Doub had not held Malik down the way they should have when he was in prison. That was something he truly regretted. Cheddar had even fucked with his girl. Then tried to justify it by saying he was only proving that she wasn't right in the first place. Either way, Malik was home now and all Pete could think about was how he just wanted things to be like they were before Phil had pulled that snake shit and snitched on his man. Since that day, they reneged on paying for Malik's lawyer, Cheddar never mentioned him. Pete and Doub reminisced about the fun times they had when Malik was rolling with them. He couldn't wait to tell Cheddar and Doub that he was home. He definitely planned to pick him up and take him shopping like he said he would. After all, Malik was still his man, and when one of your own came home from doing a bid, you showed them love. There was no doubt in his mind that like himself, both Cheddar and Doub would be willing to set Malik out real proper and welcome him home with open arms.

CHAPTER SIX

" **HEY** Doub," the girl with the pretty caramel complexion said as she opened the door.

"What up Nik? Where's Cheddar?"

"He's in the back."

"Aight," he said stepping into the apartment. Nikki closed the door behind him and walked passed him heading towards the kitchen.

"Damn Nik, you getting thick ma," Doub said seeing how healthy Nikki looked in her jean shorts. He had seen her plenty of times with shorts on and off- back in the day when he sexing her here and there. She wasn't as thick as she was now. She wasn't Cheddar's wifey, so he didn't feel as if he was disrespecting him or her by saying what he said. Any female that wasn't the main chick or wifey was fair game unless she was your main side chick. Then, she was off limits. But Nikki wasn't any of the above, so it was whatever. Besides, he knew that he could still sex her whenever he felt like it and Cheddar wouldn't care less. All their lives they slept with women behind each other and even ran trains on chicks that got down like that. He made a mental note to check for Nikki in the future to see if she could work those hips just as good as she could when she wasn't that thick. Nikki just turned around and flashed him a smile and a look as to say, "Yeah nigga I know I got my weight up!"

Doub smiled on the inside, and headed towards the back before he forgot why he really came over there.

"Knock! Knock! Knock!"

"Yo?"

"Ched, it's me my dude, you good?"

"Yeah, come in."

Cheddar was sitting on the bed counting a bunch of money. Doub knew it was that time for him, Pete, and Cheddar to get together and tally up so they could re-up again. They had been a team now for the past ten years.

"What up my dude?" Cheddar said while still focusing on the counting he was doing with the stack of 100's in his hand.

"I can't call it," said Doub.

"Where you comin from?"

"I just got back from Atlantic City, me and shortie from New Brunswick."

"Word? Who? That chick you met at Studio 9?"

"Yeah her."

"Damn, that chick was serious. Fat ass! She's a dancer right?"

"She used to dance out here when Knockers was open and before Richmond shut down, but she don't dance no more."

"That's what her mouth say. Bet'cha we can catch her ass up in Cindy's on the late night when we makin' it rain up in that piece," said Cheddar.

"I don't give a fuck."

"Oh, you must'a did you?"

"With what? Her or gambling?"

"Both nigga."

"Yeah, no doubt, I hit all around the board," Doub said laughing.

"Lucky ass nigga," Cheddar shouted, joining him in laughter.

"How much you hit for?"

"I hit' 'em for like 13 and some change on the crap table. You know they ain't want me leavin' wit that shit so they set me up wit the complimentary room and all that. When shortie seen how I did my thing and how they set me out, she threw the ass on me. So, I smashed twice that night, rolled over in the morning and beat it up again," Doub said with a smile on his face.

"Damn, I gotta step my shit up and get at her partner then. I saw her up in Richmond Beer Gardens, poppin' that thing. She wanted a nigga to hit her with some dollars but I wanted to break her off and get up outta there, broad was frontin' though. Why you ain't hit a nigga up? We could've dipped down there together and probably switched on them chicks or something or did our one two on ya little chick," said Cheddar.

"I wasn't even thinking about that, I scooped shortie on some spur of the moment shit and she just rolled wit it. But that ain't about nothing, we can still set that up for this weekend or something, cause shortie shit was good anyway."

"Yeah, that's what's up, we can do that. What up though, what made you come over here?"

"Oh yeah, I almost forgot. Yo, after I dropped home girl off, I shot downtown to get me a pack of wife-beaters and I ran into Wop from the Bricks and we started vibin' and shit. Then out the blue the nigga says when he was at parole earlier he thought he saw Malik."

The sound of the name instantly grabbed Cheddar's attention. He discontinued counting the bills, wanting to know if his ears deceived him. There was only one person named Malik that he could think of or had really mattered to him.

"Malik?"

"Yeah nigga. Malik. You don't know who the fuck that is no more?" Doub asked.

As if it just dawned on him, Cheddar repeated his question, only this time he knew who Doub was referring to.

"Malik? Our Malik? Get the fuck outta here."

"Son, that's what the nigga told me. He said he wasn't sure cause the nigga he saw was all cock diesel and shit, but it looked like him. I did hear that the nigga had got his shit all the way up to the ceiling though on some braulic type shit, so it could've been him."

"Damn, how long has it been?" asked Cheddar.

"Ten joints since that bitch ass nigga Phil crossed him like that."

"Word it's been a minute."

"Yeah no doubt, and if it's true that he's out we gonna have to holla at the nigga and see where his head is at, cause you know how that nigga was before. That's our manz and 'em, but he was on some rah-rah shit before he got knocked, and we don't need that right now. Plus that shit with Dawn, son might be feelin' some type of way about that."

"Nah son," Cheddar said. "You know that nigga was never weak for a bitch. We both knew that bitch wasn't shit. He knew that too, so that ain't about nothing, but he might be feelin' some type of way about that lawyer shit. We just got to let him know that we was fucked up back then, but it's all love now. He ain't gonna want for nothing now that he home. If the four of us hook back up, we'll take this muthafuckin town over kid. Where that nigga Pete at anyway?" Cheddar asked.

"I don't know, but I know today was his day to see his P.O. too. Maybe he seen the nigga Malik, if that was him."

"Yeah. Maybe. Call him and see where he's at."

Pete was just coming up on the Ave. when his cell phone rang.

"Yo," he answered.

"P, this Doub, where you at?"

"I'm just pullin' up around the New now, I can see your truck from here. You in it?"

"Nah, I'm in building 524 at Nikki's crib with Cheddar."

"Aight, I'll be there in a minute."

"Knew your ass wasn't far behind when Double came here," Nikki said when she opened the door for Pete.

"What's up Nikki, wit ya fine ass," Pete said, wishing he had the pleasure of tapping that like Cheddar and Doub had.

He could've had her, but he had sexed her sister. She didn't do the family thing, at least that's the excuse she had given him, and he rolled with it. Even though she still let him eat her out.

"Nothin much, just chillin," she replied.

By the way Pete looked Nikki up and down she already knew what he was thinking.

"I know. My ass got fatter. You three niggas is just alike. Always thinking wit your dicks."

Pete laughed, because that's exactly what he was thinking.

"Where they at, in the back?"

"Yeah."

"Aight, be good, and tell ya sister I said what up."

"You tell her, I don't fuck wit her like that no more."

Pete didn't comment. He just walked to the back, because whatever they were beefing over was none of his business or his concern.

"What's good?" he said giving Doub a pound and a hug, then doing the same to Cheddar.

"What up kid? Where you was at?" Doub asked.

"Just came from parole."

"That's what I figured."

"Yo, you saw Malik?" Cheddar asked.

Pete was surprised by the question.

"What? How you know that?"

Both Doub and Cheddar looked at each other.

"So it is true, the nigga home huh?" asked Cheddar.

"Yeah, I bumped into 'em and we kicked it for a minute. He was leaving when I got there. He said his moms was waitin' for him outside. I told the nigga I was gonna come scoop' em and take him shoppin'."

"What he say?" Doub wanted to know.

"He told me to come thru."

"Word?"

"Yeah, I was on my way to come find ya'll to let ya'll know, see what you wanted to do, cause I know son fucked up on the gear and shit, cause the nigga got his weight up for real."

"We heard," Cheddar said.

"What else ya'll talk about?" Doub asked.

"Nothin' really, I just told him it was good to see him and that I was comin' thru to get' em. He ain't say too much, he was on some quiet shit. He didn't look the same and he don't seem like he the same. He looks like prison mellowed him out or something."

"It's the nigga first day home, it's too early to tell what's really good," Cheddar said.

"What? What the fuck are you niggas talking about?" An agitated Pete asked.

"What's that suppose to mean? One of our manz just came home and you actin' like you don't know who it is. Nigga, this Malik we talking about, not no stranger or no bitch nigga like that nigga Phil. He the same nigga that use to bust his gun when we had beef or be the first muthafucka to hook off on a nigga if they fucked wit us. He the same nigga that hit us wit paper when we was fucked up and didn't ask for it back when we got back on board, and he the same nigga we broke bread wit, so I don't know what the problem is, but with or without you niggas, I'm going to show him mad love," ended Pete.

"Pete, cool out, ain't nobody got no problem wit Malik," Doub replied. "We just wanted to know where his head was at. When he left, we all was still young niggas trying to find our places in the game, we weren't strong like we are now. That nigga Malik always been strong, and he was wild too, but it ain't about that no more. We done came up while he's been knocked, and we wanna stay on top. So we just making sure that he ain't comin' home on no other shit like the game owe him something-getting the block all hot. You know how some niggas do when they come home, they be having attitudes and shit like they mad at the world. That's when the bullshit starts. Look at niggas like Sheed and them, trying to come out here wit their weight all up trying to take over and shit, and what happened? Either they got bodied by some young nigga who don't give a fuck about how they was doin' it back in the day or they got knocked cause they jumped back in the game too quick. We don't want that to happen to Malik, that's all."

"Yeah," Cheddar followed up.

Pete studied the both of them. He felt what Doub was saying and agreed with him. The last thing he wanted to see was something happen to Malik after being in the belly of the beast for the past ten years.

"I feel you Doub, my bad, I took shit the wrong way."

"That's aight, I know you glad he home. We are too, and we gon' make sure he aight."

"No doubt," Cheddar said. "Matter -fact, Im'ma take anything over the 50g mark of this shit and we can take him to New York. Help me count the rest of this," Cheddar said to Doub and Pete. "It should come to about 60 something."

"With the seven I took with me to Atlantic City and the 18 I won, I got 25 on me anyway Doub said.

"I already snatched 20 before I came over here so I can spend 10 on him and put 10 in his pocket," Pete told them.

"That's love," Cheddar replied. "You been around the back yet?"

"Earlier, before I went to parole."

"What was good with the lil homies around 116?"

"They said they was gonna hit me when they was ready to do something. That building is on fire,

you know them lil wild ass niggas beefin' again,"
Pete laughed.

"With who?" asked Cheddar.

"I don't know, I just told 'em to holla if they
need more hardware.

"No doubt, you did right.

"Them lil niggas stay in some shit," added Doub
shaking his head.

"Word," agreed Pete. "Oh! Rik said he spoke to
Rock and Lump."

"What he say they talkin' about. Did he say
when them dudes touchin'?" Cheddar inquired.

"Next year some time."

"Both of 'em?" asked Doub.

"That's what he said."

"The hood really gon' be off the hook for the
summer."

"I was thinkin' the same thing when he told me,"
Pete retorted.

"Yo, speaking of summers," interjected Doub.
"What was the best one for the New? Let me see if
you niggas know ya history."

"Nigga that's too easy," Cheddar was the first to
say. "92. That's when the New was the New. We
had whips parked from Plainfield Ave to Liberty St.
out this mu'fucka."

"Word up," Pete added. I was makin' weight
money hand to hand back then. I remember I came
out one mornin' and made twelve grand before
school let out, then struck' em for like six in cee'lo
in the middle."

"Yeah 92 was serious," reminisced Pete. "And all the homies was home then, Everybody was eatin', Squirm and Peter Pan, Chet and Doma, Krush and Wajdee, Money, Pookie and Ryan, Buie, Raheem, every mu'fuckin body dawg," added Doub.

"Hold on my dude," said Pete. "How you gonna forget the mu'fuckin big dawg?" he questioned.

"Who?" Doub asked puzzled.

"Who?" repeated Pete. "Nigga, the red Volvo, the white one, the 745. Is you stupid? Tizzlamallah-b-god, that's who."

"Oh shit. No doubt," replied Doub as if it had just dawned on him. "Tizz. Can't forget the big homie," Doub admirably said.

"Aight that's enough of all that shit," Cheddar interjected. "Those days are over. Love is love but let's focus on handlin' this right here so we can get up outta here. We can bounce as soon as we finish this, but what about that other thing though?"

"The sun won't go down without that being taken care of."

"That's what it is."

CHAPTER SEVEN

" **DAMN** lil nigga why you runnin' with the paper?" Dee voiced as Ski collected the large stacks of bills he just won off the table.

"I did what I came to do daddy, I'm out," was Ski's response without even looking up. He was too busy shoving monstrous knots of cash into each available pocket of his North Face snorkel.

"Scared money don't win no money youngin," Dee's partner Al followed up, in hopes that Ski would change his mind about leaving. Thanks to Ski's strong arm tonight, Al too had lost. Combined, in less than an hour's time, Dee and Al had dropped and lost over 15grand at the gambling spot to Ski. Now, they were chasing for some get back. Normally, it would be them who had other gamblers trying to convince them to stay until the sun came up so that they could at least win some, if not all that they had lost that night. Tonight was Ski's night. Ever so often, Dee would watch the take that Ski would scoop over to him after rolling an unbeatable point on the dice. He estimated that Ski was up at least 20 grand for the night. It really didn't matter to Dee one bit though. That was chump change to him, Dee told himself. Especially since he was getting keys of coke for 10 grand and moving them for 21- four and five at a time. His thing was gambling; he enjoyed it, which is why he only hated losing to someone who wasn't a true gambler like he thought himself to be. The thrill of gambling for Dee, whether he'd won or loss, was knowing that he would see those who he had beaten out of their money or had loss to again. This was his first time ever seeing Ski in the gambling hall and was sure that it would be his last and didn't like the fact at all, but still he brushed it off and chalked the few grand he lost up as a loss.

"Punk ass," Dee couldn't help but mumble before letting it go.

Ski ignored the comments and side bar of the other gamblers, particularly Dee's. He knew who Dee was as well as his reputation. Nothing or no one was going to intimidate or bully him into staying to continue. After geeing off on the block earlier Ski shot up to the east end of town to a known spot, where he could get his gamble on, in hopes to add to the 16 hundred he made on the block. Never did he think he would have such luck and leave out of the gambling hall nearly 20 gees richer. Ski remembered hearing stories about some of the town's major money getters like Azzie, Devine, and Bisquit from the Bricks, and Money Kev hitting for major paper up in the historical spot. Now after tonight, his name would be mentioned among those veterans. Ski grinned at the thought.

"Aight, old head, I'm gone baby," Ski said to the owner of the establishment, embracing the elderly man.

"You good?" the owner asked.

"Definitely," Ski replied already knowing what the man had been asking.

"Okay then, see you around young blood."

"I should rob ya lil punk ass," Dee yelled with laughter in his words to camouflage his seriousness. He just couldn't let the young kid walk out without feeling uneasy. Occasionally, in his younger years, he had done exactly what he had just said he should do to Ski to others. But Ski paid the threat no mind. He knew Dee was short tempered and would try to carry out the threat if he felt the mood, but unbeknownst to Dee, Ski was itching to test out the new Desert Eagle he possessed under his North Face.

The door buzzed open and Ski exited the gambling hall, making his way to his Expedition. It was cold out. Colder then when Ski had first arrived at the spot. To minimize the chill breaking through, Ski zipped up the neck of his jacket with one hand and deactivated the alarm on his SUV with the other. As he reached the front of his truck, something out of the corner of his left eye caught his attention.

Turning in the direction, out of reflex, Ski reached for his weapon.

"I wish you would," the un-identified voice spit. Give me a reason."

Ski instantly dropped his intended gun hand, not wanting to be a hero or statistic.

"You know what it is," the voice said stepping in front of Ski's view.

It didn't take a genius to figure out that Ski had been caught slipping.

"Nigga open ya mouth," the gunmen snarled, forcing the muzzle of the chrome pistol into Ski's mouth as he unarmed him. Between the black mask the perpetrator wore, the darkness of nightfall, and the blind side he'd been caught on, it was impossible for Ski to get a visual clue on the violator. Whoever it was had hell to pay whenever word leaked out on the streets thought Ski.

"Fuck you was gonna do with this?" the gunmen taunted Ski, shoving Ski's Desert into his waistband. Ski remained silent and stood stoned face.

"Oh, you a lil tough nigga huh? Let's see how tough you are in this backyard mu'fucka," the gunmen growled grabbing a fistful of Ski's jacket. At the sound of the words backyard, Ski's mind instantly began to go into over-drive.

Think Ski. Think. Ski told himself. There was no way he was going to be lead or forced into someone's backyard. This was not the way his final fate was intended to be, he thought. With that at the forefront of his mind, Ski sprung into action.

"Yo, I got a lot of paper on me. Just killed' em in there. Take this shit daddy, we ain't gotta go to no back," Ski tried to reason, but to no avail.

"Shut the fuck up," the gunmen growled, raising his gun hand in attempts to assault Ski with his pistol. It was either now or never thought Ski. Again, reflexively Ski reached for the burner to avoid the blow.

"Nicca, fuck you doin?" the gunmen spit through clenched teeth, caught by surprise as he and Ski fought for control of the weapon.

Feeling his adrenaline pumping a hundred miles a minute, Ski began to feel an extra sense of strength over his intended robber. Ski was now applying massive pressure on the gunmen's wrist in hopes that it would be too much to bear and he would release the weapon. As they tussled, Ski could almost see the nozzle of the huge chrome pistol pointing in his direction. Seeing that, Ski shifted and attempted to maneuver to derail the view of the nozzle. He felt his grip on the gunmen's hand slipping and fought for control once again.

"Boom!"

Bright light and thunder was the last Ski had saw and heard before total darkness fell upon him.

CHAPTER EIGHT

" MA, I don't know what you did to that meal, but it was bangin," Malik said.

"Banging? Boy you home now, don't be talking that jail talk up in here."

Malik laughed. "Ma you crazy, that's not jail talk, I've been talking like that, I was just telling you that I enjoyed the food."

"I know what you were trying to say, and that's how you should've said it."

"You right ma," Malik understood where his mother was coming from. She didn't raise him to speak the way he had. Malik had learned that lingo in the streets- the same streets he once ran and the same streets that landed him in prison. After hearing his mom reprimand him on his choice of words, he realized that he still had to work on those same things that he worked on in jail, especially if he wanted to stay out of trouble.

Malik got up from the table and gave his moms a kiss on the cheek.

"Thanks ma. I have to go make my prayer and then I'm gonna take a bath."
She smiled. "I don't know if you're going to be able to fit in that tub with your big self."
Malik couldn't help but to smile at his mother's remark. He was a big guy, but nothing could stop him from doing what he dreamed about the entire time he was away. Being able to soak and wash the prison stench off of his bodies in a nice hot bath.

"If you can fit in there then so can I. After all, I take after my momma," Malik said laughing.

"Malik, don't make me hurt you," his mother jokingly replied. It was good to share a laugh with her son after having to share ten years of pain. Many nights after visiting him or speaking to Malik on the phone she prayed to God to return him back home safely. She cried herself to sleep blaming herself for all that Malik was going through. Over the years, she turned to God and became a very spiritual woman. It pleased her to hear that Malik found God while in prison. Even though they had different beliefs and often found themselves debating over theology, they both respected the other's religion.

It was good to see that Malik had come home and was still dedicated to his belief; it was through that his mother believed that he was a changed man, a better man and would be sincere about staying on the straight path. She knew that the devil had ways of tempting those who once worshipped him, but then broke free of his darkness

89

and entered into the light. Her only hope now that
Malik was home was that he had his head on
straight and his mind focused. But that choice was
Malik's to make, and whatever he decided, whether
right or wrong, good or bad, it would affect his life
forever.

CHAPTER NINE

AFTER being in the bathtub for almost 2 hours, Malik finished grooming and began dressing when he heard the doorbell ring. He figured his mother couldn't help it and called someone and told them the good news about him being home. He smiled and shook his head as he stared at himself in the mirror just before covering it to offer his prayer. Malik finished offering his final prayer for the evening in his mother's bedroom and began reading his Quran in it's authentic language. His years of attending Tahleem classes and Arabic classes faithfully on Mondays and Wednesdays had paid off. He smiled both on the inside and outside like he often did, at the beauty of the Arabic language and the power of its words delivered by God. He was so engulfed in his reading that he barely heard his mother's voice from the outside of her room door. It wasn't until he was bringing his reading to an end that he heard the muffled yell. Malik closed his Quran, removed the towels that he had thrown over the bedroom mirror & T.V. As he opened the room

91

door, he could hear his mother calling for him again, this time she could be heard clearer and much louder.

"Didn't you hear me calling you? "She asked, with hands on her hips as if she was agitated.

"I was reading and I just got finished praying." He detected some hostility in his mother's tone and immediately became alarmed, although he couldn't figure out why or where it was coming from. He knew that it wasn't because of what he told her he had just been doing because she out of all people could understand being the religious woman that she was. No, it could not have been that. He was sure. Something or someone had upset his mother. "Ma, what's wrong?" He asked baffled.

"Tsk! Nothing, you got company," Was her response. Malik looked around the corner, because there was no one standing in the living room besides the two of them and with the place being so small, you could scan the whole house in one spin. There was no one else in sight. "Who is it and where they at?"
Again his mother threw him a look of disappointment.

"It's that boy Pete. He's outside the door, I left his butt waiting on the porch."
Malik smiled. It was evident now why his mother, such a loving and protective mother was so upset. In her eyes, he had no right to be there. She could not believe his audacity to come around in attempts to befriend her son after all these years of

abandonment. Although she trusted her son, and
had faith in him, she didn't trust Pete. Malik was his
own man, and she had to let him be just that. Malik
had forgotten that he even told Pete where he would
be staying, and honestly thought that Pete was just
talking. Malik never thought he would show up
anyway. Especially, once his guilty conscious
kicked in and he realized how he, Cheddar, and
Doub left him for dead. Malik figured that being in
the streets, living a hardened life kills your
conscious. He was once guilty of being the same
way. It wasn't until he had gone to prison that his
mind began to clear, and remorse and regret became
a reality in his life. One thing he was sure of was
that if Pete was standing outside his mother's door
then he had already consulted with Cheddar and
Doub, because they were a team. That was the way
it had been when it was the five of them prior to
Phil flipping and Malik going to prison. He could
just about imagine how the meeting between the
three of them went. He was positive that if Pete was
standing outside that door then they all agreed to the
same thing. Instead of Malik telling his mother to
let Pete in, he approached the door and opened it.
His mother stood and watched. This was between
Malik and Pete. She could only be a spectator. Not
knowing the final outcome, but confident that in the
end Malik would come out victorious. being the
favorite. It was as though she were watching a
boxing match. She knew that mentally and
emotionally Malik had trained extremely hard for

this battle. In just the short time that he had been home, she noticed the drastic change in her son. Even though he would always be her baby, he was now a man. He was no longer a boy struggling to be a man. He had grown up; he was now a man. There was no doubt in her mind that Malik could handle the situation. Pete was standing there, with a friendly smile on his face, when Malik opened the door. Apparently, leaving Pete outside didn't faze him. He just didn't get the hint that he was not welcome at Malik's mother's house. Over Pete's shoulder, Malik could see the huge burgundy Yukon Denali, with tinted windows and large chrome rims.

"What's good my dude?" asked Pete.

"What up?" replied Malik nonchalantly.

"I told you I was comin' thru to scoop you. You ready?"

"Nah not really," said Malik feeling his mothers eyes piercing his back even before he had turned around. If looks could kill, he would've dropped dead right then and there. As their locked eyes, Malik's mother broke the stare first and walked away. She didn't have to see anymore to know the final outcome. To her, her son had just been knocked out in the first round. There was no way Malik could make his mother understand the reason he didn't tell Pete to get the hell off of their porch and slam the door in his face, without making her think that he was already back to his old ways. So, he didn't try to justify or attempt to explain why he

intended to leave with Pete. He knew he had to say
something. He couldn't just leave it as it was now.
Pete caught Malik's skepticism.

"Come on Leek, love is love. Folk and them out
there."
Malik knew who Pete was referring to, but that was
the least of his concern.

"Pee give me a minute, I'll be out."

"Yeah, no doubt," Pete replied with relief. He
had no clue what was going on. He didn't realize
just how much of a problem his presence caused. It
was between mother and son. Malik went to his
mother's room in attempt to enter, but the door was
locked, so he knocked on the door.

"What Malik?" she answered as if she had been
crying already.

"Ma, open the door." After a few seconds you
could hear the lock being unlocked, and Malik
opened the door, entering his mother's bedroom.
Ms. Jones sat there, with her Bible in her hand
reading.

"Ma, I'm stepping out for a minute, and I'll be
back, but I need you to trust me on this one, I know
what I'm doing, alright?"
Ms. Jones said nothing.

"Ma, say something." Still she said nothing,
instead she waved her hand in the way one does
when they are being bothered and wanted you to
leave them alone. It was not what Malik wanted or
expected, but he had to respect how his mother was

feeling right now. He turned around and began exiting the room.

"I Love You Ma," he said closing the door. A tear dropped onto the Psalm Ms. Jones read as the door closed.

"I love you too baby," she whispered, wishing Malik heard her. Malik put his sneakers on and headed out the door.

"You ready?" Pete asked.

"Yeah I'm ready." As they approached the truck, Malik could see images in the front seat through the tint of the SUV's windows.

"That's Cheddar and Doub in the truck right?" Malik asked making sure.

"You already know," Pete said making his way to the SUV.

Malik snickered to himself at how predictable the three of them were. After all these years they were still the same cats he remembered them to be, only older. Both Cheddar and Doub got out the SUV just as Malik reached it.

"Welcome home Leek," Doub was the first to say coming from around the drivers side.

"Yeah, welcome home my dude," Cheddar followed. Although he had grown up with the three of them, the situation seemed awkward. He studied Cheddar and Doub's faces, sensing uncertainty in them. The ten years had definitely put a strain on what they once thought to be an unbreakable bond. Although he didn't see a change in them, besides their financial status, Malik knew that *he* was a different person. Maybe they saw it in him as well. Their facial expressions confirmed it all. Silence filled the air for a moment as they all stood there, until it was broken by Pete.

"Yo, what up? Let's get up outta' here before the stores start closin' and Malik don't have nothin' to wear."
They stepped to the truck all at once.

"Yo, you wanna get in the front with Doub?" asked Cheddar.

"Nah, I'm good I'll play the back," replied Malik, as he opened the back door to the Yukon Denali. Everyone hopped in and Doub pulled off. Doub popped in his Dip-Set CD and turned up the volume. Malik could tell that Doub added some speakers and an amplifier by the surround sound effect of the music as Jim Jones' lyrics blared through the SUV. *"We fly high-No lie-you know it--- Ballin!"*
Being a music lover, the acoustics in the truck sounded good to Malik. Doub definitely had a nice truck. He saw that there were televisions in each headrest, one in the middle, between the front and the back that popped out from the roof, and one in the front seat which Cheddar was playing PS3 on. The middle television was playing the movie *The Inside Man.* Malik wasn't home when the new accessories for whips came out, but he liked the glamour of it all. The biggest SUV's out before he had left were the Land Cruiser, Wranglers, and Range Rovers. Malik was convinced that he wanted

an SUV after seeing the road runners on hip-hop
and R&B videos on BET, like Excursions, Yukon's,
Navigators, and Tahoe's. On television SUV's
looked huge, but to actually be inside one made you
realize just how large and spacious they really were.
Malik pondered, as they glided down the highway.
They continued to ride in silence until Doub pulled
out a blunt from the sun visor in attempts to light it.

"Yo, what the hell you doing nigga?" asked Pete
tapping Doub on the shoulder. Doub turned the
music down, not hearing what Pete said or why he'd
just tapped him.

"What up?" He asked puzzled, wanting to know
why Pete had interrupted his chill mode.

"What you mean what up? How you gonna try to
spark that shit up and know Malik just came home
and he on parole?"
Knowing that Pete was right, Doub took the
marijuana filled blunt from out his mouth and
placed it back in the sun visor.

"My bad yo, I'm buggin'. I ain't even think like
that, my bad Leek."
Malik gave Pete an appreciating look.

"Don't worry about it," Malik said to Doub. He
knew it wasn't intentional, but Pete wouldn't let it
go though. You know that shit get in your system
Doub. You remember I caught that dirty when I first
started taking urines before I started back smokin',"
Pete squawked.

"Yo, I said my bad kid, breathe easy," Doub
responded.

"Aight, it's over both you niggas chill." Cheddar interrupted as if he was their father. It has always been like that and Malik laughed to himself at how Pete and Doub still allowed Cheddar to control them. That was something he could never do with Malik or Phil. Out of the five-man team, they were the only two that ever stood up to Cheddar and voiced their opinion. Malik and Cheddar had two fights growing up and both times Cheddar had lost. Although Cheddar wasn't afraid of Malik, like the others had been, deep down inside Cheddar knew that Malik was much more thorough than he was. Cheddar caught the smile on Malik's face, knowing what it was about and used it as a door opener. "Malik, these two niggas still go at it like two little kids and I still got to break that shit up like pah-pah." Cheddar said. At that, Malik let out half of a laugh seeing how Cheddar said what he himself was just been thinking.

"Fuck you Ched," said Doub.

"Yeah nigga, fuck you. You ain't nobody fuckin' pah-pah. Don't be frontin' for Malik," Pete said turning on Cheddar.

"Yall niggas know yall my sons," was Cheddar's come back as he laughed.

"Yeah whatever dad," Doub said laughing to himself. "That nigga can't even have kids with his sterile ass, talkin' about some pah-pah."

"That come from getting burnt too much nigga," spit Pete as they all laughed. Cheddar was notorious for catching Gonorrhea back in the day when they were younger. The statement caused Malik to think about the time he and Cheddar had pulled a train on one of the project chicks and they both got burnt. Even up until this day Malik believed Cheddar gave it to the girl and since neither one of them used a condom, she in return gave it to Malik. They didn't come from an era where condoms were mandatory. AIDS wasn't an issue then. The only thing you could catch that wasn't curable when they were growing up was herpes, and even with that they had something you could take that minimized it. Malik had educated himself on diseases while in prison. Hearing so many horror stories while in prison, Malik felt you almost had to wrap your entire body up with a rubber just to be safe in this day and time. Despite being a foreigner to condoms, it was better to be safe than to be sorry he reasoned. There were countless times he put his life in jeopardy for a night of passion and pleasure, but Malik knew those days were far behind him. Hearing him laugh, Pete directed his words to Malik.

"I know you ain't laughin'? You and Cheddar use to be runnin' neck and neck on the clinic visits. Me and Doub use to bet to see who got burnt next. You two niggas probably got the V.I.P. treatment as much as your asses got stung up." By now they all were hysterically laughing, and for a brief moment Malik enjoyed the reminiscing session with his old friends, but in an instant he was shutdown remembering where he just came from and who he was now with. This was not about a reunion it was about getting what he could get while he could. Sensing the change in Malik, the laughter died down.

"Malik you alright?" Doub asked.

"Yeah I'm good," was all he said. Malik continued to contemplate his situation. *Malik, just maintain, you know they're trying to feel you out and see where your head is. You know they feel uncomfortable around you right now because they don't know what type of dude you are or you were. They know they did you wrong in the past. Set them at ease so they can relax, make them think everything is everything. You have the upper hand because you know what they're thinking, but they don't know what you're thinking. Capitalize off of that and use it to your advantage. You're a smart brother. So, be smart!.*

By now Doub had changed the CD to a local DJ by the name of DJ Phat Rodney and turned the music back up. Malik tapped him and gestured to turn the music back down.

"What up? It's too loud?" Doub asked.

"Nah, I just want to holla at you brothers right quick," answered Malik. With saying that, Doub turned the music completely off and Cheddar turned the Playstation off as well. They gave him their undivided attention.

"Yo, I just want to say that I ain't mad at you cats," Malik started out saying. "In the beginning I was feeling some type of way, but if anybody knows how the game goes it's me. How things went

down was all a part of the game, and I respect the
game to the fullest." Before Malik could continue
Cheddar tried to interrupt, but he cut him off.

"Nah, hold up. You don't have to justify nothin'
to me. What's done is done. That was then, this is
now. It is what it is. How that cat Phil went out on
me back then had nothing to do with any of you.
He's the crab, but even with that, I ain't mat at him
because he did what he did because that's how he
was. It just took a situation like that to bring it out
of him. It's a million plus Phil's in the game, so
that's that. As far as my lawyer, at the time you did
what you could. I can't be mad at you because it
could've been worse. Bottom line, he got paid and
that's what's important. When I was lockdown, I
became Muslim, and I been Muslim for a little over
nine years now, so a lot of things that once made me
bitter I have forgotten, and instead of being the wild
brother that you remember me to be, I am now
humble so, like I said before, what's done is done
let the past stay in the past," Malik, ending what he
had to say. No one spoke. Each man deep in his
own thoughts, trying to take in what Malik had just
said. They all knew that being the strong individual
that they knew him to be, he made it without them
and came out on top. They would never realize the
depths of what he had gone through while in prison.
There were things that would test a man's sanity.
They were glad that he presented everything the
way he did because they didn't have a clue as to
how to approach the matter, let alone defend their

actions. They respected Malik for that. And though
he never mentioned it, Cheddar knew that Malik
was also referring to the situation with him and his
ex-girlfriend when he said 'what's done is done; let
the past stay in the past'. Cheddar was relieved
when he heard him say that, as Malik looked him
dead in the eyes. Malik was so focused on his
thoughts and what he had just said to Pete and the
rest of them, that he hadn't realize that they just
entered New York.

"Yo akh, I thought we were going to the mall?"
he asked somewhat uncomfortable about being in
New York. He knew that one of his conditions
while on parole was not to leave the state of New
Jersey.

"Mall? Them joints are closed, plus as big as you
are, you can't fit nothin' in there anyway. The
biggest shirt they got is a 3X and you about a 5X.
We taking you to where we shop, where they sell
the hard shit." Doub had a good point as far as the
mall, but it still didn't put him at ease about being in
the city. He would have preferred to shop in Jersey
the next day. True, he was a big dude, so certain
stores didn't carry his size, but shopping for clothes
wasn't worth getting violated and sent back to
prison for. He wouldn't have ever been able to wear
what they bought him.

"Yo kid, I don't suppose to be in no New York
while on parole. You should've told me this where
we were going and gave me the option to turn the
offer down," Malik firmly stated to the three of

them. Not wanting to laugh at Malik's paranoia, because he understood, Pete spoke up trying to calm him down.

"Malik, I'm on parole too kid, and I'm in N.Y. seven days a week. Our P.O.'s ain't followin' us like that B. That shit they tell us is just policy." As long as we don't catch a new one, don't give up a dirty urine, report when we suppose to, and pay our fines, we good. Trust me. I've been on parole for a minute now and I know." Malik knew that Pete was only trying to help. The same mentality Pete had, was the same way of thinking Malik heard many violators displayed as they returned back two and three times while he was still finishing up his same prison term. There was always someone who thought they were slick and could out beat the system. What they weren't aware of was that the system was designed to be invincible. You may get away the first time, maybe even the second and the time after that too, and a few other times but eventually you'll get caught up. When that time came, it would be when you least expected it.

"No disrespect Pete, but I don't like taking chances like that. Those days are over with, feel me?"

"Yeah, I feel you dawg. I respect that" This was indeed a side of Malik that they had never seen before. He had always been the risk taker out of the team, always coming up with new ways and ideas to get ahead. This surprised them, but like Pete said, they felt where he was coming from and had to respect that because they respected him.

"Yo, you want me to turn back around?" asked Doub. Malik grinned at Doub's suggestion. He knew that they all just wanted to accommodate him on whatever because of their deep guilt. Malik intended to ride that out for as long as they made it available to him.

"Don't worry about it, we're out here now, I ain't mad at you brothers'. Your intentions were good. Go where you going." At that statement,'they all relaxed. Malik was definitely a changed man they all thought. The old Malik would've barked them out for putting him in this position. In some way they were all stuck in the past, reflecting back to their childhood, coming up in the game. Malik had always been a thorough individual in their eyes, and even now as they rode in the SUV with him, it was apparent that regardless to how big and bad the three of them thought they were, or how much money they had, they knew that Malik was still more thorough than the three of them combined. When they arrived at the first store, it was evident that they were regulars there. Malik was sure they spent a lot of money with the short, slicked haired Italian man. He shut the store down just for them to shop. His store was furnished with the latest and hottest gear and footwear. By the looks of the displays, he mainly carried big sizes. By looking at Hip Hop magazines like XXL, The Source, And Vibe, Malik saw how the styles of clothing had changed in fashion. Clothes were much baggier than he remembered. Before he left, the hustler's wore name brand like Guess and Gibauds jeans, with Tommy Hilfiger, Polo, or Nautica multi color shirts, and Coogi sweaters. These names were now replaced with Akademics, Miskeen, Roc-A-Wear, and Sean John. While Pete, Cheddar, and Doub were picking out what they believed to be hot outfits, Malik was in the footwear section. He was mesmerized by the different flavors of Air Force one's and Beef and Broccoli Timbs they had on display. They didn't have all the colors Malik saw before his eyes when he was home. Those were all that he really wore on his feet, and now seeing them made him want them all. He remembered he used to have conversations in the big yard when he was in prison, about gear, and he always brought up how if someone made the swamps in all flavors they'd get paid and when he saw that his thoughts became a reality, he couldn't wait to cop them. Some of the guys that were ballin' in the jail or had people holdin' them down strong on the outside had them. Malik only had his mother and he refused to ask her for $140 for a pair of boots, when he knew that she had been busting her ass to send what she could. Sometimes, even sending her last if Malik needed. "Malik, what you think about this?" asked Pete holding up a cream colored Sean John velour sweat suit.

"Yeah that's cool," Malik nodded genuinely liking the sweat suit.

"Aight, they got it in black too, you want it?"

"Whatever yo, it's cool with me."

"No doubt," responded Pete snatching a black one off the rack identical to the one he had just showed Malik. As Malik watched, he noticed the stack of clothes that were already piled up on the counter top. To him, it looked as if there were at least 40 outfits up there. Pete and Cheddar were still snatching items off the racks. Doub approached Malik.

"You still into Air One's and Timbs huh?"

"No question," Malik replied as he held a pair of burgundy and cream Timbs in his hands inspecting them.

"Yo, they got the ill Washington Redskins Jersey to go with them. Dallas still your team? 'Cause they got the blue and gray joints to go with the Roger Starbauch throwback. We going to an official sports gear store after this, so you might as well cop them."

"Yeah, these is serious, I'll get these and them Cowboys joints you were talking about." Doub smiled knowing that Malik really didn't understand. "Man, I'm not sayin' to just get them, I'm just telling you that them joints go with a Jersey. Pick the joints you like though. Matter of fact just pick 15 pair of Air Forces and 15 pair of Timbs, then when we go to the shoe store you can pick 15 pair of hot gators and ostrich to go with suits you gotta get. Malik looked at Doub when he mentioned the suits and shoes as if he had heard him wrong. He had no objections to what he had said; he just couldn't believe he had said it. He thought back to the times when he used to invite them to some parties and clubs that required them to dress up in shoes and suits. He couldn't pay them to go to anything like that. The closest they would come to dressing casual was a button up or Coogi, with some jeans and Timbs or Wallabee Clarks. Now here it was Doub had spoke about suits and shoes as if he had been dressing that way all of his life.

"When you brothers start wearing suits?" asked Malik. Doub laughed.

"I knew you was gonna ask that. It's been a few years now. Every since these chicks started throwing these Black and White parties where you gotta wear black and white. We tried it, 'cause all the official chicks we wanted to holla at be up in there, and the first time we went all the honies was on it, so we stayed with it. Plus they be on it like that at The Elks now too, so we can go out and chill, have a good time without getting into any fights or shootouts with knuckleheads. You know how niggas from the town be at the clubs and shit. Comin' straight off the block on some bullshit, you smell me?"

"Yeah, I've been tryin' to get you brothers up on this style of dressin'."

"Yeah, I remember, but don't get me wrong, we still go to the regular spots too, cause we ain't no strangers to danger." Doub said as Malik laughed to himself. Malik knew that he only made that statement to make himself seem more gangster than he really was. He knew that he couldn't impress Malik with his words and he didn't have to because that's not what their friendship was ever based on. Malik was always the gangster of their crew. After hitting the sporting gear store, the Italian shoe store, and the tailor shop, the shopping spree had ended, bringing the total amount of love on the gear tip for Malik to over $25,000. Malik was appreciative but not impressed. No amount of money in the world could make up for the lost years. Like with anything else in life, Malik felt that no loss could ever be made up. He thought no matter how much you gained that initial lost would still be there, just like with their friendship he thought. The whole time Malik was in New York he felt a little edgy, but seeing the N.J. sign relieved him as they exited the Holland Tunnel. Once he saw that he was back in Jersey, heading for Route 1 and 9, Malik closed his eyes. All that shopping had worn him out. He awakened at the sound of his name being called. He opened his eyes. It felt as if he had just closed them five minutes prior. He couldn't believe how quickly they had reached Plainfield. As he ran his hand across his face and tried to adjust his vision, Malik overheard several unfamiliar voices outside of the truck that belonged to both a males and females. By the sounds of all the commotion going on, Malik knew that he was not in front of his mother's house and to confirm his guess, he asked Pete about their location.

"Yo where we at?" asked Malik not recognizing the area. The darkness of the tint on the windows and night sky combined made it almost impossible to see out of the SUV. As he peered out of the tinted windows, seeing the crowd of people, it was evident to Malik that they were at some sort of club.

"We're at Hugo's. Don't tell us you been gone that long that you don't recognize your spot?" Pete said with a little laughter in his voice. Honestly, Malik really didn't recognize the all too familiar spot that he enjoyed frequenting in the past due to the name change. When he was home, it was called Lily Green Leaves. He had often chilled at the club drinking Hennessey so much that it had become like a second home to him. Malik had some good times up in the old Lily Green Leaves, as well as some bad ones. He remembered the many fights and shootouts he had been involved in after the night winded down. He had been intoxicated with shot after shot of his favorite cognac, chasing them with beers. On a few occasions he had escaped life threatening situations. His reputation in the establishment as well as other spots he dwelled in exceeded him. Once upon a time, he recalled being labeled a real ladies man and a thug all rolled up in one. Now, he no longer drank and had no desire to be a womanizer. Nothing inside Hugo's meant him any good. He was sure of that. He reflected back to when he was incarcerated attending drug and alcohol and substance abuse programs, how recovering addicts always testified that in order to work on their recovery and be successful at it, they had to change the people, places and things they did. Malik used to always find humor in their stories, but at that moment it finally dawned in him the significance and truth behind those brother's statements. In just a half a day, with his so-called manz and them, he had already managed to upset the one person who loved him unconditionally and wanted to see him succeed. He had broken the conditions of his parole by leaving the state, traveling with a convicted felon, traveling with drugs in the vehicle, and now he was contemplating entering a place where they served alcohol, indulged in drugs, and was most likely filled with dudes who were strapped. This was definitely not a part of Malik's plan. He began to regret taking Pete up on his offer to take him shopping, as everything was happening so quickly. Malik was now determined to slow things down a bit.

"Thanks for the gear and all of that, but the club scene just not my thing right now. I just got home and I ain't even chilled with my family a full 24 hours yet akh. So, I definitely ain't trying to chill up in this spot. Besides that, I ain't new to this, I know how cats get when they get liquored up. They start actin' stupid and I don't need that in my life right now, feel me?"

Doub broke in, "Yo, ain't nothin gonna happen my dude, not while we up in there," Doub announced reaching under his Polo shirt. "A nigga breathe on

you wrong dawg they getting laid down," he said
revealing the 40 caliber he had tucked underneath it.

"No doubt," yelled Pete patting his waist
indicating that he too was also strapped.
So, there was no doubt in Malik's mind that
Cheddar was as well. This was one of the things
Malik feared. Not only did he ride to New York
with his manz and them with drugs in the truck, but
also with the guns. Again, he knew it wasn't
intentional because that's how you had to roll if you
were from the streets, especially if you were seeing
money the way he heard they were. It was the same
exact way he used to roll.

"I'm not worried about that, you should know
that," Malik said. "I'm just saying it's been a long
day and I'd rather be home than in the club."
Pete, Cheddar, and Doub all looked at one another
and understood, but at the same time they still
wanted Malik to make a special guest appearance to
see the expression on faces up in the spot when they
stepped in with their man. Although they were
known as major figures all through the town, Malik
had a different shine than them, one that they were
unable to compare to. They all had signs of living a
good street life, but seeing Malik you could see that
he had been living a good life, looking healthy and
bright like so many other brothers who came from
prison after doing time. Each block always had one
or a few of their boys come home and bring that
flavor back to their hood. Pete and the others had
never experienced that. Phil had come home almost

three years prior but he brought a bad name to the hood and was banned from coming around because of how he crossed Malik. Now Malik was home, and regardless to whether he was done with the game or not, they felt he would always be apart of their hood and their team. His presence alone would be enough to turn heads and start a rumors. Pete, Cheddar, and Doub wanted to be a part of that. They remembered how close Malik and the owner had been.

"Leek, you don't have to stay long kid, we understand, but you know who spot this is right?" Doub asked knowing Malik didn't. Seeing the puzzled look on Malik's face, Doub continued. "This that nigga Hugo spot."
Hearing his old friends name caused Malik's face to soften. Hugo was an old friend of his from back in the mid 80's stemming back to the Jamaican club days over The Strand Theatre. It felt good to hear a name that he still had genuine love for. Doub instantly caught the surprise.

"You know that dude still got love for you. He's been askin' about you for year's dawg. At least come thru and holla for a minute; then we'll be out and drop you back off at moms," Doub said hoping his man would reconsider. Doub referring to his mother as his own had Malik feeling some type of way. For the second time today, he heard one of them make the reference. He couldn't believe that they had the audacity to use the term so loosely, knowing that they didn't represent it in the proper manner. Despite their negligence, Malik still had unconditional love for Pete, Doub, and Cheddar's mother's as if they were his own. The thought of how the years had played out while he was away was enough to leave a bad taste in Malik's mouth, but what he was faced with today was what he had worked so hard on. He knew that he was changed man and it took him a long time to realize that two wrongs did not make a right. This was what Malik had to convince himself of because had he not, none of the three men who sat before him would be breathing the air that they were at that moment. Wanting to bring the night to an end and against his better judgment, Malik agreed to go into Hugo's. Malik knew his manz and them all too well. He had practically raised them in the game. He knew that Pete, Doub, and Cheddar all just wanted to show face and show time, just by how persistent they had become about him going inside. On many occasions in the past they had always felt the need to showboat and be flashy. The fact that Malik was considered to be a gangster only added to their arrogance whenever they went out because they knew that he always had their backs. Tonight, that was not the case for Malik though. He couldn't care less about any façade the three were trying to present; he really did want to see one of the few people in his hometown that he still considered a friend.

"Yo, once I holla at Hu I wanna be out, that's my word akh," Malik said with sternness in his tone sounding somewhat annoyed.

Although Pete and Doub had missed it Cheddar had caught Malik's annoyance and understood.

"We got you yo," replied Cheddar, who hadn't really said too much to Malik all evening.

Malik was surprised that Cheddar had answered knowing the reason behind his silence.

Yeah akh, I know that situation with my ex- eating you up inside. You know you were dead wrong for that and a crab. Knowing you, you probably thought you were proving a point or doing me a favor or something. And you were right, she wasn't any good, but it wasn't your place to decide. Real brothers do real things and you ain't real akh. Malik thought to himself.

As they exited the SUV, Malik observed the beautiful females, who looked as if they had just come from featuring in the latest Rap video, making their way into Hugo's. Most of them had spoken or waved to Pete, Doub, and Cheddar, but none to Malik. Malik was not in the least bit offended. After all, he had been away for a long time besides, as he got closer, he noticed that none of the girls appeared to be older than 19. They had to have been babies when he got locked up.

"Them chicks ain't nobody," Pete said, seeing how Malik looked at them. "You wanna fuck one of 'em?"

Malik didn't answer Pete's question. Instead he just shot him a blank stare. One of the girls in the clique heard what Pete had said and turned around. She zeroed in on him and gave him the finger just as her girls were entering the bar club.

Pete just smiled and grabbed a fistful of his jeans along with his crotch. Malik took immediate offense to the gesture.

"Chill P, ain't no need for all of that akh."
The smile on Pete's face instantly erased at the sound of Malik's voice.

"You right yo," Pete said knowing that he had gone too far with his actions. Doub and Cheddar didn't say a word. They themselves had gotten on Pete about his behavior towards women publicly and were in agreement with what Malik had said. It was good to have their man back home, they both thought to themselves. Doub activated the alarm on his truck as the four of them entered Hugo's.

"Damn. You big than a mu'fucka my dude!" Doub exclaimed as he walked behind Malik seeing the width of his back and broadness of his shoulders for the first time. "What the fuck was you liftin' homie, the whole jail?"

Malik let out a chuckled. Even in prison people had commented on the size of his back and shoulders. He was known at Northern State Prison as "Big Muslim" because of his physique and the fact that he was a work-a-holic when it came to exercising.

"Something like that."

"Ya shit is up folk," added Pete.

"A dime in the joint will do that to you," Malik
dryly replied, and again his words flew right over
Pete and Doub's head.

"I feel you yo, but you home now baby and we
gonna make sure you never go back," said Pete.
After paying the entry fee, they stepped in the place
one after the other beginning with Doub and ending
with Pete. The bass engulfed them as they nodded
to the music. For a moment, Malik just stood there
looking around as he admired the new changes of
his old hang out. The first thing he noticed was that
the bar had been moved from where he remembered
it to be in the front, off to the left as soon as you
entered. He also noticed that it was being tended by
5 beautiful different shades and heights of women
who were all well endowed up top. They were
adorned with black t-shirts with gold letters on them
that said "Hugo's." Where there was once open
space to dance and socialize now sat tables to dine
and drink. His friend had definitely stepped it up
and invested some money into the place, making it
more spacious, Malik concluded as he observed the
jammed pack establishment. Women of all shapes,
colors, and sizes, out numbered the men by three to
one he noticed.

"Leek come on," yelled Doub, snapping Malik
out of his trance.
They began making their way through the club with
Doub leading the pack as the clubbers watched
them glide across the room. All eyes were definitely
on them, most of them on Malik as he made eye

117

contact with several women and caught some fake ice grills from guys. He laughed to himself, because he knew what it was all about. Externally he kept a stoned face. Some things never change he thought. He knew the reason he was receiving all the stares and attention up in the club; it had always been that way. To those who were regulars up in Hugo's, he was a new face, and new faces always drew attention. He recognized some of the people he had passed by, but didn't acknowledge that he knew them. He was sure that they had no idea who he was by their expressions. Just as they reached the bar, Malik saw out the corner of his left eye that someone was approaching him, apparently someone who had recognized him. Instant regret for agreeing to come up into Hugo's had flooded his mind, thinking back to how much he had done to people in the past in this very same club. Those very same people may have still hung out here. It wasn't fear that overcame him, because he was capable of handling himself physically and besides that, he knew that Pete and them were strapped. He just didn't have time for the drama.

"Malik!"

At the sound of his name Malik turned in the direction of the figure prepared for whatever, just as it reached within a foot of him. He saw the gigantic, dark-skinned, bald headed individual who now stood before him. He cracked a genuine smile, as the strong looking brother, who towered over him, threw his arms around Malik and embraced him.

"Malik!" the thick bald headed brother yelled for a second time over the music as everyone around them watched.

"What's good beloved."

"What up Just," replied Malik. He openly returned the man's embrace. He was actually glad to see the big man.

Justice and Malik had done time together and had befriended each other in prison. If you asked Justice about Malik, he would tell you that Malik was the brother who saved his life in prison. Justice had been a small time hustler who had a heroine addiction doing a five-year bid. When he got to the prison, and found out that there were just as many drugs in prison as there were on the streets, he jumped right into the scene head first, adding to his addiction. At the time Justice was about 230lbs, and some of the jail hustlers were either skeptical or just afraid to sell to him. No one wanted to take the chance of getting robbed or beat out of their product by Justice, and risk jeopardizing their jailhouse reputation. But though he looked the part, Justice wasn't like that. He was straight up and he respected every man's hustle. Rather than try something grimey, he would tell you straight up that he didn't have the money right now to pay you but when he got it he would pay, and his word was good to most. One particular weekend, while Malik was on the yard, doing pull-ups, Justice came over to the pull up bar where he was working out. They had known each other from the town. They were both from Plainfield but traveled in two different circles. Even in the prison system it was like that. Malik was Muslim, Justice was a Five Percenter, and while Malik stayed away from drugs, Justice indulged in them. Malik was living a positive and productive life in prison, while Justice traveled in a different direction.

Malik had no idea why Justice had come over to the pull up bar where he was. Although Justice was a big guy, Malik had never seen him work out. It surprised him that Justice wanted to borrow a carton of Newport's from him to purchase a $30 jailhouse bag of heroin. Everyone knew that Malik was known for having cigarettes to buy food, Muslim oils, and whatever else he enjoyed, because cigarettes were money in prison. Malik also didn't smoke so he always kept them. Justice told him how he had no one else to turn to and he was willing to pay him back with interest as soon as he got paid next month from his institutional job. Malik listened as Justice talked and was empathetic. Prison was suppose to be a place where you could escape all that and take time out to better yourself, yet you were faced with the same choices and decisions you were faced with in society. A lot of brothers weren't strong enough to make the right ones. Malik was thankful that he had gotten himself on the right track, but knew that for brothers like Justice it would take more time. After pondering over Justice's proposal, Malik came up with a proposition of his own. Malik agreed to lend Justice the cigarettes trusting that he would pay him back. Rather than paying him interest, Malik wanted Justice to come and work out with him and the rest of the brothers for a full five days. The catch to the deal was that throughout the time Justice wouldn't be able to use any type of narcotics or intoxicants whatsoever. Justice laughed at Malik's conditions but was up for the challenge. A small price to pay to get high he thought. He knew that he could last the five days without getting high because he had gone longer, and naturally, he was as strong as an ox. He agreed, giving his word, which Malik felt was good. Starting Monday, he would begin his workout. That Monday, after a strenuous workout, Justice vomited. In spite of his God given strength, he was no match for Malik and his Muslim brothers; He was filled with embarrassment as he watched how hard the other brothers worked. He knew that his stamina and endurance was at an all time low, but he was determined to build it up. Each day, all the way up to Friday, Justice vomited after every workout, but he gutted it out and hung in there, never complaining even once about how sore everyone knew he was. At the end of their workout that day, Malik shook his hand and expressed how proud he was of him for hanging in there the way he did. In return he shook Malik's hand back and responded back surprisingly, telling Malik that it wasn't over, he'd see him back in the weight pile next Monday, and from that day on Justice never got high again at least not to Malik's knowledge. He also became one of the biggest and strongest brothers in the prison. He and Malik became close and he often expressed to Malik how he appreciated him saving his life, and how he would never forget it. Now, two years later the two friends had been reunited.

"Damn nigga I see you still got ya shit up. Look at me, I got all fat and shit from drinkin' and eatin' good," Justice joked.

"You still a big dude Just," said Malik. Everyone continued to watch as the two big men conversed as if they were long lost brothers. People who knew Justice wanted to know who the stranger was that he was showing so much love. Doub, Pete, and Cheddar wanted to know the connection between the two. Like a Tupac song, All Eye's were definitely on the circle of men by the bar. As if sensing everyone's curiosity, Justice threw his arm around Malik nearly knocking a bystander to the floor, and yelled, "This brother saved my muthafuckin' life," Justice shouted with admiration. Those who were able to hear Justice formed immediate respect for Malik, not even knowing the details or the extent to Justice's statement. Because Justice was highly respected by all and made the statement, his words rapidly spread through the club like wildfire. Everybody who was somebody had known about Malik saving Justice's life although they could not imagine the depths of the statement.

"Yo what you drinkin' akh?" asked Justice.

"Water."

"Water? Not tonight beloved, we goin' hard," Justice insisted. "This is a welcome home celebration," he then announced.

"Come on akh," Malik humbly sighed. Instantly Justice understood. He had been around Malik long enough to know when to disengage.

"Aight beloved, next time," Justice replied respectfully.

Those closest to them had hung on to Justice's every word and had drawn the conclusion that Malik had just come home from doing time. By now a bunch of video and model type females had flocked around them. Justice, Malik, Doub, Cheddar and Pete were now the center of attraction in the local hot spot.

"Hey Just," one group of women said in unison.

"What up ladies?"

"Hey Doub, Cheddar, and Pete," they all spoke again. Doub, Pete, and Cheddar all spoke back.

"Who's your friend?" one of the females asked Justice.

She looked familiar to Malik but he couldn't place her. They all did.

"You don't know who this is?" he asked her.

"No," she replied. The rest of them shook their heads indicating that they too had no clue.

"This is my strong peoples Malik, from the New Projects." Justice's words instantly rang a bell in the girl's head.

"Malik? Jackie and Mandy's brother Malik?" she asked as her eyes lit up.

"In the flesh," Justice answered seeing the evident. Malik could see in the women's eyes that they had heard about him or knew who he was. Yet, he still could not place any of them. It had been a long time. They were younger than him by at least four or five years, but they were definitely grown women. Interrupting the conversation, Doub interjected,

"Yo Malik, you said you not drinkin' right?" he asked as one of the female bartenders waited for their order.

"Nah just spring water is good."
Doub Just laughed.

"Come on akh, you home now, at least one shot for a toast." He said sounding as if he were pleading. Standing his ground but not wanting to seem offensive, Malik declined again. Just as Justice had Doub left well enough alone and accepted that. The brown skinned girl held out her hand as she introduced herself.

"Hi, I'm Meesha, you probably don't remember me because I was little when you left, but I'm Troy's sister."

As soon as she mentioned who her brother was it all came back to him. Malik remembered who she was. He and Troy had come up in the game together as young bucks. He remembered being over their house seeing little Meesha going back and forth to the kitchen just to be noticed. She was all grown up now; he was sure that she was always noticed, because she was gorgeous. While Malik was in prison he heard about how Troy got stabbed outside a club in town over a female.

"I remember you," Malik spoke as he shook her hand. "Sorry to hear about your brother, he was a good dude."

"Thank you," she replied. Feeling the dirty looks her girlfriends were giving. Meesha introduced them.

"These are my friends," she began to introduce then "This is Crystal, that's Tee-Tee, Nikki, Monique, and that's Yolanda."

Upon being introduced, all the girls waved and spoke to Malik, each with their own sexy smiles on their faces. Malik didn't smile back, but he returned their greetings. They were all pretty girls he thought, with their hair and nails done, sporting stylish outfits. There was no disputing, hands down, Meesha was the most appealing one out the bunch. Not making it seem too obvious, Malik studied her. He hadn't noticed it at first, when she and her friends had approached them, but Meesha had beautiful bright hazel eyes, setting off her flawless caramel skin tone. They were slanted a little giving him the impression that Meesha may have been mixed with a little Asian. Her hair was also a glistening jet black as it hung down in a nice shoulder length style. The fullness of her lips was enhanced by the Mac Lip Glass she used to neatly accentuate them. Give or take she stood at 5'3 thanks to the three inch heels. He could tell that without the leather boots she wore her natural height was about five feet even. Even through the clothes she had on, anyone with eyes could see that she had a firm body. Everything properly proportioned, as if she had been working out all of her life to get it that way. Malik had been so thrown by Meesha's beauty that he hadn't noticed Doub trying to hand him his water.

"Malik?" Doub called again, tapping Malik with the bottle of spring water. Malik turned around and accepted the bottled water from Doub as Doub leaned in to his ear.

"She's the truth right," Doub said sensing Malik's interest. Malik grinned, and turned his attention back to the direction of Justice and Meesha. Just as he turned around he saw another familiar face approaching. One that he felt he could have done without seeing at that very moment. She reached him with open arms, stepping in between both Justice and Meesha. Although they both knew who she was, only Justice knew the connection between Malik and the girl. Malik told him about her on numerous occasions when they were in prison together. Malik didn't want to cause a scene so he embraced her giving the girl the half of a hug she deserved.

"Oh my God, I can't believe you home!" she expressed excitedly. Malik just looked at her but said nothing. It had been a long time since he had seen her and he was well over her.

"I was at the back of the club and I heard somebody sayin' some guy named Malik just came home, I didn't believe it was you. I mean I wanted it to be you, but I had to come see for myself," the girl rambled.

"Yeah, it's me Dawn," replied Malik feeling a little awkward at hearing himself say his ex-girlfriend's name.

"Look at you, lookin' all good and big. How you been?" asked Dawn as if she really deserved to know.

"Good and you?" was Malik's response, not really concerned, but extending the courtesy.

"I'm good. It's so good to see you baby!" she said, hugging him for the second time. Only this time Malik didn't return the hug. Picking up on his discomfort, Pete spoke up.

"Yo Malik, I'm gonna go up and get ole' boy so we can be out."

"Yeah no doubt akh," Malik said relieved, appreciating Pete's bail out. This was an awful way for him to end his evening. By now, everyone had gotten irritated and fed up with Dawn's performance, so they began breaking off. It was evident that there was nothing between the two of them. Meesha could see that, but she refused to stand around any longer and watch Dawn's tired ass throw herself all over Malik. She saw in Malik's eyes that he was interested in her. She heard Pete mention leaving so, she herself planned on making her exit with her girls as well. She moved in closer to say her goodbye to Malik as Dawn watched with hate all over her face.

"It was nice talking to you Malik, I'll see you around," were Meesha's parting words. "Oh, and welcome home," she added.

"Yeah, thank you," Malik replied. "I'll definitely see you again," he added loud enough for only Meesha to hear. The rest of Meesha's friends said their goodbyes and began walking off. Dawn shot Meesha a dirty look that she caught, but Meesha just smiled. She knew that Dawn had nothing on her. Meesha thought to herself as she walked off with her girls. Malik saw the look that Dawn had given Meesha. He couldn't believe she had the nerve to pull a stunt like she had. Furthermore, he couldn't believe that she was up in his face the way that she was, like everything between them was all good. Malik laughed to himself at her boldness, stepping to him like that with Cheddar right there. He could only imagine what was going on in Cheddar's mind. That thought again humored Malik. Dawn turned her attention back to Malik after she finished grilling Meesha. She saw how Malik had been looking at her, and that he was attracted to her. She remembered how he had looked at her in that very same manner. The way his eyes lit up and sparkled would tip any woman off to his interest. The looks Malik gave her made her feel a little uneasy inside, but she shook the feelings off. In her heart, she felt she could have Malik back. She knew that she had done him wrong in the past, but in her own sick mind she thought that she could be forgiven. Throughout the years she regretted sleeping with his man Cheddar, who happened to be sitting two seats over from him. Malik had been the best thing that had ever happened to her and since their break up she had gone down hill. She was passed from hustler to hustler like a blunt of goodness in a cipher of veteran weed smokers. She thought, if Malik would only give her another chance and take her back, she could regain her status and respect in the streets again. What she didn't realize was that she had already lost the most valuable thing of all, her own self-respect. There was nothing that Malik could do to help restore that, even if he did decide to rekindle their relationship. It was something that Dawn would have to do on her own but she no idea about that, so instead she continued to stay in Malik's face and play herself.

"Malik, for what it's worth, I really did miss you," she said sounding as sincere as she possibly could. She sensed that it meant nothing to Malik.

"Yeah?" Just as Dawn was about to respond, she was interrupted.

"Well god damn! If it ain't the devil himself!" yelled the West Indian man as he walked up on Malik. Although he came from the side, Malik recognized the voice, as he turned and smiled. He saw that life had been good to his old friend. With the addition of some gray hairs, the man still had a head full of hair, and not a wrinkle on his saffron complexioned face. He had put on a few since their last encounter, but like Malik, he was a muscular man who looked to be in excellent shape.

"What's good old timer?" Malik asked smiling, as he reached out to shake his friend's hand.

"Shit! Ain't nothing old on me but my eyes brethren," Hugo shot back, as he took Malik's hand and pulled him towards him, embracing him.

"Damn it's good to see your ass boy!"

"You too friend," replied Malik as they shared a hug. By now the entire club was convinced that Malik was someone of importance in the town by the company that surrounded him. Even though the Hugo's owner was not in the streets, he was still respected by all in streets, for having an establishment where they were able to come hang out, drink, party, and have a good time. One could have easily thought that the owner and Malik were father and son by the emotional reunion the two had.

"Boy, you feel like a tank and you look like one too." Malik's friend asserted as they released one another.

"That's ten years of working out," replied Malik.

"It's been that long huh? Damn!" Hugo responded shaking his head.

"Yes my friend, a long time right?"

"Long time bro, but glad you made it out in one piece though. I heard a lot of horror stories, especially about where you were."

"Well enough of that, what you drinkin'?"

"Water," said Malik holding up his spring water bottle. Hugo laughed.

"Yall always come home with that no alcohol policy, sippin' on water and soda and shit, then next month yall be right back up in here throwin' back shots of Hennessey chasin' it with Corona's." Malik smiled. He knew Hugo was right, just being around the alcohol and on the club scene made him crave his favorite cognac. He had been resisting the entire time he was there. He wasn't so sure how long he could continue to come in there just ordering water. Maybe it would only take a month, or maybe even less he thought. If he stayed any longer it might've been that night, so he decided to call it a night.

"Yo Hu, I only came here to holla at you and pay my respects. It's good to see you brother, but it's past my bedtime, so I'mma be out. I'll see you again though, you know that."

"Yeah I know friend, it's good seeing you too. Take care yourself and don't be a stranger. If you need anything and I got it, then you got it, just let me know." Malik smiled at the man's generosity. He knew that his open offer was genuine and he respected Hugo for that.

"Aight, I'll get up, and if I need you I won't hesitate to holla." said Malik shaking Hugo's hand again, giving him another hug.

"Yo, Doub I'm ready akh."

"Aight, let me finish this drink and we out."

"Yeah, okay"

"Yo, Just, hold it down akh, I'll see you again, aight?" said Malik.

"True, here take my cell number. Matter of fact this is my crib joint too. Get at me anytime dawg for whatever, feel me?"

"Yeah, I feel you akh, and I'll get at you, that's my word," Malik replied.

Dawn stood there waiting to see what Malik would say to her. She was hoping that he would tell her that he would see her some other time as well.

"Dawn, you take care," was all he said to her.

Doub handed Malik the truck keys.

"Yo, I'll be outside waitin' in the truck," he told them as he gave Justice a pound and a hug and walked off, leaving Dawn where she stood. Doub and Pete started cracking up with laughter.

"I know you ain't think my manz was gonna come home and fuck with you after that snake shit you pulled?" asked Doub as he continued to laugh.

"Fuck you Doub!" She yelled storming off.

At that, they laughed even harder. Cheddar couldn't help but to join them.

Just then Doub's cell phone vibrated on his hip.

"Yo," he answered.

"Aight. One." As he hung up, Doub glanced over to Cheddar, who was already staring in his direction. A simple head nod told it all.

CHAPTER TEN

IT was two in the morning when Malik entered the
house and reached the pull out couch. He fell right
out, drained from the long day. Exhaustion had
overcome him. He had no strength to even undress
himself or get under the covers.
Like clock work, when he opened his eyes it 5 A.M.
the same time he woke up for the past nine years to
make his early morning prayer. He noticed that the
cover had been thrown over his body and wondered
had his mother come out in the middle of the night
and put it over him. He got up, went to the
bathroom, and prepared himself for prayer. He then
came back out into the living room, snatched up a
sheet from off the pull out couch and folded it up so
he could use it to pray. When he finished his prayer,
he headed to the kitchen in search of something to
snack on. Hunger pains had taken over his stomach
and he felt light headed. It felt good to be able to get
up and be able to open the refrigerator, one of the
little things you learn to appreciate after doing time.
After finding some cold cuts, Malik closed the
refrigerator door, and to his surprise, his younger
sister Mandy was standing there. Malik was
startled.

"Girl you scared me!" he whispered not wanting to wake anybody else assuming he had awakened his sister. Mandy giggled the way a little girl does when they find out a boy likes them, but nothing about her indicated that she was a little girl. She was developed for a younger teenager, and looking into her eyes Malik could see that she had already experienced some things that should be foreign to a girl her age.

"Big as you are, how you gonna be scared?" She joked with her brother.

"Shut up," he said smiling.

"What you doin' up?" he asked her

"I couldn't sleep, and I heard you out here talkin' in your sleep so I was comin' to wake you up." Malik was confused, because he had been up for a little while, but then it dawned on him what she was talking about.

"Nah, I wasn't talking to myself, I was praying!"

"Praying?"

"Yeah to God, you still know who God is right?"

"Yeah boy," she answered sarcastically.

"Well, that's what you heard."

"Why are you praying so early though and out loud?" Mandy asked curiously.

"Because that's how a Muslim prays. Five times a day," he added.

"Muslim? I didn't know you were a Muslim Malik. And you gotta pray five times?" she said surprised.

"Yeah, I've been Muslim for about nine years."

"Oh."

"Oh what?" asked Malik sensing that his sister had wanted to ask him something.

"Nothing."

"Who do you think you talking to? Mommie? This is me, you can't fake me out," he said recognizing game. Mandy smiled. She was glad that her big brother was home. The past couple of years had been rough for her, hanging out in the streets. She had no idea what she was getting herself into when she became fascinated with the game and began experimenting with older guys. By the time she had realized what the streets consisted was not what she expected, it was too late. She had no one to turn to at the time and peer pressure had gotten the best of her. She had immersed herself in drinking and drugging, gave up her most prized possession due to running the streets. Mandy had experimented with weed, E-pills, and alcohol, and had been sexually active for the past few years. When she really needed someone the most she felt she couldn't turn to her mother knowing she just wouldn't understand. She wished that her older brother had been home to show her the proper guidance and school her on the game. He was from the streets, and was very knowledgeable about what went on out there. She also knew that if Malik had been there she would not have been in the predicaments that she had been. She was very naïve to the things that she could get involved in. She knew that back then, if her brother had been home,

none of the guys that pursued her would have ever
uttered a word to her or her little sister. No one
wanted to feel the wrath of her big brother. Not
even his so called friends, who had tried on many
occasions to bed both her and Jackie. Mandy
regretted ever falling victim to one of them. She
knew that if Malik ever found out murder would be
the case. Mandy could not understand why her
brother's so-called friend preyed on the innocence
of his little sister and treated her like she was just
another notch on his belt. She hoped that Malik
never found out. She didn't want to see him go back
to jail. And she knew for something like that, he
would. He had only been home for one day and
already his presence was being felt she thought. She
wasn't old enough when he was home running the
streets to know the depths of Malik's reputation.
Many people male and female who knew that she
was his sister always spoke highly of him either out
of respect or just plain old fear. All she knew was
that her brother was considered a *somebody* in the
streets. She wasn't going to tell him the real reason
she couldn't sleep was because her phone had been
ringing off the hook all night with her friends telling
her how her fine ass brother was up at Hugo's. He
saw right through her and knew that she was
holding back. Some of the chicks had gotten her
number from their younger sisters who knew they
were friends. There were other chicks she had no
clue as to who they were or how they had gotten her

number, but either way they all wanted to know
what was up with her big brother.

"Nah I heard you were up at Hugo's earlier,"
said Mandy to him. Malik was surprised by his little
sister's comment. He wondered who could have
told her that so soon.

"Where'd you hear that at?" he wanted to know.

"Come on now, this is Plainfield. The question is
who didn't I hear it from? You know how the
streets talk."

"Yeah, I know but your butt ain't got no
business being out in them streets anyway."
Mandy put her head down, she couldn't even look
Malik in the face, shame and embarrassment had
spread all over her face.

"I know, but that ain't where I heard it, I was just
sayin'. My phone been ringing all night with girls I
don't even know asking me about my *fine ass
brother*," she repeated what some of the girls had
referred to him as. That put a smile on Malik's face,
and he couldn't help but to laugh at his sister's
mockery of the women inquiring about him.

"And what you tell them?"

"I told them that I was little when you left so
some of the things I don't know, they'd have to ask
you when they see you, but I'd let you know that
they had asked about you."

"That was cool. Luckily it wasn't mommy cause
she would've cursed them all out, talking about,
'Tell them little hot tail girls don't be calllin my

house all hours of the night!' " Malik mocked his mother, as both he and Mandy shared a laugh.

"Malik let me ask you something? If you Muslim now, what were you doin' up in Hugo's anyway?" Mandy asked concerned. Malik was caught off guard by his sister's question, knowing it was a good one.

"Honestly, I should have never been in there, but Doub and them took me and I wound up agreeing to go in and holla at the owner on the strength that we was cool before I got knocked. I was only in there about an hour and a half, then I broke. I wasn't drinkin' though, so to answer your question, you can be Muslim and go anywhere you want, you just have to always maintain your humility and self-respect, understand?"

"Yeah, I understand," she replied, as the kitchen light came on.
"What are you two doin' up this time of morning? Both of you get back to bed," their mother said with her hands on her hips. They laughed. Both Malik and Mandy got up and gave their mother a kiss and did as they were told.

CHAPTER ELEVEN

MEESHA had just finished getting her hair done at
Alnisa's Creations. Normally, she would get her
hair done at Heads Together but the owner, Kim,
who happened to be her friend, was out of the
country on vacation. So, Meesha called her other
girlfriend in town who also had her own shop. At
times like these Meesha appreciated having
professional friends. The shop was packed and she
had no appointment for the day. It was busy for a
Friday, and Meesha was grateful that her girl was
able to pencil her in. She couldn't go another day
with her hair and nails looking the way they were.
Alnisa always took care of her, and hooked her up.
She made sure before Meesha left the shop, she
always looked hot. Tonight it would be Studio 9,
where everybody that was somebody would be.
That was Meesha and her crew's destination for the
evening. Meesha was just finishing up, when she
heard the side bar conversation not too far from
where she stood.

"That's the nigga Malik that just came home
right there?" the honey complexioned girl asked a
brown skinned girl.

"Um-hm. That's him."

"Girl that nigga look official," Kitten said. She was an exotic dancer from New York who frequented Jersey to dance.

"You ain't never lied, and he got his weight up too," Cocoa replied. She was also an exotic dancer from out of New Brunswick.

Most of the women in the shop had turned their attention toward the salon window. They were all admiring Malik as if he were on display. Even Meesha's girlfriend Yolanda was checking out the scenery and then turned back in Meesha's direction and smiled.

"Hurry up," she managed to whisper as Meesha paid for her new do. She knew why her girlfriend was rushing her and she was already on point thinking the same. It had been five days since the last time she had seen Malik and was interrupted at Hugo's. He was alone now and Meesha intended to take advantage of the situation. None of the other girls had caught on to Meesha intentions besides Alnisa. She knew her friend all too well and knew the only time she ever rushed out of the shop the way she was doing now was when she had a hot date or was pressed for time. As Alnisa eyed Malik herself, she thought he and her girlfriend would make a good couple. She didn't know him but knew of him. She had heard that he was a brother that was about his business when he was in the streets. She could see how Meesha would be attracted to Malik. Any woman would she thought, including herself. Nevertheless, she was not a hater she was a congratulator and in her mind wished Meesha all the best. She admired Meesha's boldness and her persistence. She knew good men were hard to find, good black men anyway.

"See you later Alnisa and thanks again," Meesha said as she and Yolanda made their way to the exit of the salon.

"Anytime girl, do ya thing," Alnisa replied giving her a smile letting her know that she knew what she was up. Meesha waved her off and smiled back as she headed for her white 550i BMW.
As Malik passed the shop, the women continued what they were doing before he walked by. Malik saw the Beemer pulling up, but he continued walking. When he heard the soft voice coming from the car only then did he come to a halt. He realized who the voice belonged to.

"I said do you want a ride?" Meesha repeated thinking Malik hadn't heard her the first time.

"I heard you before," said Malik smiling. "That's why I stopped."
Meesha was a little embarrassed by her own aggressiveness. She knew the second time she asked she sounded kind of annoyed.

"Oh, excuse me. I thought you were ignoring me," she apologized.
Yolanda was cracking up on the inside, she had never seen her girlfriend act like this, let alone apologize to a man before. She couldn't wait to replay the scene for their other friends.

"It's okay," said Malik. "And I'd appreciate the ride."

Yolanda got out of the front seat and proceeded to get in the back, Malik tried to stop her.

"Nah its aight, I'll get in the back."

"It's no problem." replied Yolanda "Besides you a big brotha you know you ain't fittin' back here anyway," she said as she climbed in the back. Malik laughed at her comment and thought that she was definitely right.

"Where you headed?" Meesha asked.

"I was on my to my mom's crib."

"Where are you coming from?"

"Jumah," Malik replied.

Meesha knew that if he had been coming from Jumah then he had to be Muslim. In her opinion Muslims were decent brothers. She had dealt with one before, and for the most part he treated her well. But she felt that he was too controlling and tried to turn her into someone that she wasn't. She was never the type to judge one person by another, so she refused to put Malik in that category. Besides, Malik didn't seem like the type of man Khalid was.

"Oh. Where does your mother live?"

"Over on Second Street and Leland Ave."

"Wow! That's a long walk." Meesha was surprised at the distance in which he had to go.

"Not really, it's cool, I need the exercise anyway."

"Yeah right, you look like you never have to work out again." She said not realizing what had just come out of her mouth. Malik smiled.
"Did I say that out loud?" she asked shocked.

"Yep," Yolanda said from the back.

"Shut up girl!" she told Yolanda shooting her a look through the rear view mirror. Malik laughed again. He hadn't laughed in the presence of a woman in a long time.

"It's cool, I know what you meant," he said putting her at ease. Changing the subject, Meesha asked.

"How long you stay at Hugo's after we left?"

"Maybe another 20 minutes. The owner is a good friend of mine. So after I paid my respect, I left. That was too much for me just coming home." Malik sensed that she wanted to say more figuring it had to be about Dawn so he felt the need to clear the air. He could tell that Meesha was somewhat interested. He may have been incarcerated for a long time but there was nothing slow about him. He dealt with enough women in the past to know when one was trying to get at him. He was used to being the aggressor though. Since he had been away, women had been stepping up and telling men what they wanted. They had evolved in this new millennium and Malik was definitely feeling the transition.

"That situation at Hugo's wasn't about nothin', that was my ex in case you were wondering, but

she's nothing to me now," Malik replied without
going into any detail.

"No. I wasn't." Meesha left it at that. That was
all she needed to hear anyway. She knew that if he
had wanted her to know more he would've told her.
He seemed to be a straight forward individual.

"You goin' back to this weekend?" she asked,
hoping to see him back at Hugo's.

"Nah, I doubt it" was his response even though
he knew why she asked.

"Oh," she answered disappointedly. Malik didn't
want her to think that he didn't want to see her
again.

"You know I'm just comin' home, and I haven't
spent time with my family in a long time, even
when I was home before, so I'm trynna to do the
family thing right now, you know?" Meesha perked
up at his statement.

"I understand, and I'm not mad at you either. I
respect that. More brothers should think like that."

"You right about that girl," Yolanda added from
the back.

"How are your little sisters doing anyway?"
asked Meesha. "I know they're happy that you
home. You were all they used to talk about."

"Is that right? Yeah they're glad I'm home and
they're fine. How do you know them though?
They're younger than you."

"They get their hair done at the same shop as me
and my friends, and occasionally they hang at some
of the local spots me and my girls chill at. We just

clicked. They are like my little sisters. I look out for them when I see them; they too young to be hanging out like that." Malik noticed the sincerity in Meesha's voice as she spoke about his little sisters and appreciated it.

"Oh. Thanks for trying to look out for them. Those are my intentions too now that I'm home." Meesha smiled, because she knew that Malik meant what he said. She also knew that he had his work cut out for him. Maybe not so much with Jackie, but Mandy, she was in too deep. It would be difficult to pull her out. She thought back to a few occasions when some no good hustler had succeeded in getting her all drunk and trying to take her out the club. She came to her aide and intervened many times, subjecting herself to being called all types of cock blocking and player hating bitches. To her, that was a small price to pay to help a young sister out, even though she couldn't be there all the time to hold Mandy's hand. Meesha turned on East Second and headed towards Malik's destination. When she reached Leland Avenue she made a left turn. Malik pointed.

"Right there behind that black truck." Meesha pulled over and parked.

"Thanks for the ride."

"No problem." Meesha responded, wondering whether he would make the next move.

"Aight then, you ladies enjoy the rest of your day," Malik said as he reached for the door handle.

145

"You too," Yolanda responded, ready to get back up front after being cramped in the back seat of the BMW. Malik opened the door, got out, and lifted the front seat up for Yolanda. Meesha knew that it was a now or a never situation and she wasn't going to let the opportunity pass her by.

"Since you won't be at Hugo's this weekend, there's no telling when we'll see each other again. So, why don't you take my number and give me a call when you have some time. Maybe I can come get you and we can hang out or something." Malik had been so caught up in the topic about his sisters that he had forgotten to ask for Meesha's number, which he had intended to do. That was a good sign he thought as he closed the car door.

"Yeah, that sounds like a plan." Meesha wrote her information down on a piece of paper and handed it to Yolanda to hand to Malik.

"Make sure you call me," she said.

"Definitely," Malik replied.

CHAPTER TWELVE

" **YO** after we finish baggin' this shit up and countin' this money we bouncin' right." asked Doub. "Yeah nigga we said we was goin', didn't we? Calm the fuck down them pigeons gonna still be up in there when we get there waitin' for your trick ass to splurge on them," said Cheddar. Pete laughed

"Word," you is actin' kinda thirsty right now my dude."

"Fuck both you niggas. I get pussy and I ain't gotta pay for it either." Cheddar, you the nigga that be payin' them broads. You know, I know. Hittin' 'em chicks at the club with two and three bills for the night. Yeah nigga, you thought I ain't know about that huh?" Doub said laughing.

"And the funny shit is I be fuckin' the same ones you be payin' for F-R-E-E! Cause I gotta big D-I-C-K!" Doub chanted. Pete continued to laugh, but Cheddar found no humor in what Doub had said. He was tight on the low behind Doub knowing his personal business about the strippers. He knew that Doub had to have gotten his information from the horse's mouth because he was always extra

147

precautious when it came to creeping with a chick from the strip club. If he had to bet money on it, Doub's resource probably was Kitten's monkey ass, because she had a big mouth and liked to run it too. Doub had caught a vein with his words, but that was his man so it wasn't about nothing, but he knew from here on out he had to be more careful with his extra curricular activities with exotic dancers.

"Yo what's up? Yall wanna swing by and see if Malik wanna slide with us to Studio 9?" asked Pete.

"He probably tired of being in the crib by now. He been home like five-six days now, feel me?"

"Yeah we can do that," said Doub.

"But I doubt if he gonna roll though. He don't seem like he with the partying shit like he use to be."

"Maybe he just don't feel like partying with us," added Cheddar.

"What? What you talkin' about nigga?"

"Why you say that?" asked Pete.

"Come on kid. I know I'm not the only one that picked up on that shit that day we was all together. I mean, what he said and all was cool about not holdin' no grudges and shit. But, I wasn't 100% convinced that it was love- feel me? Don't forget, I fucked the nigga girl yo. Then the bitch got the nerve to try to be all up in the nigga face up at Hugo's. I know that shit had him tight on the low. I wanted to smack the shit out of that silly ass bitch that night, but I didn't want to cause no scene. Either way, I know that nigga had to be feelin' some type of way about that shit." Both Pete and Doub pondered over Cheddar's words and thought that there was logic to what he was saying, but still they didn't believe that to be the case. They believed that Malik was not the same man they knew years ago and that he had put the past behind him.

"I feel what you sayin'," said Doub. "But I don't think it's like that, you know that nigga Malik be straight up with his shit. If he had beef with us or was feelin' some type of way he'd let us know from the door. It may not be all love right now because that nigga just comin' home and we did shit on him but it ain't no beef either."

"Word, I'm with Doub on this one kid. Malik on some new shit and it ain't bullshit either. He on some real live humble shit and I'm feelin' that," joined Pete. Cheddar just shook his head as he submitted. He knew that he was out numbered and hearing his friend's point of view made him question himself. He wondered if he was over reacting. He felt strongly about his opinion, but at the same time hoped that both Doub and Pete were right about theirs. Malik was a very dangerous and vindictive individual before he thought. They all were aware of that and if he felt any inclination that you had violated him, he would be out for blood. There was one thing Cheddar did want to address before he sided with his manz first.

"You see how the nigga Justice was on dawg sack though?" he asked in relation to the night at Hugo's.

"Yo that's crazy," Doub was the first to say. "Cause I was wonderin' myself what was really with ole' boy and my dude."

"Yeah, I wasn't gonna say nothin' but I wasn't feelin' that at all," added Pete.

"Probably some jail shit though. You know the town stick together in the joint."

"That's what I was thinkin'. Plus the nigga said Leek saved his life. He probably banged a joker for that black ass nigga. You know that nigga Jus a pussy, and you know how dawg get down so you do the math."

"Word. I can see that," agreed Doub.

"To be on the safe side, look into that, smell me."

"On it," answered Pete.

"Doub you hear anything on that other thing?"

"Nah, everything's - everything."

"That's what's up. Aight, let's finish up this shit so we can be out."

Malik could feel the heat from his mother's eyes on his back as she turned and noticed Pete at her door once again.

"Yeah what's good P?" Malik asked opening the screen door. Pete took it as Malik speaking though. "What it do big homie?" Doin the family thing," Malik replied.

"That's what's up. But check it. Me and the
homies on our way to this spot out in Woodbridge.
We wanted to know if you wanted to roll? It's
gonna be serious," Pete stressed. Without hesitation,
this time Malik instantly turned down Pete's offer to
roll with them to them to the club.

"I'm good akh," he answered dryly.

"Aight. Just checkin' my dude. We out, but holla
if you need us," understood Pete. Malik didn't
respond. Instead he closed the door behind him.
When Ms. Jones heard Malik refuse Pete, close the
door, and turn around to come back and finish
watching the movie they were watching together,
her heart melted as she managed to smile at her
son's decision. That was all she wanted him to do
when he first came home. Better late than never, she
thought. It was bad enough that her two daughters
were God knows where, and she was worried about
them. Though Malik was much older than them, and
could handle himself ten times better than Mandy or
Jackie, still she was more concerned about him at
all times especially since he was just coming home.
Ms. Jones knew that her son could easily go either
way at this point in his life, which is why she got on
her knees every night and prayed that Malik stayed
focused. She forgave him for leaving with his so
called friends his first day home. She was grateful
to find him fast asleep that first night. He was fully
clothed, snoring like a grizzly bear, when she
checked on him. She kissed him and placed a sheet
over him. They hadn't discussed the matter the next

day, but all had been forgiven. She was proud of
him for the way he went out each morning in search
of work, coming home with job applications, filling
them out and returning them the next day. She knew
how difficult it was for Malik to be doing what he
was doing because he had never earned any income
working an honest day of work in his life. He had
hustled most of his teenage years all the way into
adulthood. She watched her son on a daily basis as
he sat at the kitchen table with discouragement in
his eyes. Each time she made attempts to motivate
and encourage him. Assuring him that there would
be brighter days ahead, and that, "God would never
place any burdens on you that you could not bear."
That always put a smile on Malik's face, and kept
his sprits up. Between his prayers and his mother's
support, he knew in his heart that he would be okay.
Still the demons from his past still lived within,
waiting for the opportunity to be released.

Tonight was the night to be up in Studio 9 if
you wanted to get your shine on. As Pete, Cheddar,
and Doub entered the hot spot, it was apparent to
them that this was where they should be.
"This joint rockin'," Pete yelled as he threw a
double shot of Hennessey down his throat and
began chasing it down with a Corona.
"Word, this shit serious tonight," Doub followed
in agreement.
"Yeah, I'm definitely feelin' this piece," said
Cheddar as he sipped on a glass of George Vessele

mixed with Alize from one of six bottles they had
sitting in buckets of ice. This was actually the club
Cheddar and his crew was at when they first
switched from popping their usual bottles of Cristal
to George Vessele the night Wendy Williams
promoted the new drink. Instantly when Cheddar
tried it he enjoyed the smooth mixture of the
Champagne and cognac. Doub and Cheddar had
been smoking weed ever since they left the crib so
the combination of alcohol was adding to their high,
enhancing the potency of the exotic Cush they
burned. Although the two of them smoked weed on
a daily basis, the three of them were considered to
be heavy drinkers. So their tolerance level for
consuming alcohol was to the sky. They drank an
abundance of cognac and cases of Corona's and
Heinekens throughout the course of a day. In any
other case they would be considered alcoholics, but
if you let them tell it they didn't have a drinking
problem. Some years back though some would beg
to differ. Before their tolerance levels were at an all
time high, they were once at an all time low. On
several occasions all three of them had been in
situations either as individually or as a team, where
they over-reacted and put themselves in life
threatening situations that would cause them to lose
their freedom or their lives. Doub had been drinking
heavily one particular night while trying to push up
on a hustler from 3rd street's girl. When the dude
noticed how Doub was all up in his chick's face and
how he was handling her, he approached the scene

with the intent to break up what he saw. Although
he noticed that it was Doub from the New Projects,
and the fact that the block where he was from on 3rd
didn't get along with either project. The kid didn't
have any intention on getting into any type of
confrontation with Doub. As he intervened, and
whispered something into his girls ear, Doub began
to get tight as the alcohol in his system began to
heat up inside, causing his blood to boil. Without
even thinking, Doub push the kid away from the
attractive girl he was trying to take home with him
for the night. Had he been sober he would have
realized that he was her man. The kid stumbled
back from Doub's push, and bumped into a couple
of other females, breaking his fall. Having had his
ego bruised, the kid regained his balance and
charged at Doub. Since Doub was drunk, he never
saw the kid from 3rd and Monroe coming. By the
time he had, it was too late. He was sucker punched
in the jaw by the kid. Luckily, there was no real
power behind the kids punch and Doub wasn't
knocked out. Before Doub was able to sober up
from the blow and having things escalate to a fist
fight; bouncers were already in between the two
trying to defuse the situation. Doub wasn't trying to
hear it, so the two big bouncers escorted him
outside the club. Normally, he would have called
his boys and they would have jumped the kid and
pounded him out, but since he had his glock in his
whip and the Hennessey had him feeling invincible,
he sat outside the club and squatted on his attacker.

When the club let out Doub spotted the kid who
now had his arm around the girl that he was trying
to bed for the night. The alcohol spoke to Doub
playing all sorts of tricks on his mind. He was now
determined to show the kid that he had played
himself. The girl was the first to spot Doub and
yelled it out to her man. Instantly the kid from 3rd
and Monroe sprung into combat mode as he drew
his 357 and began letting off canon sounding rounds
in Doub's direction. But it was no use because
Doub had already gotten the drop on him and was
out the line of fire as he too began letting loose
from his semi-automatic. Being sure that he had hit
his target, Doub fled to his whip, jumped in, and
sped off as his adrenaline pumped rapidly. That was
Doub's first time ever busting his gun at such a
close range. When he had sobered up and gotten
calls from both Cheddar and Pete about the prior
night incident, the only things that was on his mind
now was whether he had caught an unnecessary
body last night. Miraculously, out of the five shots
Doub let off, only one hit the kid, grazing him on
the shoulder. Fortunately for Doub, the kid was not
a snitch, but a stand up dude from the streets who
respected the game. He knew not to involve the
authorities, just keep it to the street, which he did.
When he bumped into Doub one day downtown he
shot him a fair one. Even though Doub lost the
fight, he and the kid still squashed the beef. Doub
continued drinking heavily, even after Cheddar had
crashed his Benz up, and Pete burned his whole left

side up from falling off his 1100 Katana, both from having too much to drink.

"Yo, ain't that Nikki and them over there?" asked Doub.

"Nikki who?" Pete wanted to know.

"Bad ass Nikki. You know, Meesha's home girl."

"Yeah that's them," joined Cheddar spotting the five pretty chicks.

"Oh yeah, over there, Damn them broads is hot for real my dude," said Pete. Now seeing what Doub and Cheddar both saw.

"Hot ain't the word, them lil muthafuckas turned into something real decent," Doub corrected.

"No doubt," agreed Cheddar.

"Yo, you see how Meesha was checkin' Malik though? She was feelin' son," said Pete.

"Yeah, I peeped it," answered Doub.

"Me too," said Cheddar.

"I don't hear about her fuckin' wit mad dudes like some of her partners. Matter of fact I ain't heard about no dudes out the way. She must do her shit out of town or something," Pete said to them.

"You right, I don't ever hear her name like that," said Doub. But I did hear her girlfriend head game was serious. My little man Wheels said she be deep throatin' that shit *and* she swallow.

"Damn! Which one," chimed Pete grabbing the crotch of his jeans at the thought.

"Crystal."

"I believe that shit too, look how big her mu'fuckin lips is,"

"Word her shits is crazy big and Monique got some nice big ass lips too," joined Cheddar staring at Monique.

"What about Yolanda?" asked Pete. "You ain't hear nothin' about her?"

"Nah yo," answered Doub "Oh matter fact yeah, I heard shortie a dick teaser and a virgin. Heard she be talkin' that waitin' on marriage shit. Fuck outta here. She probably a dick teaser but I ain't rollin' with that virgin shit though. She look like somebody smashin' that," said Doub. Both Pete and Cheddar laughed at Doub's last comment.

"You shot out nigga," said Cheddar.

"What?" asked Doub as if unaware why Cheddar had said what he just had?

"Nothing my dude, forget it," replied Cheddar not wanting to get into it with him.

"Yo, let's go holla at 'em," suggested Pete.

"Man I'm tryin' to get at some definite skins for the night, I ain't tryin' to waste my time on nothin' suspect," voiced Doub.

"I'm feelin' that," said Cheddar, "I'm definitely try'nna smash."

"What you think I'm tryin'?" asked Pete. "Them chicks ain't no different than any other chicks we get at. The way you niggas be trickin', it might be cheaper to try to fuck with Nikki and them anyway."

Cheddar and Doub couldn't argue with what Pete
said because they knew that he was 100% right.
When it came to trying to persuade a female or
females to have sex with them, there was no limit to
the extent they would go to proposition the chicks
they intended to sleep with. They were well known
in many strip bars for how generous they were
when it came to dealing with the strippers on a
sexual level. They put out as much as $1200 at
separate times, leaving a club with two dancers, or a
dancer and her female lover. Both Cheddar and
Doub cracked smiles as the thought of Pete's
statement marinated in their brain because they
knew that they were two freak ass tricks.

"Aight, fuck it let's go holla, but if we strike out
nigga, you goin' wit us to Cindy's and coppin' two
chicks for us," said Doub.

"Word," agreed Cheddar. Pete just looked at
them and shook his head.

"You two niggas shot the fuck out, but that's a
bet. If we can't bag three of them then we'll bounce
to Cinderella's and I got you. Trick ass
muthafuckas!" he ended as he laughed.

"Ain't that Cheddar and them comin' over
here?" Crystal was the first one to ask. The five of
her girlfriends looked to see three male figures
making their way over to them.

"Yeah that's them. Look at Pete with his fine
ass," expressed Tee-Tee.

"Girl you ain't never lied, but I heard he ain't got no work in the bed," Crystal offered.

"Now Doub, I heard he suppose to be holding."

"Yeah girl, I heard that too," Nikki joined.

"I heard that about both Doub and Cheddar, and I heard that they some freaks too. They done fucked damn near every stripper in the Tri-State area and then some," said Monique.

"I don't care about all that, I heard they be puttin' that money out, shit I don't mind a brotha breakin' me off if the dick is good!" Crystal said with a little laughter.

"Okay!" Nikki said in agreement.

Meesha listened as her girlfriends carried on about the three that were moving in their direction. At times she could not believe that these were her friends. When they were all growing up together they were not the way they were now. She and Yolanda were the only two out of their crew that were not attracted to or fascinated by what hustler's could do for them. They valued their independence too much. That was the reason why they were so close.

"Ssh! Here they come," whispered Monique hoping they hadn't heard her.

"What's good?" Pete said addressing not one in particular but all of them leaving his options open. They all spoke back, but Tee-Tee, Crystal, and Nikki, addressed them individually by specifically using their names. They wanted them to know who they were interested in. Tee-Tee spoke to Pete,

Crystal spoke to Doub, and Nikki spoke to Cheddar.
Sensing their interest, Pete, Doub, and Cheddar
decided to pursue the three that had spoken their
names. Doub immediately moved in for the kill
after they offered to buy all of the women drinks.
"You leaving with me tonight?" he asked loud
enough for only Crystal to hear. Her smiled
confirmed her answer.

After a lot of conversation and a few drinks,
Cheddar and Pete were confident that they too
would get the response that Doub had gotten. They
wanted to move the party to a more secluded area,
with less noise, less talking and more importantly,
less clothes. It was definitely time to get their freak
on. The night was winding down; Cheddar, Pete,
and Doub were ready to head to the nearest motel.
Meesha and Yolanda knew what time it was, even
before their friends began saying their goodbyes.
They were use to their girls stepping off with men
they were attracted to. As the girls were getting
situated, Doub stepped to Meesha with the
intentions of picking her brain.

"Yo Meesha, what up?" Meesha gave Doub a
puzzling stare. Sensing her confusion, Doub came
at her differently.

"Yo what you think about my man Malik?" At
the sound of hearing Malik's name, Meesha's whole
demeanor changed. She had been thinking about
him the entire night, causing her to turn down
several dance offers, conversations, drinks, and
numbers, the things that most of the men and

women in the club come for. Not really knowing why Doub had asked, Meesha decided to tap dance around the question.

"What do you mean what do I think about him?"

"I mean, yo, I seen the way ya'll was vibin' at Hugo's, and I know my man. I can tell when he feelin' a chick and it looked like you was feelin' him too, so what up?" asked Doub. Convinced that his question was genuine Meesha gave in.

"Yeah, I like him, and I guess he like me too. We were together earlier today."

"Word?" asked Doub surprised at Meesha's statement.

"Yeah, well not really together, but I dropped him off at home. He was walkin' from Jumah and I was across the street at the shop."

"Oh, yeah he Muslim now, that's cool he tryin' to stay on his Deen, I ain't mad at him," Doub said admirably.
Meesha caught the admiration and respect for Malik in Doub's tone. This intrigued her even more, but there was something else mixed in as well; she just couldn't place it. Had Meesha known the history between the four of them it would have been apparent that there was a bit of guilt in Doub's words as well.

"Yeah, it is. That's good he's trying to do right. I respect him for that." Meesha wanted Doub to know her opinion of Malik. She knew like women men also gossiped and knew whenever he got the chance he would let Malik know she was interested.

"Oh yeah, no doubt. Malik's a good dude and I want to see him do good, no matter what. I'm just sayin' he deserves to be doin' good cause the dude been gone for a minute. He deserves to have a good chick on his team too," Doub stated. "Hope I'm not out of line," Doub then paused. "But I think that you a good chick. Not like that snake broad Dawn he use to fuck wit. So if you really feelin' him, then handle ya business."

"Thanks Doub."

"I know you will. Aight yo let me get up out of here before your girl change her mind," Doub grinned. Meesha shook her head and smiled again. She knew what Doub meant. It was none of her business though. She too was now ready to call it a night. Everyone said their goodbyes and went their separate ways.

CHAPTER THIRTEEN

MALIK awoke on a positive note, feeling better than he had for quite sometime and he had every reason to. After being home for almost two weeks and filling out one application after another he had finally caught a break and landed a job interview. He continued to make Duua's in his prayers, asking that Allah open a door of opportunity for him, and here it was on this bright Wednesday morning. As he groomed and prepared for his big day, he thought about how this would be the first time in his life that he had gone on an interview. And if all went well, this would also be his first legal gig. He was somewhat nervous, but he was really looking forward to acing the interview and landing the job. He was not concerned with the work, the pay, or the hours because he was determined to do whatever it took to stay out of jail. The same determination, energy, and passion that drove him when he was in the game, was the same thing he would use to try to establish himself in the work force. Anything was better than nothing any day Malik felt. He knew that he would rather get the job at Sears in their warehouse than to get back in the game and have to look over his shoulder constantly. At least he would be able to sleep peacefully at night knowing that the money he made wasn't any type of blood money or food money being taken out of little mouths. His mother was so proud of him when he shared his good news with her about the call he received from the Sears representative. She always believed that something would come through for her son, and now that day had come. She thanked God for watching over her baby boy and keeping him on the straight path. She promised to add more money to her offering at the church for the blessing sent down to her son.

"Malik, boy get your butt in here and eat this breakfast, so I can get you up there early," Ms. Jones yelled towards the bathroom area. "You don't want to be late for your interview. It doesn't look good. Besides you been in the bathroom for over an hour. You're worse than a woman."
Malik smiled as he finished lining his beard up. Even in prison he had often been accused of hogging up the bathroom and was teased in the same way that his mother just had.

"Here I come now ma," he yelled back.

Malik shoved the last bit of toast in his mouth and put his plate and glass that was once filled with orange juice in the sink.

"Thanks ma, I needed that," he said to his mother, kissing her the cheek and snatching up his jacket.

"You're welcome baby, you can repay me by taking me out to breakfast when you get your first pay check," she said confidently.

"That's a deal."

CHAPTER FOURTEEN

" MR. JONES, Mr. Solomon is ready to see you now, the red haired, freckled faced white secretary advised Malik, flashing him her best phony smile. Malik saw right through her but didn't care he was caught up in the moment. *I'm happy to be here.* He said to himself as he smiled on the inside.

"Thank you," he replied as he got up and walked by returning her smile. Only his was genuine, because he was really happy to be there. Noticing the warmth in his smile, the red head added, "Good luck."

"Good morning Mr. Jones my name is Mr. Solomon, have a seat he extended his hand in the direction of the chair. Malik figured he stood at about 6'1 with the frame of a basketball player. He looked no more than about 35 years old with a student type of look. His office was put together in a way in which one could tell that he was a man who dealt with organization because everything looked as if were in its' proper place, neatly positioned. There were several different plaques and framed certificates on the walls and a few trophies off to the left confirming Malik's guess about Mr. Solomon's educational background. He sat before Malik with what he believed to be his own application that he submitted. After about two minutes of silence Mr. Solomon spoke again.

"Mr. Jones, I was just looking over your application that you submitted to our company, and I have to say with all due respect that I don't see any consistency or any type of previous job references at all listed on your application, and based on how you answered number seven when asked have you ever been convicted of a felony, you answered 'yes'. Would you like to explain in person? I assume that you spent a lengthy amount of time incarcerated, am I correct?"

"Yes sir," answered Malik making eye contact with Mr. Solomon. Something his mother had suggested.

"How long were you confined for?"

"Ten years."

"When were you released?"

"Almost two weeks ago."

"Prior to your incarceration have you ever had any work experience?"

"No sir,"

"So this would be your first employment if hired, is that correct?"

"Yes sir, that would be right," replied Malik unable to read Mr. Solomon's demeanor.

"I noticed that you put that you'd work on holidays and weekends, and you are a hard worker."

"Yes sir, I am, and I will."

"Tell me about your incarceration, what were you convicted of?"

At the sound of that, Malik heart began to pump a little faster. The last time he had to repeat the crimes he had committed was the day in court when he entered his guilty plea and the judge told him to state what he was been guilty of. Although he committed the crimes, he was accused of and even some he hadn't been caught for, he always had a problem with admitting them to anyone. To him it was almost like telling on himself, but he knew that if he had any chance of getting this job he had to answer the question.

"I was convicted of manslaughter," was all Malik had because there was nothing else that he could say with it that would make it sound any less that what it was. Up until that point Malik could get no reading from Mr. Solomon's facial expression, but hearing what his conviction had been, it was apparent now what Mr. Solomon was thinking.

"Mr. Jones, the way we determine hiring employees here at our company is based on their resumes which consists of their experience, skills, and previous job references, and things of that nature. There are some positions that require minimum experience, if any at all, but at this time we have none of those positions available, and as an employer I have to make the best as well as the proper decisions when hiring employees. In an event that one of our positions that I mentioned has an opening, you will be kept in mind for future positions. The best of luck to you though Mr. Jones and I appreciate your time and patience with us," ended Mr. Solomon.

Before Mr. Solomon had reached the final verdict of the interview, Malik had already known what the outcome would be. He was disappointed because he really needed the work, but he was not surprised. He knew that number seven would be the turning point of the interview and was surprised that he had gotten as far as an interview with answering the question truthfully. At the bottom of all the applications he filled out they all said the same thing, *Please answer number seven truthfully, you will not be discriminated against by your answer.* After today's interview, Malik believed that the statement on the application was put on there to aid businesses that were actually prejudiced. What started out as a good day began to quickly turn into a gloomy one for Malik. It was at that moment that he heard the whispers of the demons that were locked away in the back of his mind. Malik ignored the whispers that echoed inside his head but, there was no doubt that he had heard what the whispers were saying. Ms. Jones tried to console her son, reading the disappointment in his face when he exited the building and headed towards the car. Malik fell silent and remained that way the whole ride home. Malik went straight to the couch and stretched out as soon as he entered the house, deep in his own thoughts. There was nothing that his mother or anyone else for that matter could say that could assure Malik that everything was going to be all right. He had worked so hard in prison to prepare himself for the work field and now everything he did was shot down in a matter of minutes. No matter how honest he was on his application or how eager it appeared that he wanted to work, and would work hard, the only thing Malik felt that the employer was concerned about was the fact that he was convicted of manslaughter. He was often told that when he got home and tried to establish a legitimate way of earning a income he would already have two strikes against him, one being a black man and two being a convicted felon. He thought that the brothers used those reasons as a crutch or to justify why they chose the illegal route. Experiencing it first hand, he believed those two strikes that the brothers told him about were true. Getting back in the game was not the route that he wanted to take, and he would fight it for as long as he could. He wanted so bad to do the right thing but the continuous struggle was becoming so overwhelming for him that he began to question his capabilities as a working man. He had never felt so insecure in his life and he was uncomfortable with the feeling. Malik knew that if he didn't find work soon the demons locked in the back of his head would eventually find a way to persuade him to do their bidding. All types of thoughts ran through

Malik's head as he lay there. So many different images flashed before his eyes to the point of giving him a migraine. He didn't realize he had dozed off until he heard his sister Mandy's voice. He opened his eyes to find Mandy standing over him with the cordless in her hand.

"Telephone," she said extending it in Malik's direction. Half asleep, Malik asked.

"Who is it," Mandy smiled pleased about who was on the other end of the receiver.

"It's Meesha."

"Meesha?" he asked as if he never heard the name before, not recalling giving her his mother's number.

"Don't act like you don't know who she is Malik," his sister replied with a smirk on her face. Wiping his face, Malik stood up and took the phone from his sister as he stretched.

"Nah, I know who it is, I'm just half asleep that's all."

"I wasn't going to wake you up, but Meesha my girl and she good peoples, and I know you would like her," Mandy spoke excitedly. Malik grinned. "Oh you do huh?"

"Yeah I do," now talk on the phone boy and stop tryin' to act all hard," Mandy told her big brother. Meesha laughed on the other end of the phone, enjoying the conversation between sister and brother. It made her think back to her own brother, Troy. She felt the love between Malik and Mandy

171

and wondered if one day he would possess that same type of love for her.

"Hello?" Malik waved Mandy off. Mandy exited the room sticking her tongue out at her brother.

"Hey," answered Meesha.

"Pardon me for the hold up, I just woke up."

"Yeah, I know. I heard." Meesha said with laughter in her tone.

"Oh you heard all that huh?"

"Yeah," she replied still laughing.

"My little sister crazy, with her grown self," said Malik.

"No, its okay, it was cool I know it was all in love, but I apologize for waking you up though."

"You don't have to apologize, besides you didn't wake me she did,"

"Yeah, but she woke you up for me."

"It's cool, I'm sure it's worth it." Meesha smiled at Malik's comment.

"Thank you."

"You don't have to thank me," Malik replied. It had been almost two weeks since he had seen or heard from Meesha. He had been so busy and caught up trying to find a job that he forgot that he even had her number. Like his little sister had said, he definitely liked her and by receiving a phone call from her today, Malik assumed that it was mutual. It was going on a month now that Malik had been home. Besides the time he had spent around the house with his mother and attending Muslim services, he really didn't have a social life. He hadn't taken any time out for himself to enjoy his freedom. He was so focused on finding work. Hearing Meesha's voice on the other end made him realize that he had been lacking female companionship. Even as a free man, Malik was still a ten-year virgin. The thought humored him. Speaking to Meesha had sparked something inside of Malik and lifted him up from the slump he had been in earlier. He thought that Meesha was exactly what the doctor ordered for him in his life. He intended to take full advantage of the dosage prescribed. From the first time he laid eyes on her in Hugo's, Malik knew that there was a connection between the two of them. At the same time, he was just coming home and didn't have time to really adjust to his freedom or even get his feet fully planted for that matter.

"The reason I called was because I hadn't heard from you and I thought by now I would have, so I wanted to make sure that everything was alright?" Malik couldn't believe her words. It had been along time since a woman had spoken to him with such concern besides his mother. In that instant, he built a certain admiration for Meesha and had to agree with Mandy that she was good peoples.

"I appreciate that, but yeah I'm good and I didn't forget about you, I really did intend to call you but the past two weeks have just been hectic for me, trying to find work and all." Malik didn't want to go into detail about his present situation.

"I understand. I know how hard it is. I mean, I can imagine how difficult it is just coming home after so long trying to get reestablished out here. I mean it's crazy. People that have never been to jail are out here struggling and can't get established. That's why there are so many brothers on these street corners, you know?"

Malik was impressed with Meesha's words. He could tell that she had a good head on her shoulders, which Malik thought was an advantage in life. The way she spoke made Malik know that she truly did understand. She felt where he was coming from. He was grateful that she made him feel comfortable discussing an uncomfortable topic.

"Yeah I know exactly what you mean and I agree, but it can't stay like that forever," Malik spoke trying to restore his self-confidence.

"You right. So what's up stranger?"

"I can't call it, just taking it one day at a time, you know? What's up wit you?"

"Nothing, just wondering when we gonna go out together, that's all," Meesha bluntly stated. Malik couldn't help but to laugh at Meesha's cockiness. The same aggressiveness she displayed now was the same she had in their last two encounters. She was indeed his type of woman, intelligent, sexy, and straight up. Besides going to Hugo's his first night at home, Malik hadn't gone out since, which is why he considered the offer. Who, in their right mind, would turn down such an offer from someone as

fine as Meesha? No one he could think of- in their
right mind. He jumped at the opportunity.
"Whenever."
Meesha was surprised by Malik's response but had
no complaints. She had only thrown the question
out there to make conversation. She never thought
that Malik would take it serious, even though she
really did want to go out with him. What woman
wouldn't as fine as he was and as thorough as she
heard he was, Meesha thought. She decided to see
whether or not his response had been just thrown
out there like her statement was.
"You don't want to go out with me."
"Why you say that?" asked Malik puzzled
"Because your schedule is probably booked up
for the rest of the year," said Meesha trying to
sound serious. Malik was confused. He had no idea
what Meesha was talking about.
"What?"
"Don't act like you don't know."
"Know what?" asked Malik confused. He really
had no clue as to what Meesha was referring to.
Unable to hold it any longer and sensing Malik's
irritation, Meesha brought her game to an end.
"You know every chick in town talkin' about
you and wanna get at you. I know your mother's
phone has been ringing off the hook with dates,"
she said as she laughed a little between her
statements, hoping that what she had said had no
truth to it. Malik's confusion was now replaced with
laughter. He wanted to smack himself for not

realizing that Meesha had been playing the entire time. Seeing that Meesha had only been playing, he felt a little embarrassed about not being able to recognize a joke, but where he had just come from was no joke. It was a very serious environment, serious as a heart attack. Although you shared occasional laughs with your immediate circle, the tension in the air at the prison was so thick that the majority of the time, you could hardly breathe. But he was home now, and it was time to lighten up and live he told himself.

"Aw you got me, that was funny," said Malik giving Meesha props for her Academy Award performance.

"But I hope you know it's not even like that at all. I don't have any women coming at me like that. If they're trying to get at me then they must be dialing the wrong number," Malik offered, adding his own humor to the topic.

"As a matter of fact you're the only one that dialed it right."

If Malik could only see the big grin that Meesha had plastered on her face, showing her perfectly set white teeth, he would have known right then and there that he had the key to her heart. No man had ever made her feel the way that Malik had at that moment with mere words.

Other men had tried to spit game in attempts to get a spark out of her or pique her interest, but Malik's words came out natural and sounded genuine, as if he were the first to ever say them.

"Well if you not just saying that to just to gas me up then I'm glad that I'm the only one who got it right," Meesha responded back.

"I'm not trying to gas you up, I'm dead serious," replied Malik wanting her to know.

"Okay then, I believe you."

"Good, cause it's true."

"Now that we got that out the way, how does this weekend sound?" she asked

"Sounds like a plan," Malik said without hesitation.

"Alright, what time do you get home from Jumah?"

The fact that she remembered he attended Muslim service on Fridays impressed Malik.

"I should be home by 2:30 because one of the brothers drops me off at home now."

"Okay, I'll call you and we'll take it from there."

"That'll be cool, just make sure you call, cause your schedule might be busy," Malik slid, giving her a dose of her own medicine.

"You just make sure you answer the phone," Meesha shot back smiling from ear to ear.

"If I don't then that means it's out of order."

"Funny. So, until then."

"Until then," Malik repeated.

Malik hung up with Meesha feeling ten times better than he had before. He was looking forward to the weekend rolling around so that he could spend some time with her. He wondered where they would go, and what they would do because he hadn't been out

with a female in almost ten years. As he thought
about that, something else popped up inside his
head. It dawned on him that he had no money to go
out on any type of date with Meesha. The thought
of being broke turned his stomach and dampened
his spirits again. His original feelings that he felt
earlier that day after the job interview slowly began
to seep out as he continued to dwell on his financial
status. He continued to hear the whispers and
knocks of the demons locked away. They were
much louder than they were earlier which made it
harder for Malik to ignore them, but he tried his
best. Each time he questioned himself as to what he
could do, the demons would answer back, *You know
what you can do. You know what you gotta do!*
Malik fought the unwanted advice. Thinking back
to his night at Hugo's, Malik remembered his man
Justice giving him his number to reach him. Back in
the day when he was younger, there was no way
that he would ever considered asking for help
outside his hood, especially someone from the 3rd
St. area, which had been his project's street rivals
for as long as he could remember. Growing up in
prison taught him some of life's most valuable
lessons. One, that where you were from did not
define who you were. He knew that Justice was a
genuine dude and would loan him a few dollars
until he got situated. Ironically, Malik felt more
comfortable with reaching out to Justice over
Cheddar, Doub, and Pete. Besides, he wasn't
looking for any handouts; he just needed something

to hold him down until he got on his feet and found work. There was no way he could see himself asking his manz and them because they had let him down once before when he needed them the most and he refused to let that happen again, or give them the satisfaction of thinking that he needed them. He had more love for Justice, who was considered an outsider because he was from another block, than he did those he had come up with. One of the things you find out about men in prison is there were thoroughbreds from all over, just like there were snakes from all over too. One of the most popular statements in jails throughout the world was what rapper Rakim had said in a rap song, *"It ain't where you from it's where you at,"* thought Malik.

Malik pulled out Justice's number, picked the phone back up and dialed the seven digits that were on the piece of paper.

CHAPTER FIFTEEN

" **YO**, we gotta turn it the fuck up kid cause our flow ain't like it use to be," said Doub.

"Word, shit is slow around the way B. Every time I check on our young boys around the way to see if I gotta re 'em up, they still sittin' on the last package I hit 'em wit for two and three days," added Pete.

"You know why right?" asked Cheddar as if he had the missing piece to the puzzle, but both Doub and Pete already knew the reason why. It was no secret who was behind the drought in their projects. That night they saw him at Hugo's they exchanged stares, neither man saying anything to the other, but the ice grills they shot him and he shot back in return said it all. On both parts, out of respect for Malik's presence and his just coming home, both parties decided to let it ride for the time being. Doub, Cheddar, and Pete wondered how Malik had saved Justice's life in prison and what he was doing even dealing with Justice like that in the first place. He wasn't from the projects. What they didn't know was that on many occasions Malik confided in Justice about how his so called manz and them had

left him for dead, and that night Justice also
wondered what Malik was doing was doing with the
three niggas that had abandoned him in his time of
need. Ever since Justice had started selling ounces
of coke for $750 and his bricks of dope for $225,
plus his workers selling crack 3 for $20 and $7 bags
of diesel, Doub, Pete and Cheddar couldn't compete
when their own ounces went for $850 and their
bricks of heroin for $275. Their workers took
nothing less than 3 for $25 on the crack and straight
$10 off the bags of dope. They knew that Justice
had to have a proper connect in order to move his
product for such prices. To top it off Justice had
good product, which made it that much harder for
them to compete. They refused to drop down to
Justice's prices. At the cost they were paying they
were guaranteed to lose, so that was not an option.
Instead, they had to come up with some other way
to slow Justice's flow down and increase their own.

"Yeah, that nigga the cause of all this bullshit,"
Doub was the first to say.

"Yeah that nigga killin' em right now with them
seven dollar bags of diesel and that 3 for $20 shit,"
said Pete.

"And the nigga got o's for dirt cheap."

"I know, that mu'fuckin doin' it up big right
now," said Cheddar.

"They gotta be at least pullin' in 30 to 40 G's a
day out that piece on the ground alone, and niggas
coppin' them onions from the nigga for $750 like
hotcakes."

"Word, that's damn near New York prices, and you know niggas don't try to dip over there like that anyway fuckin' wit the tunnels and the GWB. I heard niggas from the east end just got knocked comin' out the Holland. They were comin' thru Jersey City with two birds and three pounds of smoke. Niggas shook right now to go over so they tryin' to find the best deal, so they ain't gotta go to NY," said Doub.

"I heard about them niggas getting knocked a couple of days ago, and I figured that would have niggas getting at us, but I only got rid of like 24 o's since then. You know I was good for at least a brick and a half every two to three days," said Cheddar.

"Word, I only moved a little over a quarter in four days. I'm still workin' on my first brick out of the five you gave me last week," said Pete.

"Yo, shit is crazy right now kid, something gotta give," demanded Doub.

"I'm wit you Bee, that nigga is a problem, and he need to be solved, nah mean?"

"No doubt, but how we gonna handle it?" asked Pete. They all pondered on Pete's question for a minute, then Cheddar spoke.

"However we handle it, it gotta be on some mu'fuckin street shit, nah mean? Let niggas know that The New run shit. Niggas think cause a nigga seeing paper he can't be touched. Yeah aight, that black mu'fucka can get touched and I ain't never seen a mu'fuckin armored car behind a hearse before."

Both Doub Pete nodded their heads. They knew what Cheddar meant.

CHAPTER SIXTEEN

" **PEACE** to the gods," greeted Justice answering his cell phone. Malik couldn't help but laugh at the way Justice answered the phone. He remembered how Justice always responded the same way when they were in prison whenever someone wanted to speak with him.

"Peace," Malik answered trying to disguise his voice but Justice recognized the voice and became attentive.

"Malik what's the deal Big Muslim?" Justice announced happy to be hearing from his friend, addressing him by his prison monarch.

"Nothin' much beloved, just tryin' to maintain, you know?"

"I hear that, how you holdin' up though?"

"You know how it is akh when you first come home, shit rough, but I've seen rougher days."

"I feel you yo. What's happenin' though you aight other wise?" asked Justice.

"I ain't even gonna front akh, not really, that's why I called cause I ain't have no other brother I could really holla at."

Before Malik could go any further Justice cut him off in mid-sentence.

"Say no more dawg, I got you. Where you at?"

"At my moms crib."

"Where that's at?"

"On E. Second St. "

"Second and what?"

"Leland."

"Nuff said, give me about ten minutes and I'm there. I'm on 22 right now comin' up on the Terrill Rd. exit."

"Aight yo, I'll be outside in front, it's a light blue and white house.

"Got you."

"Just, good lookin' yo," said Malik appreciating the assistance.

"Come on god, you my peoples, that's nothin'. I'm just glad you hollered at ya dude instead of gettin' at ya manz and 'em from the projects. Speakin' of that, I gotta get at you about somethin' anyway that's been heavy on the mental. I'll be there in about five I just turned off."

"Yeah, no doubt we'll poly when you get here." When they hung up Malik thought back to what Justice had said about Cheddar and them, about him being glad that he got at him instead of them. The average Joe would've looked at it like Justice wanted to make sure that Malik didn't go backwards after remembering how they weren't there for him when he was bidding. Malik was far from being an average Joe. He knew that it was

J.M. Benjamin

more to Justice's statement than he said and he had
a strong feeling that whatever it was Justice wanted
to talk about to him had something to do with his
manz and them. He went outside and waited for
Justice to arrive, curious to fine out what was going
on.

Justice pulled up shortly in his gold Yukon
XL, sitting on 26" rims. Justice was a big guy so he
needed a big truck. The SUV fit him perfectly.
Malik jotted to the truck, got in and they pulled off.
Just as Doub's truck was when Malik entered it,
Justice's was almost identical on the inside tricked
out with the TV's, DVD player and Playstation.
Malik wondered if every hustler in town with an
SUV had their truck laced like Doub's and
Justice's. He knew if he had been home during that
era in the game, he also would have a big truck,
sitting on chrome, decked out inside.

He and Justice pounded each other up as the
sound system filled the Yukon with a track off of
Tupac's classic CD *Ambition of a Rider*. Malik
remembered how Justice used to play his favorite
CD everyday in the penitentiary. Justice turned the
volume down as they rode through downtown.

"You still love that CD huh?" asked Malik.

"What? This is a classic here kid, nobody gets
deeper than the brotha Pac. God bless the dead. Big
was a ill dude and a lyrical muthafucka, but Pac was
a poet. Both them niggas was ahead of their time.
You know *Ready to Die* is the next joint in my
changer."

"I feel you akh, they both was the best that ever done it."

"No doubt, and that nigga Hov up there with 'em too, don't get it fucked up," said Justice.

"No question, but 50 cents holdin' it down for the East right now."

"Oh yeah, can't leave 50 and them G-unit niggas out."

"I know all them joints be club bangers."

"Word," Justice responded as he switched to the *Get Rich or Die Trying soundtrack*, keeping the volume down low.

"But when I wanna zone out I put my D-Block and Dip-Set niggas in. I don't give a fuck about all that industry beefing shit. I played the shit I'm livin' and survived, feel me Big Muslim?"

"True," Malik agreed. He too felt the same about the controversy and violence surrounding hip-hop.

"Here take this," Justice motioned to Malik as he handed him a knot full of money.

"That should hold you until you get situated." Without counting it, Malik stuffed the money inside his jacket pocket.

"Good lookin' Just. You know I appreciate this."

"That's nothin', you my peoples. Without your help I would probably be dead already. I wasn't bullshittin' when I said you saved my life in the penn. If it wasn't for you I probably woulda came home and started back usin' instead of slingin'. Technically, I owe all this shit to you," said Justice waving his hand in the air as in reference to his SUV.

"Nah akh, you don't owe me nothin'. You did everything on your own; I just pulled your coat on your full potential.

"However you wanna look at it you played a part in me getting back on top of my game and I'll never forget that. I got a lot of love for you Leek, that's real!"

"I got a lot of love for you too," replied Malik. Just pulled out onto the highway in route to his destination, ready to discuss what he intended to talk to Malik about. Even though he noticed that they had just entered the highway, Malik didn't question Justice about their travels because he was confident that he wouldn't put him in the same type of position his manz and them had. He knew that Justice wasn't as reckless as they were, especially with him being on parole himself. He was sure that there were no drugs, alcohol, or weapons in Justice's truck. He also knew that when you were knee deep in the game the way Justice was you could never be too sure. There was always that chance of you making that fatal mistake of thinking that it's alright to travel dirty this one time. That's when a nigga gets knocked. He refused to ask Justice was he traveling dirty. He just hoped that he wasn't, for both of their sakes. Some people would call him paranoid, but to Malik, he was being cautious. Picking up on Malik's uneasiness, Justice wanted to make sure that his friend was as comfortable as possible with him. He had a great deal of respect for Malik and felt honored to have him in his presence. He was familiar with Malik's background because they were from the same town, and he always admired how he kept it gangster on the streets before he went to prison. He could tell that Malik wanted no more parts of the streets or the game, but nothing would have made Justice happier than having someone like Malik on his team. He thought it would have been an insult to offer Malik a piece of the pie, but all it would take is for him to say that he wanted in for Justice to make him a 50/50 partner. Just knew that there was no way Malik would ever deal with his manz and them again, but to be 100% positive of that he had to ask Malik and hear it from Malik's own mouth. In prison you say a lot of things and go against them when you get out. He didn't view Malik as being that kind of individual, but when it comes to the streets you always have to cover your back.

"Leek, don't worry baby boy we ain't dirty, I'm good. I'mma shoot to Newark and drop this paper off to one of my little honey's and we gonna turn back around, aight."

"Yeah that's cool, do ya thing." Answered Malik relieved by Just's words. Switching lanes, Justice knew it was time to address what had been on his mind since he had last seen Malik with them.

"Ayo Malik. Remember when we were at Hugo's?"

J.M. Benjamin

"Yeah," replied Malik knowing Justice's next question.

"What was you doin' wit them dudes?" Justice finally asked no longer wanting to beat around the bush. Malik gave it to Justice straight up.

"Yo if you askin' me do I fuck with them cats like that the answer is no," said Malik as he replayed the whole episode from the time he bumped into Pete at parole down to when they entered Hugo's. Satisfied with what he heard, Justice felt that Malik needed to know the situation between him and his manz and 'em.

"Yo, I don't know if they told you or not but me and them cats don't see eye to eye. They ain't feelin' me and I definitely ain't feelin' them either. It's a lot of bullshit goin' on, and they startin' it. But I'mma wind up finishin' it though. You know how that shit is kid. Niggas feelin' some type of way cause I'm eatin' right now and I'm takin' food outta their mouths I guess. But that ain't my concern. I'm just tryin to do me. I be hearin' that them niggas sayin' little slick shit on the low around muthafuckas, around niggas and chicks, feel me. Come on dawg you know you not suppose to be runnin' ya mouth like that around no broads. That's one of the unwritten rules of the game. The funny shit about it though is that them dudes ain't said nothin' to me though. If you gangsta, bring it to me!" Justice expressed his tone becoming more agressive.

190

"I needed to know where you stood with them
cats 'cause you my man and I ain't tryin to have no
fall out with you over some shit you ain't, even a
part of, feel me? Between me and you, the night we
was all up in Hugo's one of my main lieutenants got
pushed coming up out of Ben's. I can't say for sure
and the streets ain't talkin' yet, but if I get any type
of wire that they had their hands in it, it's a—."

"Say no more akhi," Malik stopped Justice
before finishing his sentence. Justice had been so
caught up in his own thoughts and feelings that he'd
almost forgotten that Malik was no longer in the
game nor did he live life on the terms Justice had.
"My bad beloved, I know better than that, but you
can see how this thing is gonna turn out in a minute
and I just don't wanna see you up in the middle or
nothin' like that. You just comin' home and you
don't know what's goin' on out here in the streets.
You've been away for a while. I was the same way
when I came home, and I was fucked up for a
minute until I got back in the swing of things. I been
goin' hard every since, but you remember how we
use to always hear how niggas got out after doin 5,
7, 10, and 15 years and only home for about 30 days
and get bodied or knocked right back off and be
back in the system. I ain't tryin' to see that shit
happen to you like that dawg. Niggas like us is
gonna always be on top and stay on top cause that's
what our hands call for nah mean? That's why I
know you gonna be alright and I respect how you
tryin' something new. When I came home I was on

it the same way you on it. I gave up kid, straight the fuck up. Shit was rough. I got three kids dawg. So, I had to go out there and do what I do best. I got me a hammer from the nigga Tah-Tah, went over to New York, robbed one of the papi's on Broadway, took that shit and flipped it on another part of Broadway, came home, opened up shop, and been on every since. As crazy as this might sound, I had to come back to the place where I felt most comfortable, and that's the hood."

Malik hung onto Justice's every word, from his beef with Cheddar and them to his struggles when he came home and how he handled it. He understood Justice's position as a hustler doing his thing in the street being subjected to beef and war over drugs and money. Malik understood Justice taking matters into his own hands when he couldn't find work and doing what he had to do to get on in order to survive. Malik knew that any father from the streets who was in Justice's shoes would have chosen a similar route because no man would ever feel like a real man if they couldn't provide for their family. What they didn't realize at the time was that if caught, the only survival they would have to be concerned about is their own lives in the prison system.

Malik waited until Justice was done before he spoke. "Yo Just, I appreciate you pullin' me up on the situation and all with you and them dudes, but you know none of that pertains to me. You know I know the drill so I ain't mad at you at all, but like I said I don't rock with my manz and 'em like that no more," said Malik. " And besides I got more love for you than I got for any of them dudes even though I've known them jokers damn near all my life, you know akh?" Malik added.

"I feel you big bro and you know I got love for you too, I was just pulling you up because I didn't want you to be in the dark about no shit and get caught in the mix," Justice explained.

"No doubt, but I'm not in the game no more so I don't even think about all of that. But on some real, I hope you brothers can reconcile your differences peacefully." Justice shot Malik an indiscernible grin after hearing his words.

"I know akh," Malik continued seeing the look on Justice's face. "I know in the streets it didn't turn out like that, I'm just sayin'. I remember hearing about you when you got out, how you were out here goin' hard puttin' the pressure on dudes, muscling the block and all of that. I didn't know the depth of your madness until you just told me, but still I used to make prayer for you that Allah protect and watch over you while you were out here. I see you now and it's good seeing you, not cause you doin' ya thing in the streets but because you still alive and in good health. A lot of brother's from our era that came up runnin' can't say that. I thank Allah everyday for sparing me akh. I'm not knocking what you do or condoning it but I can't do it no more. I don't want no parts of the streets. I don't wanna take that route, right now I'm just trying to gut it out and do the right thing, feel me akh."

"I know yo," Justice replied. "And I respect you for that. I just wanna see you do good that's all," he added.

"You will akh, trust me you will." After Justice gave his young jump off her monthly bill money and allowance for her services, he and Malik headed back to Plainfield. Justice pulled in front of Malik's mother's house and parked.

"Yo I appreciate this paper akh," Malik stated as he exited the Yukon.

"You told me that already baby boy, that's nothin'" replied Just. Malik just smiled. In his book Justice was a good dude, not because of the money he had given him but because of the manner in which it was given. Malik was positive that there was no hidden agenda or ulterior motive behind Justice's generosity, like he felt would have been with his manz and them.

"Aight my brother."

"Yeah, I get up", said Justice. "And you know if you need more just holla, it's there."

"I know akh, but I'm good."

"Well just in case. And get at me anytime so we can cool out. Shortie you just saw got some bad friends I can get her to plug you in. I know they'll be feelin' you with your big pretty ass," Justice joked. "My chick looked like *she* wanted to give you some when I introduced you."

"Go ahead with that akh," Malik said as he cracked a smile.

"Yeah aight, don't let me catch you around my chick Malik, I'm telling you," said Justice with a smile.

"Get out of here Just," said Malik as he reached for the car door handle.

"Aight yo, I'm out, but if you need me just holla."

"No doubt akh," Just blew the horn and he pulled off.

When Malik entered the house the first person he saw was his mother, standing there with her back towards him. He snuck up behind her and gave her a kiss on the cheek. She smiled, spoke, and told him he was just in time for dinner. Malik went to the bathroom to prepare himself for prayer and dinner. Before he started, he pulled out the roll of money Justice gave him and began counting it. When he was done counting, the stack of hundred dollar bills the tally was $2500. Malik had no idea that the amount of money Just had given him was so much. He wasn't surprised because that was the type of dude that he viewed Just to be. He made a mental promise to himself he would never forget this day.

CHAPTER SEVENTEEN

THE weekend had arrived and the ball was in motion. Meesha and Malik had confirmed their date that Friday afternoon, and now at 7:05 pm Malik waited patiently for Meesha to come and pick him up. They both decided and agreed on going to the popular comedy club in New York, Caroline's. They had reservations for the 9:30 show, which included dinner and drinks. Malik had never been to the establishment before but he had heard how nice of a spot it was from a female who worked in the prison. Meesha had never gone before either, but had also heard the same from a few of the girls at the shop where she got her hair done. Malik was definitely dressed for the part for the evening. From the clothes that Cheddar, Doub, and Pete had bought him, Malik wore a crème colored Ralph Lauren mock neck shirt under a chocolate brown suede blazer and a pair of dark blue denim Polo jeans with almost identical chocolate suede with crème stitching Pellegrini shoes. It had been a long time since he felt such smooth fabric up against his skin. It was indeed a big step up from the khakis and yellow state boots he had become accustomed to. He was just tucking his shirt in and pulling it

back out a little when the white BMW pulled up.
Meesha was impressed with Malik's appearance
when she pulled up and saw him standing there on
the porch. She analyzed him from head to toe as he
began approaching the car. He was by far one of the
handsomest brothers she had ever laid eyes on in a
thuggish type of way.

She blushed to herself as her panties moistened at
the thought of how attractive she found Malik to be.
Other than his physical appearance, there was
something else about Malik that turned Meesha on.
It was the way he carried himself. Confident and
calm, but nothing about him was timid. He seemed
to be the epitome of strength. Meesha picked up on
it the first night they were introduced at Hugo's.
There was nothing that she loved more than a strong
black man. She was glad she was at Hugo's that
night. Malik was the last of a dying breed Meesha
thought. Brothers like him were scarce where she
came from.

"Hey," Meesha said as Malik got in the car.

"What's up," he responded scanning her
appearance

"You look nice."

"Thank you." Meesha had out done herself from
head to toe for the occasion and Malik noticed
immediately, which was a plus on his part. Meesha
was a sucker for a compliment. She had specifically
told Alnisa to hook her up with a different hairstyle
than usual this go around. When it was all said and
done Meesha looked like the poster child for a Dark

197

and Lovely ad. Meesha had gone all out on her outfit and felt that this evening was well worth what
she put on her body. She sported a mahogany
colored Roberto Cavalli suede jacket and wide lapel
and collar, along with a contour fitting t-shirt, the
matching Roberto Cavalli suede skirt that possessed
a diamond shaped cut elastic in the front that ran to
a point exactly in the middle of her thighs. She liked
the comfortable fit of the skirt as she thought back
to how she slipped in it at home, as she admired the
perfect fit in her mirror. To top her outfit off,
Meesha sported the half calf high brown and tan
fendi boots with the fendi spy bag to match. It was
if as though she and Malik had read each other's
mind the way their colors coordinated. Malik caught
an instant erection at the sight of Meesha. He had
dealt with many women in the past, but Meesha was
definitely the hottest female he ever came across.
Malik tried to block her appearance out and think of
something else to help suppress his bulge. Her eyes
had already swept across his lap. She just smiled as
she headed toward the highway.

The line wrapped around the front of the building to
the door. Hopefuls waited and hoped they could get
in. Malik and Meesha, walked straight inside and
down the dimly lit carpeted stairway. Scanning
through the guest book, the hostess found the name
"Tameesha Davis" and unlatched the velvet rope
and, welcomed them inside. The bar stood in front
of them, surrounded by groups of well-dressed
people socializing. Malik and Meesha found a small

round table that sat alone in the most intimate corner of the club. It was draped with a deep burgundy tablecloth and a short round vase filled with beautiful deep red roses. Next to the vase sat a glass candle, which glowed just enough to accentuate Meesha's true beauty. As Malik turned his full attention towards Meesha, he stared into her eyes admiring their beauty as the lit candle made them light up in the darkness.

"What?" asked Meesha wondering why Malik was staring at her. He seemed as if he were in some kind of trance.

"Your eyes," he replied. Instantly Meesha blushed. "They're beautiful."

"Thank you," she replied in a low tone. She had been complimented on her hazel eyes all her life, but the way Malik said it made her realize just how beautiful they were. Meesha was completely enjoying Malik's attention, but she wanted to lighten the mood.

"So, did you have place that you just had to go when you came home? I know when I go to visit my family down south, I already have in mind what I have to eat. People go to Philly they want cheese steak. When I go to Houston I gotta go to Timmy Chan's. I have to. So what did you want? Malik smiled at the question. "A nice slice from Ferrarro's."

"Oh yes, Ferrarro's is what's up." Malik continued to stare at Meesha.

"So what's up with you? Why don't you have a man?"

"That is the million dollar question," Meesha smiled as she subtly shook her head.

"What was that about?" Malik asked.

"What?"

"The long contemplative head shake."
Meesha smiled at his attentiveness as she quickly decided to share.

"Well, I was seeing this guy from New York. We had been seeing each other for a few months and he convinced me that the relationship needed to be a secret because of the type of job he had." Meesha paused. "One night we were at his house and there was this loud knock on the door. I'm thinking, the last thing I need was some crazy and deranged chick coming here ready to fight or possibly try to kill my ass over some dick. I was wrong." Meesha shrugged her shoulders and shook her head again. "It was actually a crazy and deranged nigga."

Meesha was crushed but found the situation amusing. What she hadn't revealed was it had been a known rapper from out of one of the five boroughs on the down low. He didn't want the media putting his personal business out in the streets; at least that's what he had told Meesha. Without major incident, she left walking far enough to call a cab to take her back to Jersey.

"He tried to offer me a lot of money to keep my mouth shut." Meesha frowned. "I turned down the money but I gave him my word that I wouldn't say anything. We are still friends." Malik was impressed with the way Meesha handled the situation. He never thought he would ever meet a woman like her. Most women want to get back at a brother and take him for everything he has. It was obvious that Meesha was different. He also respected the fact that she didn't shit on the nigga name. It said a lot about her. Meesha put her hands on the table as if she had thrown in her hand. Malik reached out and put his hands on top of hers.

"Davis party of two," the maitre'd called out, breaking up what would be considered a romantic moment between Malik and Meesha. Happy to be one of the first to be called, Meesha was still a little irritated by the interruption. It wasn't too often that a sister from the hood shared a romantic interlude with a brother from the hood or any brother for that matter. She wanted to savor the moment. Malik was enjoying the night already and they hadn't even eaten or seen the show yet. Before he went to prison his dates consisted of, meals on wheels, a drive thru at a local or out of town fast food joint, some Boone's Farm, or some Zima for the shortie and some Hennessey for him. Then it was off to the motel. He didn't have time to be winning and dinning chicks back then. They were seated on the second row; Malik helped Meesha with her jacket and then took his off. No one had ever done that for her before. *He's too good to be true,* she thought as Malik pulled out her chair.

"This is nice," Meesha said admiring the set up of the club.

"Yeah, word," Malik agreed.

After sitting and waiting, ten minutes later the announcer introduced the first comic. Five minutes into the act, the waitress came and took their order. Meesha ordered the grilled chicken sautéed' in white wine. Malik ordered the half of baked chicken and rice.

"What would you like to drink with that?" asked the waitress.

"I'll have a Long Island Ice Tea,"

"And you sir?"

"I'll have a coke."

"With what sir?" Not knowing that Malik wasn't aware of their policy.

"That's it."

"Sir all of our shows require a two drink minimum. I'm not saying that you have to drink them but you do have to order them, its' my responsibility to tell you this and to make sure that you get them served to you or it's my job." Somewhat embarrassed by his ignorance of their policy, Malik reordered.

"I understand, no problem, I'll have a Hennessey and coke, with a little ice," he said, remembering how he liked his drink. He had no intentions on drinking the drink he ordered. He just didn't want to put the waitress in an awkward position. He really could tell by the tone of her voice that she really

needed this job, something he understood, because
he himself needed a job.

"Okay," she answered with a smile

"Will there be anything else?"

"Uh yes, let me get a glass of ice water with that
too," answered Malik

"Coming right up," she replied taking the menu.
The show was entertaining, as the two previous
comedians did their thing, ripping the front row to
pieces. The room was saturated with laughter.
Malik hadn't laughed like that in such a long time
that he had almost forgotten that humor like that
even existed. He had been living such a hardcore
life for so many years that laughter became foreign
to him. The comedians had joked about everything
they could think of or seen before them from
chick's weaves, looks, and outfits to brother's
haircuts, and jewelry. They had saved the best for
last as the final comedian rocked the house. Meesha
had just finished off her second Long Island Ice
Tea. Malik could see the glare in her now tinted
hazel eyes. Although he was somewhat thirsty, he
had yet to touch the two drinks that sat before him.
He had run out of water over an hour ago and
hadn't seen his waitress since. A few times he
looked and contemplated on whether he should use
them to quench his thirst. The more parched he
became the more the smooth scent of cognac
aroused his nostrils. Reasoning with himself that the
Coke had diluted the liquor, Malik took hold of the
glass and brought it to his mouth. Malik hesitated at

first as if to think things through one last time, but then shook it off as he opened his mouth and poured the bitter-sweet mixture of Coke and cognac. The drink slid down Malik's throat and ignited an intense and warmth in his body. The drink was stronger than he expected it to be. The familiarity was good to him. Without hesitation he downed the rest of the drink. It was as though he had just discovered the fountain of youth. Although tempted, Malik refused to touch the second drink, instead he let the first one marinate as it was already beginning to take affect. In spite of all the "hooch," jailhouse made liquor, and alcohol the officers brought in to some of the inmates, Malik never indulged in any of the drinking parties. His system had been clean and dry for ten years, putting his tolerance level at an all time low.

Meesha observed Malik downing the drink and couldn't help but to laugh a little at how he was fighting with himself about drinking. Had he left them sitting there a little longer, she herself intended to dispose of the liquor because her two drinks had her feeling nice, but she knew that the two Henni and cokes would have her feeling right.

The show was ending and the waitress reappeared to clean up their table and leave the bill.

"I got this," he said smoothly. He was grateful for having a friend like Justice.

"Okay," was all Meesha said.

She hadn't expected Malik to pay for anything; it was her treat. She knew that he had just come home and probably wouldn't be in a position to afford a date like tonight, but she was impressed with both his offer and ability to pay.

Meesha had always traveled with more than enough money whenever she went anywhere with a man. She heard enough horror stories from her girls how niggas got shady at times and pulled all types of stunts and tricks like they left their wallet in their other jacket or pants at home, or wanting them to front half of the bill.

When Malik opened the flap, the total balance for what he considered to be one of the best times of his life, came to a little over $300 for the show, dinner, and the two minimum drink. He felt the evening was money well spent. He reached inside his leather jacket pocket and pulled out a small portion of the $2500 he had in it. Pulling out six $100 dollar bills he placed four inside the leather case and stuck the other two in his linen pants pocket. The show had ended and it was time to go. Malik stood up and for a split second and almost sat back down, feeling woozy from the drinks. He helped Meesha with her coat and then put on his leather.

As they were leaving, the waitress walked passed, gave Malik a big smile and thanked Malik. Meesha caught it but said nothing. Had it been any other man and under different circumstances she probably would have checked the waitress and questioned him. She knew Malik hadn't done anything tonight to disrespect her so she drew her own conclusion and figured he had been generous with the tip. She put her arm through his and they walked out.

The two drinks Malik drank had now taken its full affect on him knocking him out. As Meesha drove he laid there in a deep sleep dreaming while she contemplated him. Meesha never questioned her physical attraction for Malik as she peered at Malik as he slept. She looked at his smooth saffron skin and perfect teeth. He was perfect himself she thought. A gentleman. She thought about how he opened the doors, helped her with her jacket, and pulled out her chair. Meesha had dated all types of men from professional to street dudes but none of them measured up to Malik. His presence alone was enough for her. His strength, the respect he commanded from others and the fact that that he made her feel secure. Something she never felt before. Her mind rested on their phone conversations and how he shared with her how Islam and prison changed his life. She remembered admiring his strength. Malik groaned as he shifted in his seat. "I don't know, I don't know, everything was happening so fast, it was crazy out there, I don't know!" Malik mumbled.

"You don't know what?" asked Meesha thinking he had been talking to her.

"Huh?" asked Malik not knowing what she was talking about.

"You said you didn't know something, you must've been dreaming."

"Oh yeah," Malik replied not realizing where they were. "Where are we?" he asked.
Meesha smiled. "This is my spot." Malik got out of the car and examined his surroundings. As kind and down as he thought Meesha was, he knew of too many scandalous chicks and the drinks helped perpetuate his paranoia. He noticed the park across the street and the street sign. He was close to his old hood. He relaxed a little now that he knew exactly where he was. The vacant lot on the corner had been there for years. The rocks and grass were gone. It was now level and fenced in. The housing projects that were adjacent to Meesha's spot had been given a facelift and now looked like an acceptable place to live. Malik smiled at the memories the scene sparked. As they approached the house, the sensor alerted the lights and the porch lit up. Meesha opened the door, cut on the lights, and placed her keys on the table near the door.
"You want something to drink?"
"No thank you. I'm cool."
Malik plopped down on the couch.
"You can relax. Take off your jacket. I promise I won't steal it" Malik smiled as he stood up and took off his jacket.
"If you don't mind, I'll take that drink now. Meesha walked to the kitchen to fix two glasses of juice When Meesha walked back into the living room she saw Malik leaning back with his head resting on the back of the couch relaxing. Meesha

was glad he was comfortable. He had a thoughtful smile on his face.

"What are you thinking about?" Meesha asked. "Whatever it was, it must've been good. It had you in deep thought *and* smiling." Malik paused as if were absorbing all he could from the memory. "Nah. . . I was thinking about that park across the street. It is just crazy how your mind picks moments for you to remember certain things. I mean this is the first time I ever thought about this since it happened. It is just crazy how our mind works. "Well?" Meesha inquired. "Oh! I remember there was this little girl on her bike. It was one of those pink Huffys. The one with the square seat"

"I had one of those!" Meesha excitedly exclaimed. "Well, all my friends did."
Malik began again "She was on her bike. She was right there on the corner of Third and Plainfield Ave. in front of that rec. center. She was surrounded by these two little girls and one big girl eating something." Malik thought for a second. Meesha listened intently. "I don't know what was going on. I think they may have been trying to take her bike, beat her up or something. I don't know. But the little girl was just crying her eyes out, while they yelled in her face. I saw one of them grab the handle bars and the other girl started to push her. This is crazy. I can see it like it was a few minutes ago. The fat one just stood there eating. I felt so bad for her. I went over and made the girls leave her alone and. . ."

"You walked her home, wiped her face and told her not to worry about it." Malik looked puzzled. "Nah- that couldn't have been you? Was it you? Yall didn't live in the projects. I walked her right across the street to those projects." Malik was baffled. Meesha was in awe as well.

"We did live in the projects but we moved to Third Street. We lived in the projects for about two years."

"I know y'all use to live right here right."

"We lived across the street."

"I thought it was the same house"

"No." Meesha spoke softly as she moved closer to Malik. He put his hand on Meesha's thigh as she settled in close to him. The airy silence was calm and comfortable as the both considered what fate could possibly have in store for them. Meesha boldly leaned in and passionately kiss Malik. Malik took his hands and palmed Meesha's ass and slowly moved his hands up her shirt and caressed her back. Meesha couldn't wait. She moved his hands, stood up and reached back for Malik's hand. Meesha guided him past the sofa and down the hall to her bedroom. The room was dark when Meesha pushed the door and opened it. A few seconds later the room lit up as Meesha felt the side of the wall and located the dimmer light switch. Malik entered the large room. It was a well furnished room with a king sized bed. Meesha brought down the lights and closed the door behind Malik as he walked over to the bed. The mood was perfect thought Meesha. The smooth sound of Floetry filled the air. For a moment she stood there and watched Malik. When Malik sat on the bed and felt its softness, all he could think about was lying back and going to sleep. He had been sleeping on the uncomfortable pull out couch for a month now and prior to that, the state's twin sized, hard plastic, mattress, so the king sized bed was a luxury to him, but he had no intention on resting right now. Tonight he had every intention on doing things that he could only imagine for ten years. Malik removed his blazer and slipped off his shoes. Meesha's inner thighs moistened at the sight of Malik's physique. She hadn't been with a man in eleven months. That last experience left a bad taste in her mouth. Her hormones were in full gear and she was horny as hell. Eleven months had been long enough and tonight she intended to let it all out on Malik. He had no idea how much she wanted him. Neither of them said a word, instead Malik held out his arms in gesture for Meesha too come to him. She responded by moving towards him. Her jacket dropped to the floor as she moved in. Malik gently lifted her shirt over her head as he took in the scent of Nectarine Blossom and Honey that illuminated off of Meesha's body. As Malik wrapped his arms around Meesha he unzipped her skirt and let it fall to the plush carpeted floor. Meesha was now exposed, revealing a work of art. Malik stood there in awe for a brief moment, just staring at Meesha's body. Her matching burgundy laced Victoria

Secret's set enhanced her sensuality thought Malik
in admiration. Meesha knew that Malik was pleased
with what stood before him. It turned her on to
know that she was turning him on.
Malik ran his hands along the outer crevices of
Meesha's frame awakening her body from an
eleven month slumber. Her skin was smooth like
silk against his skin.
 Malik drew Meesha in fully and wrapped his arms
around her waist, guiding her closer into his
embrace. There bodies were nearly one as her body
was now up against his own. He could feel the heat
of her warm body penetrating through his shirt and
jeans. Gently, Malik planted a kiss on Meesha's
forehead then applied the same to both cheeks until
he made his way to her lips. Meesha parted her lips
for Malik to enter her mouth. She was aroused by
Malik's touch. At that very moment, she wanted
nothing more than to feel Malik inside her. She felt
like a high school girl all over again. Tasting
Meesha's tongue caused Malik's joint to instantly
stand at attention. Meesha felt his erection on her
inner thigh through Malik's jeans. They continued
to kiss as Meesha took control and guided them to
her bed. Without breaking their lip lock, Meesha
loosened Malik's belt and jeans. Malik jeans
dropped to his knees. He began to slide them off as
Meesha slid back on to the bed. By the time he had
peeled out of his wife beater and boxer briefs,
Meesha's kitten was purring. Not only was he put
together like a finely chiseled statue, he was also

well endowed Meesha thought. Meesha could see
what he was working with and thought he would
definitely get the job done. Malik climbed onto the
bed with the condom that he pulled out of his pants
pocket clinched in his hand. His days of throwing
his manhood on the crap table hoping he didn't crap
out were over, besides he wasn't ready to be a
father either. Considering, he could barely take care
of himself.
Malik felt Meesha's body flutter as his flesh
collided with hers. Malik kissed Meesha again, slid
down her body and planting gentle kisses. He
created a trail from her neck and worked his way
down. She parted her legs to fit the width of Malik's
wide frame as his head traveled down between her
thighs. She moaned at the touch of Malik's
moistened tongue on her. It was foreign but felt
good. Meesha's body tensed, as she climaxed
instantly. Malik sexed her with his mouth until he
knew Meesha's entire being craved for him. He
then lifted up and slid on the condom. Meesha was
impressed but not surprised when she saw Malik
sliding it on the provalastic. She had been so caught
up in the moment that she never even considered
the condom. That was not like her. She was usually
much more cautious. She had known a lot of
women who had either gotten pregnant or
contracted some type of STD from one night stands
or being with a man without using protection. She
was glad that Malik had been the responsible party
of the two. Malik positioned himself between

Meesha's legs and she reached out to guide him
inside of her. She was on fire and it felt as if she had
melted the rubber right off his flesh. He tried to
maintain his composure as best he could in hopes of
not exploding right then and there. Meesha spread
her legs wide for him as Malik sexed her with
rhythmic strokes. She began to loosen up as a
second orgasm overcame her. This was just what
the doctor ordered she thought to herself as she
thrusted her hips in rhythm with Malik.
He was trying to hold his own but he was no match
for how Meesha was throwing it on him. Meesha
climbed on top. From that point on, it was she who
dominated the rest of the evening. Meesha arched
her back and placed her hands on Malik's chest. She
couldn't help but hold on to his pecs as she rode
him. She could literally feel Malik's hardness inside
her stomach. Malik had lasted longer than he
expected. He tried to focus on he and Meesha but
the sounds of their juices coming from between
Meesha's inner thighs invaded his thoughts. Malik
knew that from her wetness and the fact that she
was riding him like she owned him that he'd be
exploding at any given minute. And he was right, as
if on cue as the sun began to come up Malik could
feel the familiar tingle he had longed for.
Reflexively, he began to meet and match Meesha
thrust for thrust reaching even deeper inside of her.
Sex and music intertwined in the air. Both Malik
and Meesha were out of breath. She had drained the
life out of him, and he had freed her. When it was

all said and done they both had been satisfied.
Though that night it wasn't stated or discussed
verbally, from that day on Meesha was Malik's
became a couple.

CHAPTER EIGHTEEN

BAM! Bam! Bam! Was the sound the door made as Pete pounded on it.

"Who the fuck is it?" Cheddar yelled agitated at the banging on his front door. It better be important he thought as he was interrupted on the down stroke, laying the pipe to a fresh new young piece he had been working on for the past two weeks.

"Yo open the door it's me!" Pete yelled back. Detecting the urgency in Pete's voice, Cheddar quickened his step and rushed to unlock the door. When he flung the door open, Cheddar saw Pete standing there stoned face and knew instantly that there was a problem.

"Yo what up kid?"
 Entering Cheddar's apartment, Pete looked around in a paranoid manner,

"Yo who here wit you? Asked Pete.

"Why what's up?" Cheddar asked again wanting to know the reason for Pete's strange behavior.

"Nigga who here wit you?" he asked again.

215

"Whoa, whoa! Nigga you better calm the fuck down and let me know what's good."
Sensing Cheddar's anger, Pete toned his aggression down to a minimum. The last thing he needed to be doing was beefing with his man when they had bigger problems on their hands.

"Yo my bad dawg, shit just crazy right now, who up in here though cause this ain't for everybody."
Understanding what Pete had meant Cheddar began to calm down.

"Yo, hold up then. I got this little freak in the back; let me go close the door."
Hearing his words Toya ran back to the bed and jumped in it. She was a fiend for gossip and couldn't resist ear hustling Pete and Cheddar's conversation. Though they hadn't really discussed anything she knew that something was wrong and she wanted to know what that something was.
When Cheddar looked in the bedroom Toya was up under the covers asleep. He smiled at the sight and had credited himself for what he believed was the way he put it down in the bedroom. He closed the door behind him and walked back to the living room where Pete was.

"Shortie sleep, what up?"

"Yo that nigga Justice violated!" Hearing Justice's name immediately heated Cheddar. Justice had become a continuous thorn in his team's side and knew that he would remain there until they did something about it. "What happened?"

"Yo, the nigga set up shop right down the street from the block, got some lil niggas on 2nd and Liberty over by Orchid."

"Say word! Up the street from the New?"

"Word!" But yo, that ain't the half. Check I was just getting around there when niggas told me about the shit and how lil Sheed and them went down there to step to the niggas he had pumping for him at the house. You know the house in the corner where all the fiends and them be up in."

"Yeah that crack head bitch Tina crib, right?"

"Yeah no doubt. Dig, while these niggas is telling me all of this all of a sudden I hear a muthafuckin' shots going off, comin' from down the way, and the first thing come to mind is that them lil niggas went down there wildin' and start bustin' off at them cats, but I see Sheed and them jettin' my way, feel me?"

"Word?"

"Word, these niggas Justice got down there was the ones that was lickin' off, bringin' it to muthafuckas. Now mind you, I ain't even got my joint on me cause you know how hot it be around the way, but my shit in the truck, so I make a dash for my shit, but by the time I get down there them niggas had already bounced, then I heard sirens and shit so I catted out. That's my word! That nigga gotta pay kid," said Pete hyped up.

Cheddar had become heated by the minute, blood pressure boiling, as Pete replayed back the scene. He knew that before they could react to the latest

217

incident he needed to be sure that Justice was the one that was in fact behind the violation.

"Yo, how you know them niggas worked for Just?"

"Cause niggas said his truck been going back and forth over there all day, and they seen when he dropped the four niggas off."

"You sure?"

"Positive."

"Aight, where Doub at?"

"On his way over here."

"Aight let me get dressed and get shortie outta here."

"Aight, I'mma wait outside for Doub."

Toya hurried back into bed as she did the last time, only this time she hopped back in more informed than she had been when Pete first came to Cheddar's crib. She closed the door back that she had cracked to hear the conversation being held in the living room, hoping that she wouldn't get caught. She wasn't afraid but she knew enough about Cheddar, Pete, and Doub to know that if they had any inclination she had over heard their discussion, they wouldn't hesitate to do something to her. Toya knew she had to make sure that she made it up out of there in one piece because someone's life depended on it.

CHAPTER NINETEEN

JUSTICE sat impatiently at his normal meeting spot waiting for his little manz and them to arrive. He was not pleased about the disturbing phone call he had received an hour ago. Without going into details he knew that something had gone wrong at the new spot. He had doubts about opening up in his rival area operating with the way that little Chris was talking in code to him. But against his better judgment, he went ahead and opened up shop, knowing the possibilities of his actions. It wasn't about whether he feared the consequences and repercussions that came with the move. He was far from being a stranger to danger. His only concern was the unnecessary drama and heat that it would bring and he didn't need that in his life right now. He was doing good, the best he ever had in his life, with two brand new houses, one in sleepy hollow and another in South Jersey, a new truck and two Benzes, and a Ducati 1100, along with a cleaners he was trying to get off the ground, all which cost him a great deal of money, money that he had worked hard for. Street money. Drug money. When he got out of prison he came home to nothing and nobody offered to give him anything either, so he went out and took it. Now he had eight dope spots and four crack houses that he supplied 24 hours a day, and moved weight to niggas from five different towns including his own. If the situation he was waiting to hear about was as bad as he thought then he knew that all that he had established would be in jeopardy or at least at a stand still. One thing for certain and two things for sure, he knew was war and cash didn't mix. He knew that it would come to this sooner or later. It was long over due. Had it not been this situation that triggered it off, it would have been something else. Justice knew what had officially begun.

CHAPTER TWENTY

" THANK you for the meal Ms.Jones, Meesha
gratefully asserted.

"Oh baby you welcome. Anytime. Even though
you didn't eat much. You ate like a little 'ole
rabbit," noticed Ms. Jones. Meesha laughed.

"Ma, be nice," Malik said coming to Meesha's
rescue

"Boy hush, I'm just messin' with the child. I can
see that she can eat as thick as she is. I remember
when my shape was like that."

"Aight ma, that's too much information laughed
Malik.

"What? It's your fault."

"What? How you figure?" Malik asked

"After I had you and your sisters I ain't been the
same, but you gave me the most problems. Your
head was so big they had to cut you outta me."
Meesha laughed again, only harder.

"Aight, I'm out of here since you done called my
lady fat and me a big headed body wrecker," Malik
joked with his moms.

"She ain't call me fat," joined Meesha

"Oh my bad," he said laughing.

"Yeah, okay big head," Meesha shot back. Ever
since their first date over two weeks ago, Meesha

and Malik had spent everyday together. They were good for each other. Meesha supported him throughout his struggles. She respected Malik more for enduring, considering all the brothers who were out in the streets taking the easy route. It wasn't about money with her; she had her own money, enough money to take care of both her and Malik if necessary. Meesha had money from her mother's insurance, plus the money that her brother made out in the streets before he got killed. She was just glad that she had a man that came home every night and spent time with her. Someone she could call her own. She knew of Malik's past but she judged him and defined him by his present. He was a good man. He was her man. It felt good to Malik to be able to enjoy a good meal and a laugh with two of the four women in his life. He felt blessed, for having Meesha in his life. She was a good woman, something he never had before. He didn't want to mess that up. He was feeling the love and support that she constantly showed him and he felt bad for not being able to truly show his appreciation the way that he would like to due to his financial dilemma. His presence in Meesha's life alone was more valuable to her than any green paper. Not being able to find work was really taking a toll on him, but he refused to allow it to put a strain on their relationship. He maintained his optimism as best he could in her presence, but on the inside, it was eating him up. He was down to his last few dollars that Justice had hit him off with, because he had given majority of it to his mother to help her with her past due bills. He never told her where the money came from and she never asked. She was confident that he hadn't done anything wrong or illegal to get it. She just assumed that it had come from Meesha, who she liked, and was growing to love. She hadn't seen her son so happy since he was a little boy, and knew that he was in love. She was right because Malik had fallen in love with Meesha the first day he saw her, but he knew that love was not enough to pay the bills, so he had to come up with a way to get an income flowing.

CHAPTER TWENTY-ONE

" THE following inmates report to the bubble for mail."
Graham, Cave, Wint, Brent, Wooten, Hall, Sawab...."
Thinking that he had heard his name being called, Kwame paused and stopped the chess move that he was about to make.
"Did you hear them call my name?" He asked Bashir
"I don't know, I wasn't listening."
"I think so," said Muhammad.
"I think they did, hold up for a minute," Kwame told Muhammad and proceeded to the officers station.
"C.o., you call me for mail?"
"What's your name?" asked the white rookie officer. Had it been anyone else they would have known Kwame's name because he had time in on the unit and in the jail in general.
"Kwame Sawab 270441," he stated
"Yeah, here you go."

Kwame reached for the envelope and checked the
return address wondering who had written to him.
It had been a long time since he received any mail.
The last time his name was called for mail call it
was for what you would call "junk mail" a chain
letter that you had to send to somebody else if you
ever got one because it was suppose to have been
bad luck, but as a Muslim Kwame didn't believe in
luck so he ripped it up.
"Alhamdulla laah," was his reaction to the sender's
name.
He went back on the unit to share his mail with the
brothers. Knowing the last time Kwame received
mail, Bashir and Muhammad asked simultaneously
who had written to him?
"Yo, the brother Malik got at me, he replied.
"Word, Abdul Maalik?" asked Bashir
"Yeah."
"Open it up, and see what the brother talkin' about,"
said Muhammad.
*"In the name of Allah The Most Merciful, The
Beneficent.*
As Salaam u Alaikum Akh,
*What's the deal? I hope when you receive this
scribe it finds you and the brothers in the struggle
in the best of health in all aspects. What's up with
Muhammad and Bashir? Let them know that I sent
the Salaams. As for myself, Allah is Akbar, it's a
beautiful thing to be home. I wish that you brothers
were here with me. Pardon me for the delay in
reaching out to you. Just know that it was not my*

intention to take this long, I've just been trying to get situated, something I have yet to do in the fullest form. Satan is indeed working overtime in trying to discourage me to stray from the straight pat), but I have not given up. Since I've been home all I have been focusing on is finding a job, filling out applications for the past two months, and still. . . I am jobless. You told me Akh that it was going to be rough, and you were right, it gets rougher and rougher each day on some real shit. I don't know how much longer I will be able to last. Remember those demons you used to always warn me about? Well those very same demons continue to whisper in my ears constantly each day. Akh, I feel myself getting weak, not physically but mentally. I still offer my prayers and attend Jumah and I ask Allah to give me the strength to weather the storm and bless me with employment because I know that this is a test. One that I don't think I will pass if something doesn't happen soon. Now I see how so many brothers come home and jump back in the game and return back to prison. It's hard out here Kwa. I don't want to go back to jail but it seems like it's designed out here for you to go back. It's crazy Akh. I need you to take on this as well as some positive feed back. Get at Muhammad and Bash with it and see what they got to say about it too. Moving onto something much more positive though, overall things are good, my moms is good. She is happy that I'm home. I told her I was writing to you, she sends her love. My little sister's alright too.

*But they out there runnin'. I haven't had the chance
to address that yet, but I will. I met a shortie. I
mean a sister, a good one too She's not Muslim but
she possess the qualities of a Muslim woman. Her
name is Meesha, she's from out here. I knew her
brother, we was cool, he got bodied while I was
there, as a matter of fact I told you about it when it
happened back in '96, you probably don't
remember. Anyway, she's definitely a good girl and
she has my best interest at heart. I didn't take any
flicks yet, but when I do I got you. Oh, check when I
came home I saw my manz and them, you definitely
would have been proud of your brother because I
kept my composure. I even let them cats take me
shopping, but since then I haven't dealt with them.
We're all different individuals now and travel down
two different paths, feel me? I also seen my ex too
while I was with that cat Cheddar, she tried to act
as if everything was everything like I was suppose
to forgive and forget like I'm Mother Love (Ha! Ha!
Ha!). You know that was our show. Like I was
sayin', I didn't disrespect her, but she knew she
ain't have nothing comin' this way. Guess who else
I bumped into, the brother Just. You remember
black Justice that use to work out with us. He doing
good, real good I mean, it depends on how you look
at it, but the brother set out to help me during my
times of struggle on the strength of the love I
showed him in there. If it wasn't for him I'd be
doing worse than I am now, feel me? Basically
that's all that's going on with me, I just wanted to*

bring you up to speed and let you know that I ain't forgot about my real mans and them. I miss you brothers and I got a lot of love for all three of you. I know you probably saying I didn't have to but I sent you $50 with this. Tell Muhammad and Bash that they'll probably get theirs tomorrow because I sent theirs a day after yours. I had $300 so I split half with you three. I know I'm out here struggling but you know what's mine is yours ain't nothin' changed, love is love holla back

Ma Salaams

Abdul Maalik.

The three of them sat there looking at each other after Kwame finished reading Malik's letter.

"Damn, that was deep," Bash was the first to say.

"Word," Muhammad followed.

"Yeah, the brother going thru it right now out there, but he trying to hold it down though, said Kwame.

"Yeah you right, but I can hear it in his words that he reaching that breaking point," said Bash.

"I caught that too," Muhammad joined.

"Man that's fucked up, them people dirty out there. They don't want you to commit no crimes or break no laws when you get out but they don't wanna give you no job either. Im'ma write Leek back tonight and get at em," said Kwa.

"Me, too," said Bash

"Yeah, me too," Muhammad said in agreement.

"He know he ain't have to send us that paper either," Kwame said changing the mood.
"Im'ma get on him about that cause he know we good, but Alhamdulla laah for his intentions though."
"I was thinkin' the same thing," replied Bash
"Word," replied Muhammad. He needs it more than we do.
"No doubt, but that's what type of brother Malik is. As a matter fact, Im'ma bout to start on that letter now."
"Aight Akh, As Salaam u Alaikum," said Bash.
"Walaikum As Salaam," Kwame responded.

CHAPTER TWENTY-TWO

" MR. JONES, I have given you ample time to find a place of employment. I've been working as a parole officer long enough to know when someone is and isn't really trying and I can tell that you are. Not only that it's apparent that you do not indulge in alcohol or drugs which is a good thing, and you always come with some type of payment to go towards your fines and restitution, but the fact of the matter still remains that you must obtain employment, enroll in some form of educational program or technical training program, as a part of your supervised release conditions. You have yet to produce any proof that you have done one of the three," the white parole officer stated as plainly as she could. Malik listened as his parole officer spoke. Although he didn't care for her personally, he had no choice but to respect how she came at him because she continued to give him a fair shake. He also could tell from the tone and firmness of her words that her patience was beginning to run out. This woman that he sat before technically controlled his life. She had the power to determine whether he remained free or returned back to prison. He despised the power that she had over him, but she was not to blame. He took full responsibility for even putting himself in the type of position that he was in. The few months that he had been home, he had tried his best to adjust and be a law-abiding citizen. Yet, his efforts and intentions were seemingly useless. He was still faced with the possibility of returning to prison even though he had broken no law or committed any crime. The thought sickened him, and as he continued to dwell on his thought. His sickness began to turn into resentment. His resentment turned into anger. His anger became so strong that it caused the door which held his inner demons to burst open, and at that point he was no longer in total control of himself as the voices began to instantly take over. *Man fuck this chick, she actin' like you ain't been tryin' and shit. It's easy for her white ass to talk all that bullshit and act like she's giving you an ultimatum and shit. It ain't her ass that's in this position. I peeped her being on some bullshit from day one when she laid all those lame ass rules and regulations down to you but I ain't wanna say nothing cause I know you was tryin' to change and I was feelin' that, but dawg come on baby. You bigger than this shit, you ain't gotta put up with this white bitch shit. Back in the day you would've murdered a muthafucka playing with your freedom like that, and that's what she doin'. She know you fucked up in the game right now, but all she thinkin' about is that fine and restitution you owe. This broad don't care if you go*

out and rob a bank as long as you get that paper to
her so she can give it to the muthafuckin'
government. Dawg trust me, this white broad
comin' at you like this cause she know how you get
money and she tryin' to force your hand. Your
whole life is in that file and on that computer, she
know how you get down baby. She already thinks
you out there back in the game anyway. You just
learn and figured out a better way to manipulate the
system so you don't get caught so easy next time. It
ain't gonna be no next time, cause you gonna do
shit right this time. Ain't no need to bullshit around;
you need paper and you need just that. Moms
struggle, you struggle, your little sisters out there
fuckin' with niggas in the street tryin to get broke
off cause they struggling You got a wifey now, so
dawg you gots to step your shit the fuck up and get
this paper. Fuck those white folks, they ain't playin'
fair anyway, so why should you? Dawg, you ain't
no dumb muthafucka, you know what you got to do
and who you got to see to make shit happen. Handle
your business, we with you we ya manz and 'em."
"Mr. Jones do you understand what I am saying to
you?" asked the parole officer as she snapped Malik
out of his delusion.
"Yes maam I understand."
"Alright, I'll see you in two weeks then."
"Yes you will.

CHAPTER TWENTY-THREE

AFTER meeting with his little mans and them, he had them replay what took place with them and his adversary's crew. Justice had a clearer perception of what he was up against now. At least he thought he did. Just as he, little Chris and the rest of them went their separate ways Justice received the strange phone call. He hadn't heard from Toya since he had hooked up with her three months ago when he had taken her to Atlantic City and Wildwood for a three day weekend. She was a bad young piece in his book and he couldn't get enough of her tenderness, but she was too high-maintenance for his taste. He was already taking care of three other young and tender chicks that would put Toya to shame, beauty wise, and sexually, especially orally. He made a mental note to keep on her reserve though just in case he had to cancel one of his starting three. His first thought was that she wanted him to hit her off with some paper for her bills or something when she said she had to talk to him in person. He started to blow her off, but when she stressed how important it was and how she didn't want to talk

over the phone, he took her words serious and asked
for her location.

Justice pulled up to the green and white two family
home and blew the horn. Two minutes later Toya
came out with a black Prada belly t-shirt on and a
pair of blue jean coochie cutters and slippers, with a
scarf wrapped around her head. Even in something
as simple as that she had Justice wanting to sex her,
which he knew he would try to do before he rolled
out even if it had cost him a few dollars. First it was
business before pleasure. He wanted to know what
was so important that she needed to see him face to
face and couldn't be discussed over the phone. Toya
hopped in the SUV and didn't waste anytime. She
immediately went to what she had overheard while
at Cheddars crib. When she was done Justice's
whole attitude changed. He no longer had sex on his
mind or anything else for that matter besides blood.
Blood that belonged to three individuals, blood he
intended to have spilled. He was thankful for
Toya's information, realizing that she may have just
saved his life. He went into his pocket and broke
her off. She offered to give him head in the whip
right quick, but he refused, telling her how he'd
catch her on the rebound. She had earned her paper
already, and to Justice it was money well spent.
Toya got out and Justice pulled off. When she got
back into the house and counted the money Justice
had given her. She counted almost five hundred
dollars. She smiled at Justice's generosity and made

a mental note that she owed him a good shot of ass and some even better head.

CHAPTER TWENTY-FOUR

MEESHA had been distracted all day at work after she hung up with Malik. She knew that he had to report to parole today and was somewhat nervous behind the fact hat he still hadn't found a job. The last thing she wanted to see happen was him being violated and sent back to prison, but she assured him that she would be there for him every step of the way until he got back out. She even offered to take off of work today to go with him for support, but he suggested and insisted that she went to work, and if he did get locked up he'd leave the keys to in the dashboard. She was happy to hear his voice and to find out that he hadn't been violated. But there was something in his tone that struck her as odd. She just couldn't pinpoint it. All she knew was he didn't sound the same. When he asked her if she would be able to catch a ride home from work with

a co-worker because he had to take care of
something and it may take the whole night, she
became suspicious. But she didn't question him.
She was confident that whenever he came in he
would fill her in on what prevented him from
picking her up from work like he had been doing for
the past couple of weeks. Malik felt a little funny
about calling Meesha and asking her to catch a ride
home with someone else without any detailed
explanation. Truthfully, he wouldn't have known
how to explain it to her. He couldn't explain how
everything up til now brought him to this point. All
he knew was that it was what it was and it was
either now or never. Justice told him where to meet
him. Malik knew that what he and Justice were
about to discuss would change his life forever. For
better or for worse. He would never know unless he
took the chance. Justice received the call right after
Toya jumped out and he pulled off. In spite of the
disturbing news he had just gotten from Toya, his
whole demeanor changed at the sound of Malik's
voice. He detected the urgency in Malik's tone as he
requested to meet with him somewhere so they
could talk. He found it ironic how he had received
two phone calls in one day that were too important
to discuss over the phone. He wondered whether the
two calls were related, thinking how Cheddar, Pete,
and Doub or one of the three may have gone to
Malik in attempts to squash the beef trying to use
Malik as a mediator. He immediately exed that
thought because he knew Malik's caliber, and knew

that even if he wanted to do something like that he would never do something like that. He would never allow anybody, male or female to use him as a middle man or a flunky. As Justice pulled into the parking lot, he spotted the white BMW Malik said he would be driving.

Across town Cheddar, Pete, and Doub discussed plans of their own. "Basically that's how we gonna do it. Feel me?"

"Yeah we with you," answered Doub.

"Yeah no question, something gotta give," followed Pete.

"Aight until then we just gonna let shit marinate," Cheddar told them both.

"Cool," they both replied as they hugged and pounded one another up.

"Yo, I'm out."

"Yeah, me too."

"Aight I'll holla late, one."

"One." Each man went their separate way knowing what position they played and when their plan would go into effect.

CHAPTER TWENTY-FIVE

MALIK saw Justice's truck pull into the parking lot as he pulled along side of him and parked. Just hopped out and got into the 550i with Malik.

"What's poppin' baby?" Justice said shaking Malik's hand.

"Same shit different day." Malik replied finding himself falling back into his old dialogue, using his street lingo.

"I know that ain't the good brother talkin' like that?" joked Justice surprised by Malik choice of words. That was his first time since he had known Malik to ever hear him use any profanity, and wondered if it was just a slip.

"It is what it is," answered Malik.

Justice looked at Malik strangely. He could see the difference and the change in his face from the last time they had met. The look was all too familiar to him. It was that same look that he saw on his own face when he had looked in the mirror and decided that enough was enough.

"What's on your mind beloved?" he asked already knowing, what Malik was about to say. As his friend and someone who loved and respected Malik, Justice wanted to tell him to hang in there and don't give up, but as a man who came from the street and knew another man's caliber and capabilities he wanted to embrace Malik whole heartedly on is decision. Although he was torn between the two, Justice knew how he intended to handle situation if what he thought Malik had to discuss with him was about getting back in the game. Malik thought one last time before he answered Just's question. For a brief moment he started to change his mind and make something up to throw Just off. But there were too many demons flooding his mind, whispering in his ear. They were everywhere and the odds were against him. Where he came from majority ruled and they had won the battle that that he continually tried so hard to become victorious. Although he had won many he had just lost one, the most important one, his freedom. "Man, shit for me it's been like a livin' hell. No matter how hard I try these crackers keep shittin' on me, nah mean?"

It wasn't a question, it was a statement, and Justice knew that. He just sat there listening letting Malik get what he had on his chest off. That's what a real friend would do.

"My p.o. stressing me the fuck out, talkin' all this job shit. I mean she been keeping it gully with me cause she could'a been violated me and sent me back, but still in all the white bitch actin' like a nigga ain't been tryin' to find a job. Then she talkin' that school and trade shit, man I ain't got time for that, that shit ain't puttin' no money in my pocket. Besides, I got my G.E.D and Black Seals license in the joint, so I wouldn't have to come out here, and have to go through this shit, feel me? Then I got mom dukes, she strugglin', my little sisters out there runnin' the muthafuckin' streets chasin' behind niggas who got paper so they can get broke off. While I'm out this piece broke as hell on some humble shit, when it shouldn't be like this. Niggas should be scared to death to even look at my little sister's dawg. I mean these little niggas out here don't really know how I play, but niggas our age and up know how I got down before I left, but niggas ain't respectin' my gangsta dawg. Shit I ain't even respectin' my own gangsta right now. I got a shortie who holdin' me down and got mad love for me and I can't even do shit for her to show her how much I'm really feelin' how she treatin' a nigga. I'm tired of all of this lame ass sucka shit akh. That's it I'm done, that's why I wanted to holla at you and see if you could hit me with something to get my feet wet and you got my word that I'll see you back with whatever and then some." Justice smiled at Malik's last statement and his heart went out to him. He felt his pain, as if it were his own, and if he ever had any doubt about his decision he had none now. "Yo son, I feel where you goin' wit it," Justice started out saying. "And that ain't about nothin'. However or whatever got you to this point is on you, you your own man baby, and I respect that So, I ain't even gonna touch on that, trust me I feel your pain. My main concern now is making sure that your next move is the right move, feel me, cause I know you ain't tryin' to go back, right?"

"True."

"Aight so let me hear how you planned on doin' things once you got some material, cause I know you thought all this out already. But you just comin' home so you don't know who's who or what's what dawg," Justice wanted to know. Malik had anticipated the question and had prepared himself with the answer.

"Basically akh, my best bet right now is to open up shop where I feel most comfortable and that's around my old hood," he started. " I mean, I know it's been a minute and things ain't the same, but I grew up around there and know them buildings inside and out, like the back of my hand. I don't plan on standing outside on no corner like no young boy or nothing runnin' up on cars and shit like it's 89. I'mma go around there and get me two of them buildings to operate out of, the ones I grew up in around the front."

Justice facial expression spoke a thousand words. Malik knew that Justice was not convinced that his story was fool proof.

"Akh, before you say anything, let me say this. It's still in me. I feel it everyday. No matter how much

or how hard I try to fight it it's there. I don't know
why but I'm built for this shit. It is what it is Jay.
All I need you to do is bless me with some material
and hit me with two hammers and I'mma make it do
what it do. Trust and believe that akh. Niggas gonna
either get down or lay down, bottom line!" Malik
spoke with conviction. By the time he had ended,
there was no doubt in Justice's mind now that the
old Malik was back, new and improved. Justice was
about to speak but Malik beat him to the punch.
"You still got access to heat right?" Malik asked
referring to the gun connects Justice once had.
"Yeah no question, but--."
"There it is then," Malik interjected cutting Justice
off. He was now feeling himself. The more he
spoke the more alive he began to feel. This was a
feeling that he had missed, and it felt good to him.
He was already beginning to envision how and on
who he would execute his plan on need be. "I know
my manz and 'em got it on smash around there right
now, but I'm one of the pioneers around them
projects too. I made it safe for them niggas to eat,
you know that akh, they ain't built like that. I don't
have to deal with them dudes, I'm from 524 too and
it's enough room and paper around there for all of
us. Them jokers is the least of my worries. It's the
lil niggas I'd have problems with. They killin' with
no regards. But either way I ain't playin' no games
with no niggas, young or old, plain and simple, feel
me akh. Some of them lil niggas gonna wanna get
down with me just on the strength of who I am

anyway. Even my manz and 'em gonna try to holla but that aint about nothin' though. You know the history behind all of that, I don't even gotta go into that."

Justice just nodded his head as Malik spoke.

"You know I got more love for you on some genuine shit than I do any of them dudes, that's why I hollered at you, I wouldn't have did it any other way."

Malik's words touched Justice. Nothing could be more than the truth thought Justice. Malik had showed that time and time again while they were in prison together. That only confirmed what Justice had in store for Malik.

"Yo Leek, I know love is love between us beloved. I never doubted that nor will I ever. Some things just go without sayin', feel me? It's crazy that you got at me like this. I was hoping it never came down to this because I never wanted to see you return back to this type of shit. Like you said it is what it is. You ya own man. I'm glad you felt comfortable enough to come to me and not them clowns you keep callin' ya manz and 'em. Them dudes ain't ya manz, I'm ya mufucka manz akh. Do me a favor and stop callin' them jokers that. But yo, I got to be honest with you big bro, I feel where you goin' with it but I'm not feeling ya plan."

"Yo Jay."

"Wait, let me finish akh. I heard you out now hear me out."

Malik couldn't argue with that. Justice now had his undivided attention.

"Them projects ain't no option beloved. Fuck going back around there and putting yourself in the midst of all the bullshit. You right, them young boys ain't playing. Say you gotta put a couple up in a few niggas who try to rebel. Trust me akh somebody gonna tell. Then it's a short career for you. Or say somebody feel some type a way about you going around there. You know when niggas go back around their old hoods after doing a bid try'nna re-stake their claim on some braulic shit they get laid the fuck down. We use to hear it all the time back in the joint. Not saying that's your fate, but why even put yourself in that type of position? Even if you don't have that problem and they show love, the type of brother that you are, when they run down it's you that's gonna go down quick and hard. Akh them projects is on fire right now. I know you been hearing about all them bodies and shit. You don't want no parts of that. We from the old school, war and cash still don't mix. Then you'd have to grind and deal with all the mechanical bullshit that comes with getting shit up and runnin', choppin' up, bottlin' up, given out samples to build clientele, showin' face so they know who shit it is, being on your workers, and the rest of the b.s you know you'd have to go thru to get ya thing up off the ground. Your hands don't call for that baby!" Justice emphasized. "You left with status so you should come home to status." Justice paused for a minute, so Malik could digest his words before he spoke again. "Akh, I'mma keep it a hundred, if it wasn't for you I don't think I'd have everything I got and don't know where the fuck I'd be in life right now. Probably somewhere sucking my own dick, that's my word on everything I love dawg. A lot of dudes get out and forget about the mu'fuckas who still in the belly of the beast, but I don't pump like that beloved. I never forgot about you. I've been waiting for you to touch, so I can show you what you helped create. Akh, all this, I credit to you, and half of everything I own belongs to you. I didn't ever think you were going to get back in the game or even want it, because I knew you were living on the straight path, but that's not for me to judge. I gotta deal with my own demons and actions, that's between you and yours. I ain't even gonna front. When I first saw you I was like damn my manz home. Even though I didn't want you back out here I was wishing that I had you out here with me cause I know how you get down. So, this shit right here is like a dream come true for a nigga, nah'mean. akh. You ain't gotta do shit if you don't want to. All you gotta do is stack paper and enjoy life. I got, nah pardon self, we got a crew a niggas hustling for us and regulars coppin' heavy from us. I would never let you go back around your old hood, not to get no doe anyway. If you feel you have something to prove and that's what you wanna do then as your brother and ya manz I'mma respect

that. Just know you don't have to take that route.
You have other and better options," Justice ended.
Malik was overwhelmed by all that Justice had just
expressed to him. He had never imagined or
entertained in his mind what he had just heard. The
way Justice had broken it all down to him made
perfectly good sense to Malik. Being the type of
individual Justice known him to be, Malik could not
just accept what Justice had said on those terms.
Like a game of chess, Malik gathered his own
thoughts once again before he made his next move
and spoke.

"Damn akh," he started out still collecting his words
in his mind, not wanting to offend his man. "That
never dawned on me that you looked at things like
that. But yo, you know you don't owe me nothin'."

"Come on dawg, I know that," interrupted Justice
feeling that Malik had taken his love the wrong
way.

"Hold up," Malik stopped him. "Let me finish."

"Pardon self lord," an apologetic Justice replied.

"All you just said I was feelin', hands down. That's
nothing but love, real niggas do real things, and ya
plan definitely sounds a hundred times better than
mine, but Just you know I just can't roll with it like
that, how you put it. I wouldn't be myself if I did."

The disappointment on Justice's face instantly
appeared as Malik spoke. Even before he finished
saying what he had to say Justice knew that his
proposal had been turned down. "I respect that yo,
but I--."

Justice cut him off again.

"Damn nigga let me finish, that's the second time
ya ass cut me off like that," said Malik with a smile.

"My bad my bad baby go ahead," replied Justice not
really wanting to hear the rest,

"Aight, like I was sayin', I can't just roll with your
plan like that. Unless!" Malik emphasized. Justice
caught the emphasis and immediately keyed into
what Malik had to say now anxious to hear the rest.

"Unless when we out this shit together whatever
paper you hit me with from out of your own stash
you let me pay you back," said Malik smiling
knowing that he had faked Justice out.

"Nigga, you fucked me up for a minute, I thought
you wasn't feeling my plan," said Just attempting to
punch Malik in the chest but not before Malik could
block it.

"I know, I was just fucking wit you, but yo just
talkin' about this shit got me feelin' good as hell. I
was stressed the fuck out before you pulled up."

"Word, I seen that shit all over your face, but fuck
all that, you aight now and you gonna be aight. First
thing we gonna do is take you to go get some
license cause I know you ain't got none, and you
definitely need them. They gonna be in your name
and all of that, shit legit. I got a shortie that work at
motor vehicle who can put your shit in the computer
too, then we gotta dip out to Jersey City and have
my man print you out some fake check stubs to
keep that p.o. broad off your back, then we'll dip to
my crib, I got a Ack I don't even drive. You can

have that until you ready to cop something or you
can keep it, whatever. I know your shortie need her
whip."
Malik grinned inside at the mention of the Acura.
He reflected back to when he first caught his case
when they just came out. How he talked about
getting one for the summer but never had a chance
to, but now he was being given one. He listened as
Justice continued to fill him in on their agenda for
the remainder of the day.
"I'll just follow you in the coupe and you can drive
me back home. Tomorrow we'll get together and
I'll introduce you to the necessaries and fill you in
on who's who and what's what. You'll pick up on
all that shit in one day. Don't worry kid I got you."
"I know you do yo."
"It's me and you baby against the world," voiced
Justice as he opened the door of the BMW.
Malik smiled at his words, and repeated them to
himself, and it sounded good to him.
"Yo follow me," Justice told him as he closed the
car door.
   The night had come to an end and Malik felt the
best he had ever felt since he had been home,
feeling good about his accomplishment, as he
cruised on the highway in the pearl black Legend
coupe with a legit valid drivers' license and a book
of pay stubs that would last him throughout the
year, along with 25 thousand in cash that Just hit
him with for what he called pocket cash. After he
dropped him off at home, and he headed back up

north since the house Justice kept the Lex at was located in South Jersey. The sound of Erykah Badu filled the car with her high pitched tone guiding him back to town. The closer he got home, the more he thought about what he would say to Meesha. He knew that she'd be up waiting for him. When Malik dropped the BMW off, to take Justice home, he could see both the living room and bedroom lights on from outside. That was a little after 9 p.m. It was now approaching midnight but still he knew that she would be up, waiting for an explanation. One she deserved. This was his first time ever coming in this late. To him it was for a good reason, he just wasn't sure that she would agree once he told her. He needed her to roll with him on his decision. Meesha heard the keys in the door, breaking her out of her nod. She had been waiting on the living room couch since 7 o' clock. Meesha hopped in the shower then prepared a meal of boneless chicken, with yellow rice, and vegetables. By eight she made Malik's plate and sat it in the microwave. She sat there flicking through the cable stations, channel surfing for an hour trying to find something good to watch. She had just gotten into the latest episode of The Wire when she heard the car door slam earlier in the evening. She knew it was Malik because she knew all the sounds of her car. But after 20 minutes, and Malik had not walked through the door, Meesha got up and looked out the front window. She saw her BMW sitting there in the front of the house but there was no sign of Malik. She glanced at her watch. The time read ten after twelve in the morning when Malik walked through the door. As soon as Malik stepped foot in the house the first thing he saw was Meesha spread across the leather sofa. He looked square at her as he closed the door behind him, looking for any indications of an attitude. The only thing he was for sure of was that she hadn't been asleep prior to his coming through the door. She looked as if she were wide awake. He walked over to her, leaned over and kissed her on the face, then lifted her legs and sat down, putting her legs across his lap.

"I made you something to eat, it's in the microwave," Meesha spoke breaking the silence.

"Aight I'll get it," Malik responded as he walked over towards Meesha, kneeling down and began massaging her feet.

It had been a long and tiresome day for Meesha at work. She had been standing throughout the course of the day and that killed her feet, so the massage was soothing. As good as it felt and as relaxed as it made her feel, she couldn't allow that to throw her off from what she had practically waited up for most of the night. Before she got too comfortable, and wound up falling asleep from Malik's relaxing touch, she initiated the conversation that needed to take place between the two. She wasn't sure if she should be angry.

"How was your day?" she started out asking.

"It was good," Malik replied.

"Is everything okay?"

This was not what Malik expected. "Yeah. . . Everything's good."

"Well, what happened earlier? Why couldn't you pick me up?"

Malik took a deep breath then exhaled. He had prepared himself to give her the answer. He was now positive that he wanted to answer the question truthfully. The only thing that he wasn't sure about was whether she would understand his decision. If not would he be willing to sacrifice their relationship by pursuing his plans without her by his side. That was not a bridge that Malik was fully prepared to cross, but knew facing that very bridge was inevitable and the only way for him to move forward was to cross it. To him that was the only path that could take him to where he needed to be, now he needed to know that Meesha would be with him when he did.

"I was with Justice," he answered Meesha, looking her directly in the face to see how she took in the name.

"Justice?" A frown instantly appeared across Meesha's face as if the name seemed foreign to her.

"Yeah. Justice."

"What was so important with him that you couldn't pick me up and was late for dinner?"

She asked not seeing how anything pertaining to Justice was more important than her.

"We had to discuss some things," was Malik's response

"Things? What things?" Meesha snapped snatching her feet back off of Malik's lap getting heated.
"Business."
As soon as the word rolled off of Malik's tongue and came out of his mouth, it all became clear to Meesha. Her heart began to pound against her chest and the blood started rushing to her head as she managed to keep her tears of rage and pain in tact.
"Oh business! I see. You tryin' to get back in the business huh? I mean just say it Malik, be a man and just tell me. You wanna run the streets again. You tired of me? Huh? You tired of this? What? I bore you?" she asked as the tears began to well up and flow down her smooth brown face.
Malik stood up and attempted to wipe her face and explain to her that she was wrong, but she pulled away.
"Don't touch me! I'm not a baby you don't have to pacify me. I knew some shit like this would happen that's why I don't deal with street niggas. All my life dudes been try'nna to--."
"Hold up!" Malik interrupted in a boisterous manner as he grabbed her by the arms.
"You buggin' out right now. This shit ain't about me wantin' to run no streets, this shit is about us. Me and you."
Meesha's eyes were as wide as they could be stretched. It was if as though Malik could see her soul through them. In a split second, he remembered that day at Hannah Atkins recreational center when they were younger and knew they were made for

each other. He loved every particle of her being and she needed to know that.

"You think I give a fuck about runnin' the streets? Nah, it ain't about that, it's about what I know and what I do best in order to survive, in order to take care and provide for my family. You, my moms, my sisters, that's what it's about. Baby don't ever get it twisted I love you and nothing will ever change that. You're the best thing that ever happened to me, that's my word," he said squeezing her arms tighter.

"Malik you're hurting me."

Realizing that his grip was too tight he released his hold of her arm.

"Baby I'm sorry I ain't mean to grab you so hard, I'm just trying to get you to see that I have no other choice. These people forcing my hand. I tried and I tried and the ending result is nothing! Not a damn thing! How you think I feel when you do something for me and I can't return the love? As a man, I feel fucked up. I know you don't do for me because you look for something in return, but you deserve something in return. Baby, if I could I'd buy you the moon I would. That's how deep my love runs for you. You should be able to have money at your disposal for whatever and so should my moms and sisters. When I was in prison, my moms bent over backwards to see to it that I had the necessities in jail from the time I stepped foot in there, til I got out, up until the time I met you. Now it's time for me to hold her down.

"You see this right here? Malik said pulling the 25 g's that Justice gave him out of his pocket and threw it on the coffee table. This is just a piece of what I can get."

Meesha didn't even bother to look at the money, as she was unimpressed. She understood what Malik was saying to her but felt that it still didn't justify what he was considering. He was so caught up right now in the value of the dollar that he over looked the value of his freedom and what stood before him, she thought as she took in all of what he was saying. If it was all about the money with Malik, Meesha felt that it wasn't too late to get him to change his mind about getting back into the game. She thought she could give him some reassurance that she was there for him.

"Malik, I love you too, and I know what you're goin' thru. I see it with my own eyes and it hurts me to see you hurting, but goin' back out there is not the answer baby," she said through her sniffles as she wiped away what tears she could. Malik extended his hand and caught the fallen tears that ran down her cheek.

"Baby I---," she stopped him in mid-sentence.

"No let me finish. All my life all I ever wanted was to be loved whole heartedly. I mean my mother loved me but she loved her work more, my brother loved me too but he loved the streets more, those very same streets that you want to go out in. These past few months you have made my dreams a reality. You have been a breath of fresh air for me.

Since I was a little girl my heart was yours even before I knew what love really was and now I have you in my life I am not tryin' to lose you to nothing or to no one. If it's about the money then baby you don't have to go out there, I got enough money to take care of the both or us until you get on your feet. What's mine is yours. That's what a relationship is about, holding each other down and watching one another's back. Malik please listen to me when I tell you this, you don't need that. You lived that type of life already and look where it got you. We gon' be alright, it gets better," Meesha ended hoping that her words penetrated. Malik's blank stare let her know that her words were useless. Malik listened as Meesha spoke. He felt all she was saying, but his mind was already made up. If she meant all of what she had said to him then he felt that she would stick by him no matter what. But he had to handle his business the best way he knew how. He just hoped that Meesha really understood. "Meesha, listen baby, I'm feeling all of what you was sayin' and I love you for that, but I gotta do what I gotta do. I know you got my back and I'm trying to have yours too, but the only way to do that is to get it how I know how to get it. This is all I know how to do that don't require a college degree and I don't have to fill out no job application or go to no job interviews to get turned down. Nah, out there your education is based on experience." He pointed to an imaginary place behind him. "And your background experience is the streets, and out there," he pointed again. "I don't need an interview with no boss. I'm my own boss, make my own hours, and I pay myself. I know ain't no longevity in this shit and I'm not trying to make a career out of it either, I'm just trying to stack some paper, so I can live comfortably, that's all. Baby," Malik's eyes pleaded.

"I need this and I need you. I need to know where you stand on this as far as us?" he asked. The tears began to well up again in Meesha's eyes as Malik spoke. She knew that he was standing firm with his decision. She didn't know what to do. Meesha knew that she loved him, but didn't want to be a part of the life he decided to live because she knew that it would cost her in more ways than one. Meesha was quiet as she thought.

"Malik I don't know, this is too much for me right now, I can't--."

Malik went to embrace her but she refused him, turning around running off to their bedroom. Malik fell back on the couch as the bedroom door slammed. It had been a long day and even a longer night. Malik was both mentally and emotionally drained. He knew it was best to sleep on the couch for the night and give Meesha some time and space. Malik layed on the couch in deep thought while Meesha cried herself to sleep in the next room.

CHAPTER TWENTY- SIX

IT was 4:30 a.m. when Meesha's cell phone rang.
"Meesha can you come and get me?" Mandy
whimpered in the phone.
"Where are you? What's wrong?"
"Nothing," she said through her sobs. "Can you
please just come and get me now?"
"Where are you?"
I'm at the Motel 6 in Piscataway but I'mma be at
the Dunkin Donuts. Hearing that, Meesha slipped
out of bed, threw on some clothes, and grabbed her
keys. For the first time she was actually glad that
Malik was a heavy sleeper as she crept passed him
on the couch and made her way out the door. By the
time Meesha reached Mandy she was no longer
distraught and crying. They rode in silence. When
Meesha first picked her up Mandy anticipated a
question or a speech about life and protecting
yourself. She had heard them all. Meesha said
nothing. Soon guilt began to sink in. Mandy thought
about how Meesha always came to her rescue, even
before she dealt with her brother. She felt bad for
taking advantage of her. As the silence grew

thicker, Mandy had to say something. "He kicked me out of the room cause I wouldn't give him none." She folded her arms across her chest. Meesha was still silent. When they got to 7th street Meesha asked, "Where am I dropping you off?" Mandy had never seen Meesha this angry before. "I'm going to mommy's house."

"Who is this guy?"

"This kid named Jason."

"Is he from Plainfield?"

"Yeah. Why?"

It is obvious you don't love yourself. Do you love your family? Your mother? Did you ever think about your brother? Do you want him to go back to jail?"

Mandy looked confused. "What are you talking about? What do they have to do with this? What does my brother going back to jail have to do with me?"

"You just don't get it. Malik loves you! What do you think he would do to this Jason boy if he knew about this?" Mandy never considered it for a minute that what she did had anything to do with anyone else. As far as she was concerned, Jason would be getting just what he deserved. The cheerful thought of revenge did not last long. This feeling was overpowered by the pain of not having a brother for ten years. Meesha pulled in front of the house and didn't expect Mandy to answer her questions. As Mandy got out and shut the door Meesha looked at her. "Next time he might not put you out. You may

not make it out. Don't put your brother in that
position, your life and his depends on it." Meesha
drove off and Mandy walked up the steps. She
never thought that her behavior affected other
people. She began to think about how she was
hurting her mother and had been for a long time.
She never even thought about the influence she had
over her sister. As Meesha drove, she began to feel
bad for being so stern with Mandy. She also knew
she needed it. Meesha's phone rang. Mandy's voice
was quiet and apologetic. "My mother said she got a
movie she wanted you to see. I was supposed to tell
you the other day, but I forgot. "Thanks." Mandy
was on the edge and slowly losing her grip. Meesha
wanted to tell Malik about his sister but she didn't
want to betray her trust. It was obvious that she was
the only person she could call on. By the time
Meesha got home it was time for her to go to work.
She took a quick shower and jetted out the door.
By the time Malik had awakened, Meesha was
gone. Normally, she would have woken him up
when she got up. He would groom, offer his
morning prayer while she was in the shower, they
would eat breakfast together, and he would drive
her to work. It was almost 10 o'clock when he got
up. Last night's events had him physically
exhausted which caused him to over sleep, missing
his prayer. Malik went to the bathroom, took a
quick shower and got dressed. Since he had missed
his morning prayer he made a mental reminder to
make it up when the afternoon prayer time came in.

Lately he had been missing a prayer or two
throughout the course of the day, sometimes making
them up before he went to bed. This was not like
him Malik knew but credited his negligence to his
present situation. Malik made a mental note to
himself to be more mindful of his daily prayers. He
made his way into the kitchen to kill the hunger
pains that invaded his stomach. He was pressed for
time this morning because he was to meet Justice at
another one of his cribs by 10:30 leaving him no
time to cook anything. Apple Jacks or Fruit Loops
would have to suffice. As he went to the cabinet to
get the cereal, he noticed a note taped to the
microwave. *"I love you, no matter what! xoxox. p.s.
your breakfast is in the microwave."* Malik's day
had officially began. The words "I love you no
matter what" was what Malik needed to get him
through the day. He warmed up the turkey bacon,
scrambled eggs and buttered toast, scarfs it down,
and jetted out the door to meet Justice. They both
arrived simultaneously. Justice was just reaching
the door of the apartment building when Malik
showed up. He waited for him to hop out the coupe,
so they could go in together. They exchanged
greetings as Justice lead the way, with a blue and
white Nike duffle bag hanging from his shoulder.
Malik could only guess the contents of the bag and
couldn't help but to laugh to himself when he saw
the apartment door reading 4B. It reminded him of
an old Jay Z song. The small apartment was decked
out with all the necessities that defined your

lifestyle as living ghetto fabulous, from wall to wall carpet and leather sofas to a flat screen t.v. and dvd player. You name it was there. Malik had a nice little crib before he got knocked, but it looked nothing like the crib in which he stood now. Some of the appliances in the apt weren't even out back then. If they were it still wasn't definite that he would have owned them because most of them were extremely expensive and Malik and his team weren't doing it that big back then. The time when he got arrested would have put them over the top to live the way Just was living now.

"Yo this piece is nice kid," admired Malik

'This shit ain't nothin dawg, this just our stash crib and a spot to bring the chicks up in when we don't feel like driving or paying for no hotel room, feel me?"

"I feel you, but it's still nice."

Don't even sweat this, ya shit gonna be laid in a minute too, but better than this. I got a couple more of these laced like this. I'm going to make sure you know where they at and you got keys for them, just in case. Yo you might as well get comfortable cause we gonna be here for a while and I need you to help me take care of something, plus I gotta show you a few things too," said Just taking off his jacket and slipping off his Prada shoes.

"No doubt," answered Malik doing the same.

Justice sat the duffle bag on the leather sofa and unzipped it, and began dumping out the contents onto the soft tan carpet. What Malik assumed the

261

bag contained was not what he'd thought. He expected bags of narcotics to come falling out, instead only stacks of rubber banned money fell to the floor.

"Yo we need to count all this shit up before the night is out," Just told him.

"We got to separate the bills and put everything in ten gee stacks. Tally up the fives and singles but don't worry about putting them in stacks like that. Do the singles in hundreds stacks and the fives in two hundred, we can take them to the strip clubs and get hundreds for them."

"I got you," replied Malik as his eyes stared at the piles of 100's, 50's, 20's, 10's, 5's, and singles. He was certain that this had been the most money he had ever seen in his life at one time. With an educated guess, he figured the amount to be at least two to three hundred grand.

"I need to do something else and then Im'ma come help you count this up, but yo I wanna show you something before you start."

"Aight." Justice went to the bedroom, opened the closet, and pulled out a medium sized gray safe.

"The combination is 5-31-17, try to remember because you gonna have to come here sometime." When Justice opened the safe Malik saw the neatly stacked bricks of what he believed to be coke in rows of five and stacks of four, with a top and a bottom part, Malik estimated at a minimum 40 kilo's of coke to be in the safe.

"Whenever dudes want birds this where you get them from. Depending on who they are and how many they want determines what to do to them. Right now a nigga want four, he a good dude and he be spendin' so I aint gonna hit'em hard. Im'ma take this three and turn them into four, but I could stretch'em to 5 ½ easy if I want but like I said son's a good dude and be spendin'. "You know how to stretch?" Justice asked Malik.

"Nah," replied Malik feeling green.

"Aight don't worry Im'ma show you, shit easy, but you Im'ma take care of this right quick and I'll be in there when I'm done."

"That's what it is."

"When I come in there I gotta holla at you about something anyway."

"About what?" asked Malik.

"I'll talk to you," forgetting to fill Malik in on what was on his mind last night.

"Aight let me start runnin' this paper thru the machine to get a count on all this shit then."

By the time Justice returned to the living room, Malik had piles of money put into ten thousand stacks, thirty grand in hundreds, ten grand in 50's, and fifteen grand in 20's but it looked as if he hadn't dented the money pile that covered the floor. When he had first spread the money all over the floor he assumed a rough estimate of the count. He had first estimated the count to be about two to three hundred grand, but it had actually turned out to be a hundred thousand more. There was in between money, up under money, over top of money. There was money every where. He found himself counting, recounting, and counting again, each ten gee stack over and over before he rubber banned them. Justice sat on the carpeted floor and snatched up a big chunk of the money pile and began running it through the counting machine.

"You double checked the stacks you got rubber banned over there?"

"Tripled checked," said Malik.

Justice smiled. He knew that it had been a dumb question to ask someone of Malik's caliber before the words even came out of his mouth.

"My bad kid, I know better."

"I know dawg, no offense taken, but yo what you wanted to holla at me about?"

"Oh yeah," said Justice remembering what he wanted to discuss with him.

"Yo, it's something you need to know before you hop back into this shit, cause I don't want you to be in the dark about the situation and something jump off, cause believe me when I tell you dawg, when muthafuckas find out we down together niggas gonna be feelin' some type of way."

"Put it out there kid, what's the deal?" asked Malik.

Justice began filling Malik in on the latest situation between his mans and them, how he had set up shop and what happened after that. Malik took it all in and when Justice was finished he spoke. "Yo, don't even worry about that akh, I'm back on the scene now. When them niggas find out we together they

ain't gonna want no problems. Matter fact I'mma
go around the way and holla at them cats and dead
that shit right now. That ain't about nothing, I got
it." Justice knew that Malik had the capabilities to
squash the beef between him and his manz and
them. It was not is intentions to get Malik involved,
he was only shedding some light on the situation.
Regardless, whether those were his mans and them
in the past, according to the street law and the rules
of the game, once Malik got down with Justice, his
beef was Malik's beef and vise-versa. At the
mention of deading the upcoming war he knew
what laid ahead. Justice began to lean towards a
peace treaty if Malik could pull it off, but in the
back of his mind he knew that there was that small
possibility that the beef had ignited far beyond
resolution. If that was the case then Justice knew
that it wouldn't be over until it was over, still he had
faith in Malik's wisdom.
"I know you got it dawg."
No question," replied Malik taking a quick glance at
his watch. "Shit let me get up outta here akh, I'm
late for prayer again."
"Peace, take care of that."
"Peace."
Meesha had been thinking about her decision all
morning long. She knew she loved Malik but she
wasn't sure that she made the right decision. Her
mom had always told her 'love is not enough'.
Experience had also revealed that truth. Being
home, Mandy running wild and not being able to

265

find work was taking a toll on him. Meesha understood and didn't want to add to that by not being there for him. His back was against the wall and she intended to be there for him as long as he needed her. "Hey Meesh, you alright gurl? You been in a daze all day," One of her co-workers noticed.

"Girl, I'm just tired. I was up late last night." Her co-worker knew that Meesha had come to work after hitting the club with three hours of sleep. This was different. Meesha's mind was traveling a thousand miles a minute playing out all of the possible scenarios of her decision. Each scenario ended with her being hurt. She just hoped he could get in and get out like he planned. Meesha never wanted anyone or anything like she wanted Malik. "Tameesha Martin please report to the information desk." *That must be Yolanda. I don't know why she ain't call my phone.* Meesha perked up. "Alright y'all, I'm goin' to lunch." She clocked out and headed for the elevators. As she rounded the corner she saw several nurses and food service workers crowding the information desk. As she got closer she tried to peer through the crowd to see what the attraction was. She reasoned it was none of her business as she searched the lobby for Yolanda's face. She wasn't in her usual spot. "Meesha!" The security guard yelled across the lobby as the crowd dispersed. "Hey what's up?" she spoke to the female security guard. "Girl you tell me!" Meesha smiled as she walked over to the counter. She knew

266

she had some type of gossip to share. She always did. "Girl, what you got down there?" Meesha was confused but still smiled. "You must got a gold, no a damn diamond mine down there!" As she approached the counter, she saw the huge bouquet of three dozen roses with a single white rose placed carefully in the center of the arrangement. "You musta' gave that brotha a big piece last night" The guard leaned back in her chair and belted out a loud laugh as she slapped her knee. The officer bent down, picked up the flowers. Meesha stood silent. Every fear and negative thought was erased when she read the attached note.

You are a beautiful woman
who deserves beautiful things.
I love you!
Everything in me loves you!
I know that you've been hurt by other people before.
The red roses represent them. I am not them. I will
do everything in my power to remain unstained in
your heart.

She tried everything in her power not to breakdown "What the fuck is wrong with you? Which one of these hoes I need to smack up in here." Yolanda was silly like that. You never knew what she was going to say out of her mouth. Meesha wiped her face and handed Yolanda the note. The guard yelled "Read that shit out loud!" Yolanda looked her in the face, turned and began walking out the door. Meesha shrugged her shoulders and followed Yolanda out the door. "That nosey gossipin' ass bitch get on my nerves." Yolanda was still mad because she had spread a rumor that she and Meesha were gay and they were dating. So, any opportunity Yolanda had to treat her bad she took advantage of it. They stood in front of the hospital as Yolanda read. "Ooooh! Girl! He love yo' ass! He sent all them roses? This is so nice. Dudes send flowers everyday but they don't put no thought into it. Look at this shit. I mean who would think of some shit like this if it wasn't from the heart." Meesha never doubted Malik's love for her but this just helped her settle into her decision. "You know you gotta give him some tonight."

"Oh! That ain't no problem!" They both laughed. What we eatin' today?" Meesha asked.

CHAPTER TWENTY-SEVEN

LATELY Pete and Doub had been hugging the block, overseeing their workers, making sure they were doing what they were suppose to be, while Cheddar conducted their business affairs on a larger scale. Ever since the situation with Justice's lieutenant and the shoot out up the street of their projects, they had beefed up their artillery and stepped their game up on the block, seeing to it that they snatched up any and all money that came through the area from all angles. Even some of the dudes who were from around there were complaining how they were being cut throated, but their cries went unheard. They knew that they were out numbered and out gunned so they let it be and sufficed for what they were able to get, while Cheddar, Doub, and Pete's crew was on the scene. They just put more hours in on the block when they eventually closed up shop for the night, so overall their block was booming because of it's 24 hour 7 days a week shifts being pulled. In spite of the previous altercation with some of Justice's crew, business had definitely increased for Cheddar and his boys. They were back to normal business and then some. The numbers they were putting up at the end of the night when

269

they tallied up were like Michael Jordan on a good night. Things were going so well for them that they even discussed post poning their decision, but decided to stick with the plan. Doub and Pete had been so caught up in a conversation that they hadn't even noticed the car with tinted windows pull up. It wasn't until someone had yelled that they became alarmed. "Oh shit it's a hit son," the one kid shouted, jetting to his stash to retrieve his glock. Instantly, both Doub and Pete drew their pieces, Doub with his Taurus in hand, Pete with a snub nose 4 pound bulldog in his. They were ready to unload on the vehicle that was behind enemy lines. If it wasn't for Pete immediately recognizing the figure on the driver's side, they would have indeed made a fatal mistake.

"Yo, yo, hold up, fall the fuck back, everybody," yelled Pete loud enough for his whole team to hear, who now all stood heavily armed. As he appeared in full view, Doub also now saw who the occupant of the coupe and was confused. At first Malik didn't notice the commotion he had caused because it has been a long time since he had been on the streets and had to be on point like that, but as he saw Doub and Pete reaching up under their shirts, it dawned on him that he was in a whip that belonged to Justice, their nemesis. There was no doubt in his mind that they were reaching for weapons and he had to make his presence known before it cost him his life. The little niggas had already strapped up, Malik saw as he stepped out the Legend. At hearing

Pete's word, everybody drew down, but remained
on point. Out of the bunch of fifteen young kids,
only four knew the body that caused all the
commotion, and in an instant Malik's identity began
to spread like wild fire amongst the crew. Both
Doub and Pete walked over towards the car where
Malik stood. Malik was not afraid, nor was he
intimidated by the scenery. He knew that if
anything Doub and Pete were the ones who were
fearful in spite of the small army that they had
backing them and the big guns they possessed in
their waist belts. After all, he was still Malik to
them, the same Malik that had put in work for the
very same block they stood on, repping it to the
fullest, and the same Malik who they looked up to.
It was not the age factor that was the issue. It was
the experience that Malik had along with his street
credibility. Everyone knew that he was a cold-
blooded killer.
They both spoke to Malik, greeting him with hand
shakes and hugs, and he embraced them in return.
Pete was the first to ask the question that needed to
be answered without offending Malik in the
process, because all in all he was still there manz.
"Yo, isn't that Just Ack?"
"It use to be, he gave it to me," answered Malik
"Word," said Doub unimpressed.
"Yeah, word," Malik shot back firmly catching
Doub's sarcasm.

"So what up though baby, we ain't seen you in a minute, what's good, you aight?" asked Pete changing the subject.

"Yeah, I'm good I just been chillin."

"A yo everything's everything, yall go ahead, do what you was doin'," Doub yelled back to their workers.

Malik laughed inside to himself knowing that Doub's performance was solely for him, to show how strong his arm was, by exercising his authority over the little niggas. Pete caught it too, but said nothing. He knew Doub was showing off like he did so many times in the past.

"What brings you around here though? You know this ain't your type of scene no more," Pete said curious to know.

"Things change dawg, feel me?" was the answer Malik gave.

"Say word," Doub said knowing what Malik meant.

"Word."

"Aw man say it ain't so," laughed Pete.

"Brother gotta eat."

"So what's up then?" asked Doub.

"You ready to make this thing official and put the team back together?"

It was if as though somebody had just stabbed Malik in the heart when he heard Doub's words, but he couldn't allow them to see his discomfort, because now was not the time to be creating more bad blood between them and his new teammate.

"I got something else in the making right now, so
I'm good, but I know if I need you I can holla,"
replied Malik with diplomacy which he felt they
really didn't deserve, but he couldn't allow his
personal feelings to get in the way of his reason for
being there in the first place. Being back on the
scene, brought back memories of how they had left
him for dead. He never would have ever thought
about teaming up with them again. It was apparent
to both Doub and Pete what Malik had in the
makings and with whom. The grills told it all. Doub
was the first to display his disappointment and
disapproval.
"You sleepin' with the enemy Leek?"
"What?" asked Malik, his tone confirming it all.
"Don't tell us that kid," said Doub with hurt written
all over his face. Pete was just as hurt. "Malik you
rollin' with Justice?" At that point Malik realized
just how deep the situation was and the extent of
hatred that his mans and them had for Justice, and
the same could be said on Justice's end. Malik knew
that he had to stay focused in order to defuse things
between the two parties before an all out war broke,
because just as Cheddar, Pete, and Doub had an
army of soldiers, so did Justice. "Yo listen, before
yall go any further I already know the history
between all of you, that's why I'm here. Yeah I'm
fuckin' with Just on that tip 'cause I know he a
good dude, not sayin' that yall not, because I've
known you niggas most of my life. So, I know you
niggas is good, but shit ain't the same dawg,

muthafuckas grew up over the years. You three
niggas stayed tight, but I was in the joint for ten
years with no contact with none of you niggas.
Justice was in there with me fighting the war in
there while yall was fighting it out here. I know
love is still love with us, but I got mad love for that
nigga too, feel me? I could've easily came around
here and got back in the game with the help of yall.
But I did all I could do around here, got knocked
and paid for it, while you niggas stayed out here
eatin', getting fat, this shit belong to yall now. I
wasn't tryin' to come in on that. When Just said that
night I saved his life in the joint, he meant that shit.
He was in that muthafucka dying, rotting away, I
gave him life and for that he felt indebted to me and
offered me something any one of you would've
hopped on if you were in my position. Yo that beef
yall got goin' ain't about nothin', niggas tryin' to
get hood rich man, and enjoy life. I came around
here to tell you to let that shit ride, son don't want
no beef on some real shit. On the strength of me let
that go dawg," ended Malik.
It was a lot to take in, but Pete and Doub heard
every word of what was said. Had it been anybody
else the words would've went unheard, but the fact
that they came from Malik's mouth made a
difference. They felt that Cheddar needed to be
there, but since he wasn't they would just have to
fill him in on the new development in the matter,
with Malik now in the equation they knew that they

had to reevaluate and reconsider their plans. They wondered whether this was a strategy of Justice's. "Yo Malik, we feel what you sayin', but homeboy couldn't come out and speak for himself?" asked Doub.

Malik made no reaction to Doub's question he expected to be asked. He knew that Justice had the capabilities of handling any and every situation that come his way. If the urge or mood struck him he would get his own hands dirty if need be. His rep was well known and highly respected. Even throughout the prison system. He was known for being thorough, and he was determined to re-educate them on all of this.

"I volunteered to come holla at you niggas on my own, so let's not get it twisted, son ain't had no problem with comin' thru and hollerin' on his own, but he ain't had no intentions on comin' down here. He ready for whatever like yall ready for whatever, I'm just tryin' to peace this shit up cause I can't stack no paper if niggas is at war, feel me?"

Convinced that Malik was on the up and up, Pete and Doub was satisfied with what had just been told to them. Still, it was hard for them to grasp the concept that Malik had teamed up with Justice rather than them. Never in a million years would they have thought that Malik would link up with anybody outside of the hood on that tip. The only thing they could see was that they were his mans and them and Justice was an outsider. He was their enemy, an enemy that posed a threat, and like anything or anyone that poses a threat when there is war it must be eliminated. But here it was an ally of their stood before them vouching for their adversary. Putting his word on it that the enemy was willing to wave the white flag and choose peace over war. This seldom happened in the streets when a situation had escalated to the level that it had between the two teams. Normally one of or many of these young soldiers dedicated to the game and lived by the codes of the streets, would become a statistic. In this case, Malik was trying to prevent that. He knew that he wouldn't be able to get a definite answer on the matter because there were only two of the three people that needed to decide on the issues. And the third party was the main vote that counted. Cheddar was who he really wished had been present because he had always been the influence over Doub and Pete. Although Malik knew that both Doub and Pete were being receptive, what they thought or how they felt really didn't hold any merit without Cheddar's input. Doub and Pete knew what Malik was thinking without him having to say it, and he was right, no matter what they agreed on, nothing could be final until they discussed it with Cheddar.

"Yo dawg we know you comin' at us on some real shit cause you ain't never gave it to us no other way, so if your man will dead it then you right ain't no need for no blood to be shed. But you know like we do that it ain't just up to us. We gotta holla at folk before we can really start talkin' about peace.

We gonna give it to him the way you gave it to us, matter fact you should swing by the spot and holla at him on your own that might be better," suggested Doub.

"Nah that's not a good idea, that's something that needs to be discussed between the three of you, just tell Ched I said he bigger than that, he'll know what I mean," said Malik, pulling his trump card assuming it would get Cheddar to lean towards deading the beef. It was what Cheddar always said to Malik when they met up one on one when Cheddar tried talking Malik out some of shooting someone or squashing a beef. In the end Malik would calm down, change his mind, and tell Cheddar how he did it on the strength of him.

"Aight yo, we'll holla at him," said Pete.

"Yeah we definitely gonna do that and then we'll get back at you," followed Doub

"Aight cool, put my cell number in your phone."

"What is it?" asked Doub.

As he called it out, they both logged Malik's number into their cell phones.

"We got 'em," said Pete.

"We'll holla at Ched and hit you up later."

"Bet," Malik replied and they exchanged hand-shakes and hugs again.

Malik hopped in the Acura coupe and drove off.

"Yo what you think Doub?"

"I don't even know son, I don't know how Cheddar gonna take this shit."

"Word, me neither."

CHAPTER TWENTY-EIGHT

MEESHA put her face in her hands as she sat on the side of the tub. Malik left out three days consecutive without eating breakfast, each time leaving early to meet Justice. Meesha didn't eat breakfast those mornings either. Instead, she pondered the difference between the streets and another woman. It was all the same to her now. She was used to competing with other women. She usually held her own. Not just because she was beautiful, but because men appreciated who she was. She didn't expect things to be like this with Malik. Surely, she had everything she wanted, even the man of her dreams, but the streets were slowly ripping them from her grasp. Meesha felt that she could not compete with the love that he has for the streets. Meesha's thoughts were interrupted by her phone. She flipped open the phone the view the text message ". . ." She knew what the ellipsis meant to Standard English but what was more important was what it meant to her. This was Malik's way of letting her know he was thinking about her. He

always seemed to know what she needed and when.
She knew what she was getting herself into when
she stuck the note on the microwave. The text
disappeared and Yolanda's face surfaced on the
screen. "What's up girl?" Meesha answered.
"Hey."
"Land hold on, Malik is that you?" asked Meesha
from the bathroom.
"Yeah babe, what's up?"
"You got a letter on the dresser."
"From who?" he asked forgetting who he had
written to.
"I don't know, somebody in jail," she yelled back.
Instantly a smile spread across his face,
remembering the one person he had reached out to
behind the wall.
"Sorry about that girl. What the hell are you doing
anyway?"
I'm chillin' getting ready to go out. What you doin'
oh! I forgot Malik got that ass on lock!" Yolanda
belted out a loud dramatic laugh. "You just mad
cause I'm getting it on a regular." No really, I'm
actually happy. I thought ya little thing was gonna
dry up."
"Shut the hell up" Meesha yelled as she laughed.
Yolanda could hear Meesha smiling. She was happy
to see her friend happy. So, she never told her that
Monique saw Malik standing outside around the
New Projects. Monique and Nikki didn't seem to
approve of Malik. *They were probably jealous.* She
thought. Monique and Nikki were the two that had

gone on continuously about how fine Malik was.
Yolanda didn't care what he did for a living though
or how Malik looked. *"If she likes it, I love it,"* she
told herself.
Well, girl when he give you your free. . . call me."
Yolanda joked as she made reference to *Amistad*.
Meesha just laughed and hung up the phone.

"Bismillaah Rahmanir Rahim
As Salaamu Alaikum Abdul Maalik,
I received your letter last week and it was
alhaamdullaah to be hearing from you. The
brothers, Muhammad and Bashir, send the
Salaams, and Shakrun for the money you sent us,
but you know we sending that back because based
on your scribe, you need it more than we do. You
know that Allah is seeing to it that we are well
provided for in here. May He reward you for your
intentions and effort. The past Jumah I told the
Ummah that I received a letter from you and they
all send the Salaams and said they would keep you
in their Duaa's throughout your time of struggles,
which brings me to my main purpose for writing to
you. Ahki, I see that the Dumjah is revealing it's
true self to you like I pre warned you but it's a good
thing that you continue to have sabr because
patience is a virtue and you know that Allah would
never place a burden on you more than you can
bear. True indeed Satan works overtime, and he
preys on your weakness, so you have to stay strong
Ahki, because you can easily fall back into that

*same old way of thinking and living. I hope that this
letter finds you in the best of health mentally,
physically, emotionally, and spiritually, and that
this letter isn't too late to serve its purpose.
Muhammad and Bashir both sent you letters along
with mine showing some love. Inshaa Allah when
you write back send some flicks of you and your
ummi, and wifey, other than that we don't need
nothing up in here. Take care my beloved brother.*

Ma Salaams

Abdul Kwame

Kwame's letter put Malik in deep thought. Shame
overwhelmed him as he reread Kwame's words and
then Muhammad's and Bashir's. These three
brothers had seen him come a long way, seeing the
growth first hand; they believed in him. But he had
failed them, not only did he fail his peers, he had
failed himself. It had dawned on him that he has
missed his prayers all day and Jumah last Friday
because of his meeting with Justice. He reflected
back on an old passage that he had read in his
Quran while he was in prison.

"Those who Allah guides none can lead astray, and
those who have been lead astray none can guide."
Malik wondered would he ever be able to get back
on the right path or was it too late for him. He had
no way of knowing his fate, because only Allah
knows best. Malik could not believe that he had
turned into one of the same brother's that Kwawe
had spoken about there last conversation, who
abandoned their prayers and belief. He couldn't

remember when the last time he had offered his five daily prayers or attended Jumah. He put the three letters back into the envelope, with the intention to write back. He went to the bathroom to shower and prepared for his evening prayer. When he got out he dried off slipped into his night wear and began offering his Maghrib prayer opening with the Al-Fatihah.

"In the Name of Allah, the Most Gracious, the Most Merciful.

All praises and thanks be to Allah.

The Most Gracious, the Most Merciful.

The Only Owner of the Day of Resurrection.

You Alone we worship, and You Alone we ask for help.

Guide us to the Straight Path.

The Way of those on whom You have bestowed Your Grace, not of those who earned Your Anger. Ameen."

After Malik completed the remainder of his prayer he went into the bedroom where Meesha lay in her bath towel. Meesha got up off the bed and put her arms around Malik's waist and pulled him closer to her and kissed him. The ellipsis swirled around her mind as she slid her hands up the back of his shirt. She untied the draw string on Malik's sweat pants as he peeled out his shirt. Malik released the towel from around her body. Meesha guided Malik back into the bathroom and turned on the water to the shower.

CHAPTER TWENTY-NINE

" I can't believe that nigga would do some shit like that," Barked Cheddar.

Pete and Doub knew that Cheddar would react in this manner. In the back of his mind, Cheddar assumed that if the time ever came where Malik wanted to get back in the game he would have come to them, in spite of their differences in the past. After all they were a team, even before all the drug shit. They were like brothers, brothers who had a falling out but made amends. Which Cheddar felt they had done when Malik first came home. To hear that he and that punk ass nigga Justice teamed up told him something different. Malik's words in the truck that day were a contradiction to his actions, Cheddar felt. He couldn't believe that Malik had the audacity to try and squash a beef that he had no idea how deep or serious it really was. He respected Malik to the fullest because that was his mans, but this was no longer back in the day, shit changed, and so did people. Cheddar was a big shot caller now in Malik's absence, so there was no way he was going to allow him to come home and after one or two days back on the scene try to come and dictate the momentum of an on going beef that was ignited before he even came home. His love ran deep for Malik, but he felt betrayed, and would never forget this. He never stopped to think how Malik really felt when he first heard that he was fucking his girl while he was on locked down. Maybe if he would have he could have respected Malik's request to dead the beef. He knew no matter what the outcome of his decision, Malik was definitely off limits, and he would see to it that his whole squad knew that. Had Malik not sent him the message about him being "bigger than that," he may have felt different.

"So you want me to call him and tell him that we ain't rollin with that peace shit," asked Pete.

"Nah, I don't want you to call him at all. Them dudes ain't no dummies they get the hint. You just make sure all the lil homies know that Malik ain't a part if none of this, as far as Justice, yall know what we discussed.

CHAPTER THIRTY

ALMOST two weeks had gone by, and still no word from Cheddar and his boys. Malik couldn't believe how they never got back to him on peacing up the beef. But now, neither he nor Justice was concerned about the matter. Business was at an all time high. In the two week span. Malik had made more money during that time than he had his whole combined time in the game. He and Justice became inseparable as he got his back watching and learning the new tricks and trades of the drug business, and refreshing resting memory on the old. Because of the amount of money they were getting he began carrying heat again. He sported a double hornet holster to hold his matching nickel plated forty five's up under his leather blazer, even though Justice was against it being as though he was still on parole. Malik was being extra precautious ever since he had heard about the two twins from B-more that was set up and followed home by a nigga who use to work for them. While he was locked up a similar situation happened out his way to two niggas from the projects. According to the streets, when there mans found them they were tied up, robbed, and shot executioner style. Come to find out it was two of their own manz and 'em that had committed the act. Malik remembered running into one of the kids from the projects named Buff who was down for a shooting at the Jamaican club, but was a part of the torturous murders of the two cats that had been the ones who murdered their manz. It was later found out that they burned them alive in an abandoned building. All of this came out at a trial that Buff testified in against his main manz Jamil, who wound up beating the bodies. On top of all of that Malik knew how he had crept niggas before, so he wasn't taking any chances because he was seeing paper like he had never seen before. He had saved up enough money to buy his mother a brand new home, which she refused. Just as she refused to have any dealings or contact with him. That hurt him deeply, but he had to respect her position and understood why she felt the way she did, and only hoped that she came around. As for his little sisters, they now wanted for nothing with the conditions that they slowed their rolls in the streets. They only found slicker ways to run them. Meesha also wanted for nothing, but she only wanted one thing. The one thing Malik deprived her of, his time whole heartedly. No matter how many minks or diamonds he brought her, none of it amounted to the value if his physical presence. Justice pushed his brand new pearl black 745i onto the Ave as Malik road shot gun. Their entire crew was in awe at the sight. Each one day dreaming about the day when it would be them pushing a hot

whip like that. The sight of the BMW with
monstrous chrome rims that shined like a freshly
cleaned piece of silver was something to see. The
ride alone put Justice in the category of being
"Hood Rich, to the kids that came from broken
homes and poverty stricken environments, Justice
was living the "Ghetto American Dream", a big
house, nice ride, fly wardrobe, and more money
than he could ever spend in one, if not, two life
times. By now everyone on the team had known
Malik by face and name, and knew that he was
equal to Justice as far as they were concerned, but
in some of their books he was respected more for
his quick come up and the fact that he had a
reputation for being a cold gangsta. Something
every little nigga out there wanted to be known for.
They studied the way that he carried himself and
tried their best to emulate him. When he spoke to
them or with them it was always with humility but
you could feel the strength of his words when they
came out his mouth. He was always trying to school
them on many aspects of the game and they were
feeling that because that was something that Justice
never tried to do. He was a good dude but when it
came to them he was all about business. Some of
them thought about bouncing to another team, but
changed their minds and stayed once they met
Malik. The head Lt. of the squad came back from
out of the building with the duffle bag of money and
handed it to Justice. A few of the younger heads
came by the BMW to acknowledge Justice and

Malik's presence. Justice was talking to one of their Lt's about his street work ethics and how he was doing a good job holding it down on the block. All of a sudden Justice became abrupt and began rushing the conversation as though he were in a hurry. The Lt. instantly picked up on it though he had no clue as to what was going on, "Aight big homie," he said to Malik before spinning off. Justice pulled off. Sensing something funny Malik became fully alert and got all the way on point. He began checking his surroundings. He knew if it had been the police on there tail Justice would've pulled his coat, so he knew that it couldn't have been anything like that. As he tried to figure out the reasons for Justice's actions, the reason had entered his visual just as clear as day, like a perfect picture from a Kodak moment.

"Yo stop the car!" yelled Malik.

"What?"

"Yo, Just stop playin', stop the car Akh!"

"Malik let that go baby, that shit is old, that aint about nothin."

Malik's blood began to boil. He had never been mad at Justice or had an argument with him since the first time they met, but he could not control his anger at the sight of the individual who just crossed his path.

"Yo Just stop the mu'fuckin car akh 'fore I jump out!"

Understanding his friend's anger, instead of stopping, Justice put the BMW in reverse. He knew

if the shoe was on the other foot, nothing or no one
would have been able to stop him. The only thing
he could attempt to do now was to make sure Malik
knew exactly how he was going to do what he knew
he was going to do.
"Malik, it's too many mu'fuckas out here dawg, you
just can't do it like that," said Just grabbing Malik's
arm before he exited the car.
"I got this yo."
"Hold up, listen to me," Justice began to reason. "If
you just hop out like that every nigga out here that
know you is gonna be on it and gonna know
something's up and they gonna be on point, ready to
roll. Let that nigga go ahead and cop and we follow
his ass to a place where there are less faces, and
witnesses, feel me? I know you wanna handle your
business, but you gotta do it right."
Malik listened and knew that Justice was right. He
was glad that he had a friend like him that was able
to get him to see things for what they really were.
He calmed down and closed the car door back.
After he made his purchase, they followed the tall
slim crack head. It couldn't have gone a better way
if they had planned it, as the crack head hiked it to
Greenbrook park, finding himself a secluded area to
take a blast. Justice pulled over and Malik got out.
He killed the ignition and turned out the lights.
Justice found it funny how when a crime is
committed there's always a nosey ass neighbor or
someone that heard something, but when you're in
the act you don't see anybody. At the thought of

that, he looked around to make sure there was no
one in sight. Malik saw the flame from the lighter as
the foul stench of crack cocaine filled the air, while
the crack head inhaled a new consciousness from
the smoke filled pipe. Malik drew one of his .45's
and continued to approach the addict. It had been a
long time since the two of them had been in the
same area together. He remembered the many times
that he had layed in his cell bunk thinking about the
many different ways to take this mans life. One of
the reasons he started working out was to get his
weight up so he'd be strong enough to kill him with
his bare hands. Tupac said in a song, "Get my
weight up with my hate up, pay 'em back when I'm
bigger," and that's what Malik intended to do.
Practicing Islam made him push those thoughts to
the smallest crevice of his mind, but like a lot of his
old thoughts, this one had resurfaced. It was time to
put an end to the madness. As he got closer he
called out the man's name that he hadn't used in ten
years.
"Yo Phil!" Startled, Phil dropped his pipe.
"Huh? Who dat?" he said in a paranoid tone.
Malik decided to keep him in suspense as he got in
plain view of Phil. He knew that he wouldn't
recognize him. "Man, you don't remember me?" he
asked with the .45 tucked behind his back. It was
too dark for Phil to see Malik's hands, but the
cocaine in is system had him paranoid. He felt
something wasn't right about the whole situation.
"Nah, I don't know you fam," he said honestly.

"Oh you don't know me now?" said Malik sarcastically. With that, Phil squinted his eyes in attempts to take a better look, and a quick thought crossed his mind but immediately exited. Had he realized or entertained the thought a little more, he would have taken flight. When he was in prison the fact that he had sold his soul and cooperated with authorities followed him, from the county jail down to prison and was marked as being a snitch. That made him easy prey. Fresh in the building some old head booty bandits rolled up on him and continuously took what little manhood he had left. After they were done with him they made him check into protective custody where he finished the remainder of his time. When he came home, he tried to shake the horrifying experience off but psychologically he was unstable, and couldn't cope with the torture he endured. What he had done began to weigh heavy on his conscious, causing him to turn to drugs as a coping strategy to help him escape reality. With the drugs he could be who he wanted to be and wherever he wanted to be from, which he was trying to do until this stranger rolled up on him blowing his high.

"Yo man I don't know how you know my name or how you even knew I was over here, but I don't know you and I ain't try'nna know you, dig?" Phil tried to sound tough.

Despite Phil finding some heart, Malik laughed out loud before he pulled the 45 from behind his back. At the sight of the gun Phil threw his hands up.

"Whoa brother, I ain't go nothing, Im'ma crack head man!" he yelled

"Nigga don't call me brother muthafucka!" Malik yelled spitting in his face.

"You a piece of shit you little cheese eatin' mu'fucka."

At the sound of being called a snitch, Phil figured he'd been locked up with the big man with the gun. Maybe even one of the guys that had raped him was coming back for more. He tried to clean up the words that were said to him.

"Yo, I aint no snitch man!"

"What?" Malik barked. "Nigga get on your mu'fuckin knees. You ain't no stand up nigga, you's a sit down ass nigga."

Phil was convinced now that this was one of the rapists from prison when he told him to get on his knees. If he had to give this nigga some head he was going to make sure that he bit this nigga shit straight off and leave it right in the park on some Lorraine Bobbitt shit.

Malik looked at the pitiful specimen who was now on his knees, and knew that he had prolonged the situation long enough. It was time to end the charade.

"Why you set me up akh?" Malik asked wanting to hear it out of Phil's mouth. He had waited all these years for an answer.

"Set you up?" replied Phil lost for words.

"Yeah mu'fucka!" Malik spazzed, angered by Phil's dumbfoundedness he displayed. "That day we was

in the house after we robbed the nigga from
Connecticut." Phil's eyes lit up as if he had just
discovered America.

"Oh shit Malik? That's you?" he asked attempting
to get off his knees.

"Bitch don't move. I'll blow ya mu'fuckin' head
off!"

Phil froze. "Yeah it's me nigga! Who you thought it
was Ronald Mcmu'fuckin' Donald?" For the first
time in his life, Phil was afraid of dying. There was
no doubt in his mind that today was going to be the
day. He had known Malik long enough to know that
he was in killer mode right now. All he could do
now was try to beg one last time for forgiveness and
hope that his words were felt. "Malik please man,
please, I'm sorry man I know that shit was wrong. I
regretted that shit ever since the day I did it. Man I
prayed a thousand times over for that dumb shit I
did. Muthafucka's raped me down in the joint,
checked me in P.C. and now I'm fucked up off this
muthafuckin glass dick man on some Pookie shit.
I'm already dead man, please let me die a slow
death, Please I beg you dawg!" he ended his speech,
but Malik was not impressed. The only thing that
stuck in his head was Phil request for a slow death.
Malik took his gun and stuck it back in his left
holster. At the sight of that Phil began to count his
blessings, thanking God for answering his prayers.
"Thank you man, word is bond thank --!"

"For what?" Malik growled as he rushed Phil and
wrapped his massive hands around Phil's puny

neck, and began strangling him. You could hear
Phil's cries lightly through the chocking sounds as
Malik applied pressure to his throat, cutting off his
passage in attempts to suffocate him. "You wanted
a slow death, well here it is. Die bitch!" he said
squeezing harder and harder as Will's eyes looked
as if they were popping out of his head. Feeling his
body go limp, Malik knew that he had chocked the
life out of Will. He released the lifeless body and
walked back to where Justice sat waiting for him,
feeling that justice had been officially served.
Justice saw Malik approaching and started the car.
Malik hopped in and they pulled off. "What up?
You aight?" Justice asked.
"Yeah no doubt," Malik answered calmly. "Damn
you was out there for a minute and I ain't here no
shots, what you let the nigga live or something?"
"Nah, the nigga wanted a slow death so that's what
I gave him." As sharp as Justice was, he did not
understand, nor was he suppose to. Justice
cautiously looked to the left and then to the right,
then pulled off.

CHAPTER THIRTY-ONE

" **YO** Cheddar check this out," Doub said while handing him the local newspaper.

"A local man was found dead yesterday in Greenbrook park by a morning jogger. Local authorities say that the incident is being considered a homicide. The victim was identified as 29 year old Phillup Burris of Plainfield, NJ. Mr. Burris had an extensive criminal record and sources say that police found a controlled dangerous substance and drug paraphernalia in his possession. Sources also say that there are no leads as of yet, but if anyone has any information about the incident contact us at 1800-CrimeStoppers."

Ah! Somebody finally slumped his snitchin' crack head ass huh," was Cheddars response. That was not the response Doub was looking for though.

"Yeah. Somebody did," replied Doub.

"You sound like you know who," Cheddar shot back picking up on Doub's emphasis.

"I think I do and you should too."

"Who?"

"Come on son think."

"Oh shit, word! You might be right kid," Cheddar
voiced as it dawned on him.
"Yeah word. Just think about it, Malik been gone all
this time, then he come home, been home for some
months now, and son been getting high since he got
out a couple of years ago, now all of a sudden Malik
back in the game and that nigga wind up dead.
Come on dawg that ain't no coincidence. Look how
the nigga got bodied. On some strangler type shit.
For a muthafucka to do that he gotta really hate a
nigga and he gotta be a strong muthafucka too, you
do the math."
"Nah you right, shit make sense, but can you blame
the nigga though?"
"Nah not at all, I'm just sayin', son back on his shit
again, and you know how Leek get when he get in
that zone, the nigga a beast. Let's not act like the
nigga ain't no killer, and let's not forget who he
down with now. All I'm sayin', he put son lights out
for getting him knocked off, who's to say he ain't
feelin some type pf way about the way we did him
when he got knocked," Doub said trying to plant a
seed in Cheddar's head.
Cheddar pondered on Doubs theory and knew why
Doub was coming at him the way that he was. All
their lives Doub had always been afraid of Malik
and jealous of him too. He wanted to be who Malik
was, but could never be. Over the years of coming
up in the game, Doub had built up some street
credibility, as well as a heart in Malik's absence.
Now, here it was, in a matter of weeks Malik was

able to shatter Doub's façade and cause him to become the same insecure and timid dude that he really was. Doub knew that the only way that he could regain his heart back was if he was able to eliminate the person that took it The only way he could even think to take that route was if Cheddar had sanctioned or co-signed it, which Doub knew he never would, but he had to try to persuade him anyway. "Yo Malik ain't got no beef with us and we ain't got no beef with him either, regardless of who he fuck with. The only one feelin' some type of way is you, and you need to dead that. Focus on what we gotta take care of next month and stop trying to personalize this shit," Cheddar said to him handing him the newspaper back. "That nigga got what his hands called for, fuck that nigga Phil." Doub was not surprised by Cheddar's response. In spite of their differences, Doub knew that although Cheddar had mad love for them, his love for Malik ran far deeper than any love he had for he and Pete. Cheddar would never condone something happening to Malik, and Doub believed in his heart that if he had did anything to Malik to bring him any harm Cheddar would do something to him in return.

"You right, I'm buggin'. Malik did what he had to do, if he did it. I ain't mad at the nigga at all, he kept it gangsta," Doub said down playing the situation.

"No question," replied Cheddar, knowing that Doub
hadn't really meant what he said. Cheddar knew
how he truly felt about Malik.
"Yo Im'ma bounce up outta here, I gotta meet Pete
at the mall."
"You two niggas stay up in there."
"Gots to, gotta stay fly."
"Yeah whatever nigga, but you if they got some
new flava beef and brocs snatch me up two pair."
"Aight, I got you, I'm out."
"One."

CHAPTER THIRTY-TWO

" IM' MA just be in and out, you aint gotta come in if you don't want to,"

"Nah I'm comin in I want one of those Cinnabon's anyway."

"Aight." Malik and Justice hopped out of Malik's new Expedition he had purchased straight off the Ford dealership lot in Meesha's name a week ago. That very same day he bought a white 600CLS, which Meesha now drove. The coupe became he and Justice's transporting hooptie. Malik hit the power locks and activated his alarm, as they walked towards the entrance of the mall. Although it was still being renovated, Garden State Mall located in Elizabeth was the biggest mall in New Jersey now, blowing out Woodbridge, Menlo Park, Cherry Hill, Paramus, and all the other malls alike, making it a good look for the Union County area. Pete and Doub had just finished up their $10,000 shopping spree to support the new mall in their county. Since more stores had opened up they had been visiting the mall more frequently, minimizing their shopping trips to New York. After getting Cheddar two of the latest pair of beef and broccoli

Timberland, they were ready to head back home, as they proceeded to the exiting door, each man with a minimum of four bags in each hand, turning heads of envious by passers, who wished that they themselves were able to splurge the way Pete and Doub just had. Females who walked along side their nine to five working square boyfriends glanced on the low. Both Pete and Doub laughed amongst themselves behind the attention they were getting. As they reached the exit, what they saw before them caused them to stutter step for a spilt second. Malik noticed them first, as they entered the mall. He tapped Justice, who had his head down occupied with his two-way pager. When Justice lifted his head up Malik nodded towards the front of them. When he focused he saw Pete and Doub coming their way.

 Not knowing what to really expect, both Pete and Doub now regretted that they had left their guns in the whip. They had bags full of clothes, and boots in hand. Doub focused his attention on Justice zeroing in on what he believed to be a two-way in Justice's hand. He saw Justice putting the gadget in his pants pocket and instantly Doub detected the bulge tucked into his waist belt, so he was for sure that Malik had to be packing as well. Pete had also noticed the gun butt print coming from under Justice Roc-a Wear shirt and a slight dose of fear entered him at the thought of his enemy having the drop on him and his man like that. He tried his hardest to conceal it and maintain his composure. The only thing that

really kept him from revealing his true fear at the
sight of Justice was Malik's presence. Although
Doub felt some type of way about Malik, he was in
agreement with Pete. Had Malik not been in
Justice's company, there was no telling how the
situation would have turned out. At least they were
in a position to keep things at bay until they were
able to get out the mall, by acknowledging Malik
and greeting him. Pete's greeting would be genuine
but Doub's would be strictly on some fake shit so
he could live to fight another day. Sometimes in the
"game" you had to bite the bullet and catch a nigga
on the come around, which he intended to do. Both
Malik and Justice were intending to walk right past
Pete and Doub and just ice grill them with twenty to
life mugs on their face. Even though they knew that
they had the drop on the two being strapped. There
was a possibility that Pete and Doub had heat on
them but it was obvious that they had their hands
full. Even if they hadn't, neither of the two man
team wanted to have an all out war up in the biggest
mall in Jersey or any mall for that matter. As they
started to come up on Pete and Doub stoned face
with the intentions of keeping it moving the
unexpected happened.
"What up Malik?" said Pete clearing his throat,
causing both Malik and Justice to pause in their
tracks.
"Pete what's good," replied Malik firmly.
"Chillin."
"What up Leek?" followed Doub.

"What up wit you?" asked Malik

"You know, slow motion," he responded.

Neither man spoke to Justice nor did he to them. Not really caring either way, Malik, put Pete and Doub on of the spot.

"Yo, did yall ever talk to Cheddar, cause you never got back to me on that?"

"Yeah we hollered," Pete said a little nervously surprised by Malik's directness.

"And?"

"You know how son is," Doub answered.

"Yeah I know," Malik shot back.

Everyone stared; never taking their eyes off of one another. The tension between the four of them was so thick you would have thought that you were in the rec yard down Trenton State Prison and anybody that knows about that spot knows that the tension could be sliced with a knife. Malik decided to end the meeting before it got out of hand.

"Yo we about to get our shop on like you two niggas, so we'll get up."

Pete and Doub took that as their cue to exit.

"Yeah no doubt, do you," Pete said giving Malik a half handshake and a hug. Doub said nothing, he only shook Malik's hand and gave him the same hug that Pete had. Justice started stepping off as the cipher broke up. He could have sworn he heard Doub call him a punk muthafucka' under his breath and started to whip put his pistol and whip the shit out of him, but he rethought his plan and decided to save it for a later date. Malik thought he had heard the same thing but brushed it off. He wasn't for sure whether Justice heard it, hoping that he hadn't because all hell would have broken loose. One thing Malik knew for sure was that Justice was like a brother to him and Cheddar, Pete, or Doub was no longer his manz and 'em.

"Damn! I can't believe we let them niggas catch us slippin' like that!" expressed Doub as he unlocked his truck.

"I should go back in there and shoot that nigga Justice right in the mu'fuckin face," spit Doub.

"You see how that nigga was grilling us?" he said to Pete as he reached under the driver's seat and pulled out his Magnum tucking it in his waist belt.

"I saw him," answered Pete doing the same with his 9mm.

"Wait until I tell Cheddar this shit, especially that slick shit Malik said about *he know*. He think I ain't catch that shit. You caught it right? Doub asked Pete, looking for a co-signer.

"Nah," replied Pete.

Whatever Doub intended to tell Cheddar Pete didn't want to have any parts of. He knew how Doub felt about Malik but he didn't feel the same. Malik had showed Pete nothing but love in the past and he had felt bad about the way he had carried Malik while he was knocked off. Pete was not really his own man or a leader, so he only followed Cheddar and sometimes Doub's lead. He allowed them to dictate his life to him, but he was tired of it, and wished that things were different between them and Malik, and even Justice too because he knew that if Malik dealt with him the way he did, then he had to be a good dude, in spite of the drama that they were going through. He understood that Justice was only standing his ground for what he believed in, just as they were doing and when there's a situation like that it's never likely that someone will stand down. Blood was bound to be shed. Pete had a great deal of love and respect for Doub, but he felt that it was dudes like him that kept shit going and cost people their lives, all because he felt that he had something to prove. Pete would never dare to voice his opinion about Doub like that, so instead he just let him talk. "Yeah wait until I tell Cheddar this shit," he repeated as they pulled out of the malls parking lot.

CHAPTER THIRTY-THREE

" HELLO," answered Meesha

"Meesha?" the voice came over the receiver. Oh hey baby sis, what's up?" Meesha said recognizing the voice instantly.

"Nothin' really, is Malik there?" Mandy asked. Her tone was a little shaky.

"What's wrong?" asked Meesha picking up on Mandy's tone.

"It's mommie, she had a stroke."

"Oh my god! No!" screamed Meesha as tears began to roll down her face. Alarming Malik from the bedroom, he ran in his boxers and white wife beater.

"Babe what's wrong, you aight?" he asked seeing Meesha sitting there in tears.

"Who's that on the phone?"

"Mandy" she said through her sobs. An instant headache over came Malik when he heard that his sister was on the other end of the line. He could see Meesha's reaction and tell that whatever it was, it wasn't good. Malik grabbed the phone.

"Mandy what's wrong?"

"Mommy's in the hospital," a little hesitant knowing that Malik would flip out.

"For what?" Where you at?" Malik yelled into the phone.

"Malik stop yelling at me," Mandy screamed as she began to cry. Sensing that he had scared his little sister, Malik changed his tone, but needed to know what was wrong with his mother.

"Mandy, stop crying, I'm sorry, but what happened to ma?"

"She had a stroke. I'm at the hospital, Jackie up in there with her. Leek I'm scared I don't know what to do, she ain't lookin' good."

"Babe just calm down, everything gonna be aight, you gotta keep it together and stay strong for mommie. Where you at Muhlenberg?"

"No, they got her out here in New Brunswick in Robertwood."

"Aight don't worry me and Meesha on our way."

"Okay," answered Mandy feeling a little better after talking to her brother. After they hung up she said a little prayer and promised God that if he spared her mother, she'd change her ways and turn her life around.

When Malik and Meesha arrived they were given the room number and directions to where his mother was. As soon as Mandy and Jackie saw their big brother they both jumped up and rushed into his arms with tear stained faces. Malik hugged them both as he saw his mother lying in the hospital bed with a multitude of tubes hooked up to her

unconscious body. The sight was too much for
Malik to bear and he himself broke down into tears.
Meesha came and took the girls from out of his
arms. She remembered how she had never made it
to see Ms. Jones after Mandy told her what she said.
Meesha maintained her relationship with Ms. Jones
even during the times she and Malik had stopped
speaking. Meesha was the mediator between the
two. Ms. Jones would act as if she really didn't
want to hear how Malik was doing, but still offering
her love and prayers, Malik, at home, eagerly
hoping that his mother had a change of heart about
refusing to see or speak with him. Meesha knew she
was their carrier pigeon. She didn't mind. Each of
them needed the other to know how much they were
loved. Meesha knew how much Ms. Jones enjoyed
watching movies with Malik. Many times she tried
to help fill that void. She knew that asking her to
come by was her way of finding out how her son
was doing. Meesha was miserable. "Come on yall.
Let your brother be with your moms."
Both Mandy and Jackie hugged Meesha as she
escorted them out of the room. Malik was grateful
to have such a strong woman like Meesha on his
side. He walked over to his mother's bedside and
kissed her on the forehead, then pulled up a chair
and sat beside her. The stroked had aged her at least
ten years thought Malik. He noticed that her mouth
was slightly twisted. Malik took his mother's hand
and put it between the both of his. "Bismillaah.
God, I come to you at a time when I really need you

to hear my prayer, like I know You always do. I know that I have strayed from the straight path these past few months, but Lord I am still a believer and I know that You are the best of planners. I humbly ask that you allow my mother to continue to make the best of the flesh that you provided for her soul. As a Muslim we are taught not to fear death but to embrace it because the only thing that we can be sure of is death., so I know that if my mother never opens her eyes up again I know that she will be in a better place, closer to her Lord, but again I ask that you allow her to live her life on earth long enough to see her children get there lives back on track. This I ask in your name. Ameen."

The doctor waited until Malik ended his prayer before he approached him. He himself felt the prayer that was shared between mother-son and God. He knew Malik was Muslim based on the ending of the prayer. He himself was Methodist. He believed that there was only one God and knew He had heard Malik's prayer. Malik felt the hand on his shoulder and turned around, seeing the black doctor towering over him.

"What's up Doc?" he said standing to greet the man.

"How are you young man?"

"I'm good, thanks for asking. What's the status with my mother?" Malik asked cutting the small talk.

The doctor understood his concern, which is why he didn't take offense to Malik's cutting their conversation short. He had been practicing

medicine for over 20 years and had to deal with
emotionally distraught family members and friends
regularly.

"Well, as you know your mother has had a stroke
and throughout that time she slipped into a coma.

"So what's the worse case scenario Doc and what
can we hope for?" asked Malik

"Mr--."

"Jones."

"Mr. Jones I'll give it to you like this. The good
thing is that your mother survived the stroke so she
is in no danger there. The bad part as she has
slipped into the coma. I don't know whether you are
familiar or not but when that happens there is no
way of determining how long it will last. It could be
anywhere from 1 day to God knows when.
Basically that's who's hands it lies in, and I know
that you are a God fearing man like myself so all
you can do now is pray."

Malik expected as much, because he had heard
many stories about when people were in coma's
how they could sometimes be unconscious for
months or even years. He remembered his mother
telling him about an uncle he vaguely could
remember, he was in a coma for a long time before
he slipped away. He was an old school stick up kid
who terrorized blocks, until one day his victims got
fed up and busted him in the head with a baseball
bat. Years later Malik had run into the guy who
killed his uncle in prison and the only reason he
didn't take the kids life or at least do something to

him was because the dude was Muslim. To put his hands on another Muslim guaranteed you the Hell fire. On top on that the dude was dying of Aids. It was just a matter of time before his day had come. He couldn't imagine his mother lying in a comma like that, but there was nothing he could do. For as long as he could remember she had always been there for him even when he served ten years in prison. The thought of losing her was unthinkable to him right now. Malik had been so caught up in the streets that he lost focus on what was really most important to him. When he had been sentenced he vowed to himself nothing or no one would ever come before his family. Yet he had done just that. He had chosen the streets over his mother. Tears began to roll down his face again as he pulled out his cell phone.

"Yo run your mouth," Justice answered.

"Just it's me Akh," Malik said through his tears.

"Son what's the deal, what's wrong?" asked Justice concerned.

"My moms dawg,"

"What's wrong with your moms yo?"

"She in a coma man," Malik said sniffling.

"Damn son! Where you at? I'm comin thru."

"Nah don't worry about it. I'm good, I just wanted to let you know what's good and to tell you that I gotta fall back kid. My moms need me dawg and I ain't tryin' to leave her side until she wakes up and even then I ain't tryin' to leave her alone, feel me? I got caught up in everything that was going on and fell off my square. I know that this is a sign from Allah telling me to tighten up. Yo, I appreciate all the love you showed me kid, I love you for that. You'll always be a brother to me, but I can't be a part of all of that no more, nah mean?"

Without hesitation Justice answered him. "Dawg I feel you on all of that, it ain't even nothin' to talk about nigga. Be there for your family beloved. You know I'm here for you and I'll always be there for you."

"Thanks man, I appreciate that."

"Don't mention it dawg, just handle your business."

"I will, and you, I'll keep you posted."

"'Bet,'" said Justice about to hang up.

"A yo Just!"

"Yo?"

"Travel safe akh."

"Always beloved."

CHAPTER THIRTY-FOUR

THREE weeks had gone by and still no progress or change in Malik's mother's condition. Mandy, Jackie, and Meesha visited frequently, but Malik never left his mother's side. The only time he stepped out of the room was when the nurse came to bathe her, or he got hungry, but after a while he began paying the nurses to bring his food to him, tipping them generously for their services, which they all appreciated. All the women young and old adored Malik and admired his dedication, wishing that their own children treated them that way. They weren't aware Malik had also been a child who neglected his mother when she was well and functioning. It had been months since he had seen or spoken to his mother because he refused to give up his lifestyle. But when she awoke, which Malik knew she would, they would have a long talk and make amends once she saw that Malik had given up the game again. This time for good he thought. It was sad to say, but Malik knew that if this had not happened to his mother he would never have thought about stopping his hustle. The money was too good. He realized that it usually took some type of tragedy to occur in order for someone who's

doing wrong or not living right to step back and
evaluate their lives, and think to do something to
improve themselves.

Malik had just finished his lunch and dozed off in
the uncomfortable chair that had become his
temporary bed for the pass 23 days. He sat up in
that same chair breaking day just talking to his
mother and reading his Quran to her. He took cat
naps in between. He could recall that at least 13 out
of the 23 days he had only gotten 2 hours of rest and
today it finally caught up to him as his doze turned
into a deep sleep. It wasn't until he felt his chair
being shaken and the commotion that filled the
room that he realized that by sleeping he had missed
something.

"Mr. Jones? Mr. Jones?" he heard the doctor yelling
as he opened his eyes.

"Huh."

"We need you to step out of the room."

Instantly Malik jumped up.

"What's going on?" he asked

"Get him out of here," the doctor screamed to the
nurses

"Mr. Jones please," the nurse said putting her hand
on Malik's shoulder attempting to escort him out of
the room, but Malik resisted pulling away.

"Get the fuck off of me, what's happening? He
demanded to know, but he was ignored.

"Alright, clear!" yelled the doctor as they prepared
the defibrillator.

"Yo Doc what the fuck is going on?" Malik asked
again although he now began to figure for himself
what was taking place. He has watched enough of
ER to know what the pads in the doctor's hands
were. Again the nurse tried to take Malik out of the
room.

"Mr. Jones, you shouldn't be in here, let them do
their job, Please." But her words fell on deaf ears
because as Malik looked to the corner he saw the
flat line on the screen and knew that Allah had
taken his mother away from him, tears of anger
formed in his eyes and began to drop. "No God!
No! Why her?" he cried out as the nurse wrapped
her arms around him and escorted him out of the
room. She too knew that there was nothing else that
the doctors could do even though they tried. All
Malik could hear was the infinite ring of the flat
line.

CHAPTER THIRTY-FIVE

"YO duck down, here the nigga come," whispered Doub noticing the truck approaching out of the side mirror of the hooptie as he, Cheddar, and Pete sat impatiently.

Justice rode right pass the old gray Buick as he drove through the back streets of town like he always did to jump on the highway that led him home. Had he not been on his cell phone at the time he may have noticed the three bodies squatting down in the abandoned looking car to his right, but Cheddar, Doub and Pete went undetected. As Justice turned the next block, Doub started the Buick with the intent to following him. For the past three weeks they mapped out Justice's routine and in the process tied up all their loose ends on the streets. The first of the months had just passed and Cheddar, Pete, and Doub had made a killing. Three days later there little mans sold the last of the two bricks of bottled up sized 58 slim bottles and moved the remaining eight bricks they had sold in weight like, eight's, quarters, half's, and better, they re'd-up only copping five bricks rather there normal ten just to keep a flow going. They knew that the

"Justice situation" would be a time consuming task and they would be unable to oversee their block like they normally did or attend to their customers who bought weight. In addition to that, they knew that there would be some repercussions for what they planned to do. They discussed their plans over a month ago, when Justice set up shop down the street from their block and his workers shot at their workers. They even had to revise their plan after the incident that took place at the mall between the rivals, which Doub hyped up making it seem more than what it really was, causing Cheddar to include Malik into the equation, but made revisions again when they heard about Malik's mother being in the hospital. They wanted to go pay their respects but couldn't chance it because they really didn't know where Malik stood in the brewing beef. By Malik not being on the scene it made it that much easier to get the drop on Justice. Justice's truck began to slow down in the area in which it always did before he hit the highway. He whipped his truck into the driveway of the house, let his wifey know he was on his way home and threw it in park as he hung up the phone. He grabbed the duffle bag which contained the day's take from his back seat. All three men exited the Buick with guns in tow as Justice pulled in the driveway. They looked around as they ducked behind car after car until they were feet away from executing their first plan. As Justice stepped out of the truck, out of the corner of his eye he caught a slight visual of some type of movement taking place.

"Boc! Boc!" By the time Justice was able to turn, the first bullet had already struck him in the left shoulder, causing him to drop the duffle bag in a matrix spin, while the second one just missed his face. "Pop! Pop!" Before Justice could react to Doub's shot, Pete had already released two shots from his 38. He put one in each of Justice's leg, adding to Justice's imbalance from Doub's first shot, sending him straight to the pavement. Justice had no time to even see who the assailants were. Everything was happening so fast. Justice layed helplessly on the cold ground on his stomach as the three men talked amongst themselves. He couldn't make out what they were saying but he knew that it couldn't be anything good. He tried reaching for the P-89 he had tucked in his waist belt but the impact of the blows from the shots had him faced down in an awkward position. He cursed himself for being so careless. He knew that who ever it was that got the drop on him had peeped his every move. He felt a sharp pain in his side as he was kicked in his ribs by one of the perpetrators. Just as he was able to make out some of the words that were being spoken he heard one of the unfamiliar voices tell him to turn over. He couldn't and even if he could have he wouldn't have. If they intended to take his life then they would do it without any help from him thought Justice as he layed in pain bleeding profusely from his wounds. He was a solider in the war of the

streets, a four star general to be exact. He knew that
by living by the gun, he would die by the gun as
well. His mother had always told him, "*You reap
what you sow*," and Justice believed the words to be
true. He was not afraid, so he wouldn't act as if he
were nor would he go out like a coward and beg for
his life. The gunmen repeated his request but it went
unanswered. Cheddar bent down, grabbed Justice
by his wounded arm and rolled him over. Just was
in pain but he maintained his composure as he was
turned over on to his back. His vision was
somewhat blurry, but he tried to focus to make out
the figure that stood over him. Soon, he was able to
see who was responsible for what was taking place.
Justice couldn't help but chuckle.
"Yeah nigga, who the shit now?" Cheddar asked
sarcastically. Justice smirked. He knew Cheddar
and his other two cronies were softer than cotton
candy but with a gun in their hands it would make
the softest grow a heart.
"Yo stop playin' wit that muthafucka and finish him
off," yelled Doub from behind as he and Pete stood
on point.
"Chill I got this,"
"Come on son," Pete now yelled, but Cheddar
continued to prolong what they came to do. Their
plan was to run down on Justice, each man making
sure their gun went off and that the target was hit.
That way they all played a major part in the heinous
act they were committing and if it ever came down
to it no one would be able to cross anyone because

to tell on one would be to tell on one's self. Doub
and Pete waited impatiently for Cheddar to finish
what they had started.

"Big bad ass Justice! You don't look all that tough
now nigga," Cheddar antagonized him. Justice just
laid there losing blood, too weak to say anything.
Cheddar thought that he was trying to play gangsta
by remaining silent. "Oh you ain't got nothin' to say
huh, with ya tough ass. Nigga if you say please I
might spare your life and let you live as a
paraplegic," Cheddar spit, laughing at his own joke.
That was all Justice could take. It took all the
strength he had to get his words out.

"Su-uu-ck –m-yy -dd-ii-ck!"

"Yeah? Suck ya dick," Cheddar repeated. "Tell that
bitch ass nigga Ski to suck ya dick when you see'
em! Boom! Boom! Boom!" Cheddar dumped two in
Justice chest, and one in his face, then spit on
Justice's body. He didn't care he had revealed to
Justice that he and his crew were the ones behind
the murder of one of his lieutenant's that night at
the gambling hall. Cheddar laughed to himself
behind the fact that Justice would be taking what
he'd just revealed to the grave with him, literally.
"Pussy!" Cheddar barked as he snatched the duffle
bag up.

"Yo let's go," yelled Doub as he and Pete were
already making their way to the get-a-way car. The
two bullets ripped through Justice chest-plate with
explosive force, barely missing his heart, but the
impact had him losing massive amounts of blood.

319

He knew that he was dying but he didn't want to go out like that without anyone knowing what happened to him. He felt his cell phone up under his right side and located it. With all of his strength he strained to get it. Just knew that he only had two options to reach out to, with there number's logged into the first two of the speed dial. Pressing one would instantly dial his shortie and two would dial Malik. Although they both were key factors in his life and he loved them both, he had to choose the one that would handle the situation properly. His thumb pressed down on the key pad and speed dialed the number as he pressed the speaker phone button. When the first ring rang out, some relief came over Justice.

"Ring! Ring! Ring!" was all Justice heard and thought to himself, *Come on dawg pick up the jack.* "Ring! Ring! Ring!" the phone continued.

Justice laid there and let the phone continue to ring as he felt his life slipping away from him. He began to reflect back on something that a brother had once told him when he had first received knowledge of self, as he recalled. "Allah is God, always has been always will be." Justice then breathed his last breath.

CHAPTER THIRTY-SIX

MALIK had taken his mothers death pretty hard, but he knew that he had to be strong for his two little sisters because he was all that they had now. Jackie and Mandy had taken it just as hard as Malik. He and Meesha did as much as they could to console them. Malik insisted that they stay with him at their place so he could watch over them. The last thing he wanted to see was his sisters going out into the streets and doing something that they would later regret because they were hurting and in pain. Regardless to how much they thought that they were grown women, they were still young girls. Malik knew that they were vulnerable and unstable mentally and emotionally right now, so he refused to let them out of his sight. When they arrived home, as Meesha unlocked the front door she heard the phone ringing and rushed in to answer it. Valerie was just about to hang up until she heard Meesha's voice. She let the phone ring eight times before deciding to hang up. She wondered why she let it ring so many times in the first place. She knew it had to be the worry for her man that concerned her so much. He had never taken that long to come home before. Especially after he had already called

her and said that he was on his way. Generally, if
something came up Justice would call her back and
inform her because he knew how insecure she was
when it came to him being out in the streets. So
every chance he got he tried to make her feel secure
and show her that she had a good man on her side.
That gave Valerie all the more reason to think
something was wrong. It had been almost five
hours since they had last spoken and when she tried
dialing his cell phone it went directly to voicemail.
That's when she decided to call Malik. She knew
that if anybody knew his where abouts it would be
him. She tried calling Malik's cell phone but just as
she had with Justice's she also kept getting his
voicemail. After leaving four messages Valerie
remembered that she had Malik's and Meesha's
home number from the first time the four of them
had gone out together. From the few times they had
talked they realized they shared the same fears for
their men. That's all Valerie could think about at
that moment.

"Hello," answered Meesha out of breath.

"Hey Meesh, it's me Val."

"Hey girl,"

"You aight?" asked Val

"No, not really, but what's up though?"

"What's wrong?" asked Val sensing something.

"Malik's mother passed away."

"Oh my God, when?"

"A few hours ago."

"I'm sorry to hear that, how he doin'?"

"Not good."

"I can imagine. What about his little sisters?"

"They're takin' it pretty hard too, you know they were all pretty close to their mom."

"I know. Justice told me that she was in the hospital in a coma. I've been keeping her in my prayers."

"Thanks girl, but what's up with you? You sound like something is wrong."

"I'm okay, I was calling to see if Malik had heard from Just. Was he up there at the hospital with yall?" she asked hoping that he had been.

"No I haven't seen Just. He wasn't with us. Maybe Malik spoke to him before me and the girls got up there. Hold on Im'ma let you talk to him. Malik!" Meesha shouted into the back room where he, Jackie and Mandy were.

Malik stuck his head out of the room.

"What's up baby?" asked in a low tone as he laid across his king sized bed.

"Val on the phone," said Meesha. "She wants to know have you seen or heard from Just?" Hearing Valerie's name, Malik approached the phone and took it from Meesha.

"What up sis?" Malik greeted Val as he stretched.

"Hey big brother, have you talked to Jay?"

Valerie was Justice's common law wife. She and Justice had been together since they were kids, through thick and thin. Though Malik had practically known her all his life, it wasn't until he and Justice had become tight while in prison that the two of them became as close as brother and

sister. "I'll go be with the girls," Meesha whispered
to Malik. "Aight babe. Sis I ain't heard from him
none today. He might've tried to get at me, I just
been out of it all day, you know."
"I know, I heard, Meesha told me about your moms,
sorry to hear about it, mommie was a good woman.
You know me and Just will be there to show our
support," Valerie replied. "Thanks baby girl. When
the last time you spoke to him though?"
"He called me about five telling me that he had just
left from around the way and he'd be home in about
two hours that was about six hours ago." Malik
paused for a second as he gathered his thoughts. He
knew Justice's daily routine from sun up to sun
down and knew that there were only a few places
that he could possibly be. He calculated the time in
which Valerie said she had last heard from Justice
and him leaving the block. If Valerie's calculation
of Justice being two hours away from home was
correct then Malik figured he'd have to be
somewhere close to the stash crib that only he and
Justice knew about. If something was wrong or
Justice ran into trouble, Malik was sure that Justice
would have called him. Even though he had taken a
step back out of the game due to his mother's
stroke. No matter what, Malik would remain loyal
to Justice and would only be a phone call away
from being there for him. They weren't just
business partners or friends, they were brothers, and
Malik was indeed his brother's keeper. "Okay. This
is what I'm gonna do," said Malik making his way

back to the bedroom. "I think I know where he might be, I'm not for sure though. Why he didn't call you and tell you he'd be late, I don't know but when I see him I'm going to get on him about that. Don't worry I got you, I'll call you when I find him."

"Thank you Leek," said Val feeling a little better now.

"You know you ain't gotta thank me, just make sure I'm the best man at the wedding."

"I wouldn't have it any other way."

"I feel you sis. Aight let me go find your knucklehead husband and see to it that he find his way home. I'll talk to you then."

"Okay bye."

CHAPTER THIRTY-SEVEN

" I knew that nigga was getting paper, but I ain't know they was eatin' like that on the ground," said Doub as they counted the money from the duffle bag they had taken off of Justice. "Word," Pete followed. "Fuck him," said Cheddar.

"Nigga ain't seeing paper no more. That shit is over he can't take it wit em were he at. I keep tellin' you I ain't never seen no mu'fuckin armor truck followin' no hearse," Cheddar stated in a sarcastic tone. Both Doub and Pete snickered at the comment.

"Yo, this the last of it right here," Pete said as he dumped the remaining money on the floor. "Aight, make sure you get rid of that duffle bag," advised Cheddar.

"Yeah Im'ma throw it away."

"Nah. Burn that mu'fucka. You know niggas get caught for being careless like that. That bag can tie us into that nigga. Look how new it look, he probably brought that shit and used it on trips or something, so it might be a paper trail on it."

"Yeah you right," agreed Doub.

"I got it," answered Pete.

Doub, Cheddar, and Pete finally finished counting
the $152,000 and split it three ways.
"Easiest 50 grand I ever made," said Cheddar.
"Yeah Im'ma splurge on something that'll remind
me of this day," boasted Doub. "What about you
Pete?"
"Im'ma just put this shit up, I don't really need
nothin'."
Both Cheddar and Doub looked at him.
"What you mean you don't really need nothin'?"
Cheddar asked. "Nigga I know you ain't bitchin' up
on us Pete?"
"Nah, nah, I'm just sayin'," Pete answered
stumbling over his words.
"Sayin what P?" Doub now questioned.
"It's just the situation and all."
"What?" barked Cheddar becoming irritated behind
the way Pete was acting. "Yo check. That nigga
Justice got what he deserved, believe me. Don't
think for one minute that nigga wasn't planning to
do something to us. We just got him before he got
us. That's how it goes down. If you got any regrets
about this shit you need to let us know now,"
Cheddar demanded putting emphasis on his words.
Pete knew better than to say such a thing because he
knew that he'd be right where Justice was at, so as
best he could he kept his composure.
"Nah Ched, fuck that dude, I know what we did had
to be done, I don't feel sorry for that nigga. I'm wit
ya'll all the way kid," he said in his most
convincing tone.

"Aight then, well act like it. Spend that paper, ain't no need of holding on to it. That shit is free, save the paper you work hard for, this shit was too easy, like taking candy from a baby."

"No doubt," replied Pete.

"Ayo Ched, what you think Malik gonna say when he find out his man got pushed though?" asked Doub now understanding why Pete was acting the way he had been.

"Who cares?" was his response.

"Yo, you seen my gold lighter?" asked Cheddar checking all of his pockets.

"Nah." they both answered.

"Damn, I must've left it in his truck."

CHAPTER THIRTY-EIGHT

JUST as Valerie said, Justice had been through the hood. He had collected today's earnings from one of their spots around the way. After finding that out, Malik pulled off and headed towards their stash crib.

Thoughts of his mother's death filled his head as he drove through the back streets. He couldn't believe that his mom had passed away at the young age of 51. There was so much he wanted to say to her, and so much he wanted to do with her and for her. She was the one person in the whole world that had been there for him through thick and thin, and had loved him unconditionally. Now she was gone. He had never really given the statement not missing something good until it was gone any thought until now. Losing his mother made him realize just how true that statement actually was. Not only was she a good thing, she was great. Tears built up in his eyes as her face appeared in his head. He smiled to himself and wiped his tears because he knew that she was in a better place. Malik turned the corner and was now on the street where the stash crib was located. He could see the silhouette of Justice's truck in the driveway as soon as he bucked the

corner, and grinned at Just's predictability. Night
had fallen and the streets were nearly pearl black.
The surrounding trees on each block Malik turned
onto denied the moonlight. The fact that this was an
area with no street lights added to the darkness,
which is why Malik didn't noticed Justice's truck
door open. It wasn't until he had gotten closer to
the house and turned into the driveway that he'd
saw the door ajar. As Malik pulled in he flashed his
high beams on the darkened driveway. When the
beams lit up, Malik thought he was hallucinating.
He could not believe what he saw. Instant rage
flooded his body. He quickly snatched the door of
his SUV open, jumped out and ran over to where
Justice laid. Reaching the truck, Malik stood over
his friend's still body. It didn't take a doctor to tell
Malik that his Justice was dead. He glanced inside
of Justice's truck, carefully making sure not to
touch anything. He checked for anything that would
give him a clue or inclination as to what happened
to his man. Upon looking, he noticed that the duffle
bag they used to collect the money was missing and
assumed that is was a robbery. Then he knelt down
and saw that Justice still had on all of his jewelry.
Malik ruled out the robbery. He knew that he had to
act fast before someone came by and noticed him or
his truck. He got up and killed his high beams then
pulled out of the driveway and parked down the
street walking back. He searched Justice body,
finding his 9mm on him, still tucked in his waist

belt. He took that along with all of Justice's jewelry. He then pulled out his cell phone.

"Val?"

"Yeah. You found him?" Val asked as soon as she answered the phone.

"Yeah. I need you to come to where I'm."

Valerie could hear the sadness in Malik's tone and automatically knew. He quickly explained to Valerie how he had found Justice. She instantly broke down, but had already thought the worse earlier, and had prepared for Malik's call. She was from the streets and knew what came along with running them. If it weren't for Justice she didn't know where she would be today. She knew she had to be strong for herself and their kids. That's how Justice would have wanted it. Malik told her where he was. He couldn't call the ambulance or police because he was on parole and couldn't be involved. Valerie understood, and hung up with Malik in route to where he and Just were. His mind raced a million miles a minute trying to figure out who could have acted this out. He continued to search the area while he waited for Val. When he leaned over he saw a dim green light coming from the right side of Justice. It was Justice's cell phone. Malik picked up the phone and out of habit checked the screen. What he saw brought more tears to his eyes as the number 222-1122 appeared across the screen. "Damn akh, my bad," Malik spoke in a solemn tone recognizing his cell number on Justice's phone, Justice died trying to reach out to him. Malik thought back to when he was at the hospital, when his mother's soul left her body, how his ears had been ringing, and wondered could that have actually been his phone he had heard. The fact that he had lost both his mother and his best friend all in the same day was overwhelming to Malik, but as he mourned his two loved ones death he vowed that this would be his last time shedding a tear for either of them. As of tonight he was all cried out. He shut Justice's phone off and attempted to put it in his pocket, but was startled by the headlights that pierced into the driveway, causing him to miss his pocket and drop the phone. Valerie killed the lights and got out of the red CLK. The whole drive over she tried convincing herself that she could handle seeing Justice, but when she saw him laid out in the middle of the driveway, her legs turned into jello as she became lightheaded. She felt faint and leaned up against the Benz, to prevent herself from falling out. She took a deep breath and regained her composure, but was unable to control her tears. Malik was still kneeled down when Val approached him and Justice. Malik reached for the cell to phone to put it in his pocket, but because of the darkness he had felt around for it. He felt a small smooth object and picked it up to see what it was. When he held it up his blood began to boil. This minor object played a major part in what went down Malik was certain recognizing the object. It was the missing piece to the puzzle.

Malik stuck the gold lighter into his pocket,
snatched Justice's cell phone up, got up and gave
Val a hug. She was trembling when he embraced
her, but he knew she'd be alright. Just had always
expressed to him how he had a trooper on his team.
"Yo I gotta go, but you got this right?" he asked
knowing the answer already.
"Yeah I'll be fine, but Malik who could've done
this to my baby?" she asked as pain swept her
beautiful brown face.
"I don't know sis," he lied. "But you got my word,
whoever did is gonna regret it!" he said not wanting
to give her too much. "I gotta go."

CHAPTER THIRTY-NINE

THE news of Justice's death swept through the town like a heat wave on a record breaking summer day. While everyone else was speculating and forming there own ideas about what may have happened. Malik was off in a secluded area with the elite warriors of their team filling them in on a need to know basis as the young angry soldiers listened attentively. Malik handed down instructions that were to be followed and carried out by any means. Malik had just come home from the funeral home with Meesha and Valerie, making arrangements to have two separate funerals, a small funeral with family and close friends for his mother, and the next day whatever type Valerie intended for his friend to have, no matter the cost. The reality had just set in on Malik that he was burying two people who he held dear to him a day a part. He felt as though when his mother slipped away and Justice was murdered, a piece of him had gone with them, and his heart began to grow cold as it hardened. His killer instinct had resurfaced causing his humility to be replaced by vengeance. He was out for blood and knew that he wouldn't stop until each of them was bone dry. He gave each individual their orders. He specifically told them that Cheddar was not to be touched or harmed, without giving any explanation, and his command was not to be questioned because whether they realized it or not he was their new leader. Their sole purpose for being there today, being chosen over all was to get instructions and carry them out, and that's exactly what they intended to do.

Five days after her death, Malik's mother was laid to rest. Only a selective few had been invited and allowed to come. The pastor of his mother's church along with his choir, the Iman from the Masjid that Malik used to attend when he first came home, Valerie and her two kids, Meesha, Jackie, and Mandy, and the three men that worked at the mortuary that Malik hired to be pallbearers along with himself. The choir sang a beautiful hymn through their sobs as they mourned Ms. Jones. Malik remembered hearing the song as a child when his mother used to listen to gospel music while she cleaned the house or when she forced him to attend church. Malik knew his mother loved that song which is why he requested it to be sung. He stood there stone faced as the choir repeated the chorus. *"I got a robe up in that kingdom, aint that good news! I got a robe up in that kingdom aint that good news! I'm gonna lay down this world, gonna shoulder up my cross, I gotta robe up in that kingdom aint that good news!"* After the song, the pastor spoke a few words and then the Iman read a passage out of the Quran about loving and honoring your mother. As they lowered the casket into the ground, Malik turned around and walked away. No one tried to stop him. The next day Malik got up ready to attend his mans funeral, but this one would be different. Valerie decided to allow anyone who wanted to come and pay their respects to Justice. Emotionally, she was drained. Valerie had not only lost her boyfriend, but her friend, her lover, her children's father, and husband. Justice was her world. Malik had no choice but to respect that and show his support. He would have preferred something similar to what he had for his mother but it was not his place to request that. There was no doubt in his mind that the occasion would be a big turn out and the funeral parlor would be jammed pack. Today was not only a big day to commiserate his manz death, but also a big day for Malik too. He promised himself his man would be able to rest in peace before the day was out. Today was the day for redemption. By the time Malik left the burial site, he figured that half the mission that he had given the order on would be carried out and complete. And before the sun came up and a new day began, he would have put the finishing touches on the plan. His man Justice would be able to rest in peace.

CHAPTER FORTY

" **YO** slow down somethin' goin' on up ahead," the
young lieutenant said to one of his manz.
"Oh shit, yo that's the jakes up there," the driver
said.
"Bust a right, bust a right."
"Fuck! What the fuck goin' on?" one of them from
the back questioned.
"I don't know dawg, but it looks like they at the
place where Malik told us them niggas would be at.
Yo Ace pull over right here."
The driver did as he was told him. In the back sat
Ness and Baby Kev, each man heavily armed with
pieces from handguns to gauges, ready to put in
work. To them it was nothing. It was all in a day's
work and all for the love of the hood. One of their
own had fallen and now it was time for those who
were behind it to pay. Their plans had been put on
hold until they were able to secure the area.
"Ayo Kev, go around there and see what's good,"
said Chris.
"Aight," Kev opened the back door of the stolen
Suburban.

"Nigga leave your joints here," yelled Ness seeing
that Baby Kev hadn't unarmed himself.

"Oh shit, yeah no doubt," he said pulling out a 357
from the front and a 40 caliber from the lower part
of his back and threw them on the backseat. Each
man laughed to himself. They knew they were
strapped that same way. In addition, they each had
pistol grip shotguns and 12 gauges on the back
floor. One would have thought an announcement
had been made on the news or radio that World War
IV had just been declared in Jersey the way the four
young killers were traveling.

After waiting for about ten minutes, Baby Kev
returned to the SUV. "Yo what it look like around
there?" asked Chris.

"Man, it's crazy around there, muthafuckin' pigs
crawlin all over the place," replied Kev shaking his
head.

"Who is it state of feds?" asked Ness.

"Take your pick."

"Yo, did you see who they ran down on? Was it the
niggas we came for?" asked Chris.

"I think so, by the time I bucked the corner they was
already putting two niggas in a car. The shit had
tinted windows so I couldn't get a good look at em,
but they definitely in front of that house."

"Damn! Malik gonna be tight when he find out we
aint slump them cats," Chris cursed.

"Yo lets get up outta here."

CHAPTER FORTY-ONE

AS soon as Cheddar received the call from a chick that lived across the street from Doub and Pete that he was banging, he got up and gathered up all of the money that he had in the house and headed out the door. He knew that it was just a matter of time before they would locate his where abouts, if they hadn't already. They would surely come for him, if they had Doub and Pete in custody already. He was glad that when he moved from his old address he hadn't put in a change of address with the post office, which had most likely brought him some time because he had just moved into his new home ten days ago. He was almost positive that no one had known where he laid his head at now and that was the way he had wanted it. Looking around one last time to make sure he hadn't forgotten anything. Cheddar picked up the $120,000 in all hundreds, and headed towards the door. As thoroughly as he thought he had checked the area, Cheddar was sure he had everything.

Malik couldn't believe his eyes when he pulled the stolen Honda into the empty parking space. Cheddar was just stepping out of the house with a book bag thrown across his shoulder as paranoia filled his face. The way Cheddar looked around walking down the porch steps, you would have thought that he had known something was up, but Malik knew that he was just being cautious because he had always been that way since they were kids. They used to tease him in the hood calling him "Scary Harry", but years down the line his scariness turned into a survival skill, keeping him on point in the game. The book bag made it obvious to Malik that Cheddar was on the move, but why didn't he didn't have a clue, he knew that he had to act fast though because this may be his only chance to catch Cheddar like this so out in the open. His intentions was to enter Cheddar's home and torture him before he took his life, but that plan had been exed out once he saw Cheddar coming out of the house. It was either now or never thought Malik, as he hopped out of the Honda with a 9 mm in each hand. Before Cheddar had realized what was going on several shots from the guns poured into his body. Automatically, he reached for his Taurus but came up empty handed, remembering he had never snatched his gun up from off of his bedroom dresser.

"Boom. Boom. Boom. Boom." Malik ran full speed ahead letting loose the twin cannons as he saw Cheddar reach under his shirt. Once he saw that Cheddar's hand quickly revealed itself without a weapon, he continued to dump round after round at him. Hot slugs entered Cheddar's flesh with powerful force in succession knocking him to the pavement. When Malik reached him and he saw who it was, Cheddar began to laugh.

"Oh this how it is huh? You was suppose to have been my manz and 'em," he manage to get out. Malik didn't want to waist anymore time than he had to so he brought this chapter to an end. He pulled out the cigarette lighter he had wrapped in a handkerchief.

"Yeah this how it is, and nah nigga you ain't my manz. You took my mu'fuckin' manz from me," he said throwing the gold lighter he found next to Justice on Cheddar's chest.

"You left something," he told him as he pointed the 9's to Cheddar's head.

"Boom. Boom." Malik emptied the remaining bullets into Cheddar's face. Cheddar died instantly from the impact. Malik scooped up the book bag, made his way back to the car and hopped back into the stolen Accord. For a spilt second he was remorseful for killing someone he had known his whole life, but shook it off because he knew that when you were in the game friends easily became foes. Now his manz could rest in peace.

CHAPTER FORTY-TWO

MALIK woke up bright and early with a clean conscious. What took place the night prior was now a thing in the past. Everything he had built up inside of him was released into Meesha, bringing her to her sexual peak repeatedly, as she enjoyed the intensified orgasms. Malik kissed her on the cheek and then hopped in the shower. He had almost forgot that he had to meet up with his four lieutenants to congratulate them on what he believed to be a job well done and break each young trooper off with some paper that he had taken off of Cheddar for the part that they played in the avenging plan. As the hot water beat the top of his head and poured down his back, Malik relaxed. He had only been home for six months and it had felt to him like he had gone through a lifetime of situations. He thought about how the average dude coming home from prison getting back into the game didn't even get a six month run before they had been murdered or back behind bars. Here it was out of the six months of being home he had only been back in the game 90 days and accomplished a lot in that short period of time. He had come to the realization that there was no longevity in the game and he wanted no more parts of it. When he met up with his little mans and them he would tell them that the team and the block was their's to do as they felt fit, he was done. He had reached his breaking point. An old head had told him years ago when he was locked down that "Everyone had a limitation, you just have to figure out your." Malik had found his limitation and intended to take full advantage of it. It was now up to his little manz and 'em. He was handing the business over to them until they found theirs.

After his mother's death and the murder of his manz, Malik told himself once he avenged Justice's death he would get back on his Deen and become more responsible, living his life according to the ways of his belief.

He was determined to make Meesha his wife and be a better companion to her, take care of his little sisters, including Valerie and be a better brother to them, and just be a better man in general. Malik began rinsing the soap off of his face when he heard his name, but was alarmed at the fact that it had been a man's voice. Getting the soap out of his eyes Malik stuck his head through the curtain with caution.

"Mr. Jones? Malik Jones? I'm with the DE--."
Before the man could finish his sentence Malik's heart dropped into his stomach. He could not, rather did not want to believe his ears, despite the inevitable standing before him.

"DEA, you are wanted by the United States of America in connection to drug trafficking and racketeering. We have a federal warrant for your arrest. You have the right to remain silent, anything you may do or say will be held against you in a court of law."

As Malik was being read his Miranda rights a multitude of thoughts traveled at lightening speed through his mind. How could this be? He had done everything right since he'd gotten back in and out of the game he thought. How could they have gotten on him so soon like this, he wondered? His chain of thought was broken by the agent's voice.

"Mr. Jones I'm going to ask you to please step out of the shower slowly and only place your bottom items on your persons," the agent instructed with his weapon drawn and pointed at Malik. To emphasize the seriousness of the scene, the agent's partners also had their weapons drawn as well backing their colleague.

Malik complied and did as was told to him. He slowly exited the shower one foot at a time, careful not to alarm any of the agents. He was handed his boxer briefs followed by his sweatpants. Each piece clung to Malik's dripping body.

"I'm going to now ask you to turn around and face the shower and place your hands on top of your head." Again, Malik complied. Immediately, the agent moved in and cuffed him. As they escorted him out of the bathroom, Malik saw Meesha sitting on their bed wrapped in their bed sheet, her eyes were filled with tears. Malik could not muster up the words to even attempt to console her. He could see the embarrassment all over Meesha's face. Not to mention the pain in her eyes. Rather than say anything, Malik gave Meesha a wink of the eye along with a slight smile in attempts to assure her that everything would be fine. The reality of the matter was that from the accusations alone a parole sticker would be placed on him and he would have to sit it out. The more he thought about it, the clearer it became in Malik's mind that it was pretty much over for him even before he had stood before a judge. There was no reason for him to kid himself. His two sisters stood in the living room as the agents made a path to the door. They also were crying and expressed their love for their big brother, as he told them not to worry. When he reached outside you would have thought it was Federal Agent Day or a Police function considering the amount of agents that stood outside near their SUV's, waiting for Malik to be brought out. When they got him to the truck to be placed in, as the agent opened the back door he shot a remark at Malik.

"So you wanna be the man huh?" Malik ignored him as they helped him into the Black SUV and whisked him off.

CHAPTER FORTY-THREE

MALIK had been put into the same county jail he had been in, in Union County ten years ago. Then he was housed on a federal holding tier in the old jail. The tier was just a regular tier noticed Malik. There was nothing special or anything different from what he could see. They ate the same old bullshit small portion meals, same phone system, same recreation, same time you lock in, same everything.

Malik couldn't believe that he was back in the system after being home for only six months like so many others. But he knew by getting back in the game, going back was always an option. Only this time he was now on a higher level of the judicial system because the Feds was the last stop. He was arraigned two days later and when he appeared in court Meesha, Mandy, and Jackie were sitting in the courtroom with a paid attorney that Meesha had hired. It was like deja'vu all over again seeing his sisters behind him and Meesha only difference was that they had been little girls back then and instead of Meesha, it was Dawn who was his lady, and the one person who held him down was missing, his mother. The judge denied Malik's bail and remanded him to the Union County jail because he had been on parole and had been violated by is parole officer. His attorney had a copy of the parole violation detainer along with the complaint that justified Malik's arrest. Malik reviewed both copies. He figured he's been violated by state parole because of his arrest, but as long as he wasn't found guilty as of yet the P.V. was the least of his worries. What stuck out to him the most was what he saw on his complaint. It read at the top page United States of America vs. Malik Jones, and then there were two other names up under his own, but they were blacked out by magic marker.

"Who's names are these?" he whispered to his attorney.

"As of yet I don't know, but don't worry we'll find out."

"Aight, but why they crossed out like this?"

"Most likely I would assume that they are 5K1.1."

"What's that?"

"That means they are co-operating with the government in exchange for a lesser sentence. "Do you have any idea who they could be?" the attorney asked him.

Malik thought for a minute. He didn't know who had been picked up from his team of young heads. It was well over 50 young dudes that hustled for him, so he couldn't just take a guess.

"Nah."

"Well whoever they are they are being held in the same building as you are, only not on a different floor. I will try to find out this week by filing a motion to suppress the evidence on your behalf, and let you know. That is if you don't know by then, which I'm sure you will. It's not that hard just keep your ears open, but promise me one thing though," said the attorney.

"What's that?"

"Do not discuss your case with anyone, because if you do it will be your biggest mistake."

"You got my word, but why you stress it like that?" said Malik.

"Have you ever heard of "jumping cases?"

"No," Malik answered puzzled.

"Well, that's when some of your fellow inmates use your case to get them better deals. Sometimes they let you tell on yourself while they listen and then in other cases they sneak into your cell and rummage through your paperwork, and before you know it you have a new co-defendant who was there with you when you committed the crimes you are being accused of, so they say, and the rest is history."

"Damn!" replied Malik.

"Damn is right, so keep to yourself."

"No doubt."

"Well, the Marshalls are ready to take you back to the county. I'll be there to see you soon. Your fiancé told me to tell you that she'd be to see you also this week."

"Aight."

"Okay then Mr. Jones," the attorney said as he rose to leave.

The Marshalls told Malik it was time to go. As he exited the courtroom, he shot Meesha and his sisters all a smile of assurance and all three smiled back to do the same for him.

CHAPTER FORTY-FOUR

AS soon as Malik arrived back on the tier and entered his cell, his cellmate opened up with a dozen questions. He too was being federally detained, not to mention the fact that it had been his first time ever locked up. Malik brushed the kid off. He was in no mood to be talking. Remembering his own first time in court four months ago, he understood.

Malik had just made it back in time for dinner. Had he not he would have had to eat a cheese sandwich and milk for the night. When they called for trays Malik noticed there was a new trustee who was serving the meal. Someone he had recognized but hadn't seen since he had first caught his state bid. As Malik came through the chow line, he and Crook made eye contact and acknowledged one another. When Crook handed him his food tray, Malik noticed a folded up piece of paper on the side of the tray. Malik cuffed the note and kept it moving to his cell, hoping that no one had seen what just happened between him and Crook.

After he had finished eating, Malik brought his tray back out and told his cellmate that he would be using the bathroom. He then took his towel and threw it over the top of the cell door to cover the little 36 by 8 window, pulled the yellow piece of folded jail paper out.

Peace beloved. I know you probably wonderin' who shot you this missive. But check, what I'm about to say is some real shit. To prove to you that this ain't no set up or nothin', just know that this is on the strength of the God Justice. I know you two dudes was like brothers, but dig this. The two clowns that's flippin' on you is up here wit me. They think a muthafucka stupid but the god far from that. Yo, basically my life on the streets is finished, I ain't gon' never see day light again. That's why I'm getting' at you. All I got out in the world is my older sister and that's who gonna ride with me, but she ain't no street chick, she's a square, so her paper ain't tight out there, so it's up to me to help her help me, feel me? Yo, I ain't got nothin' to lose, so if you feelin' me then I'll handle these hot ass niggas up on this end for you. I can't guarantee that I'll get 'em both, but you got my word that the one I do get will have to be flown up outta this muthafucka in a helicopter and the other will be so scared that he'll forget what he told them people. Incase you interested I'll give you the address at the end of this scribe. Cost you 10 a head. If I don't get 'em both I'll have 5 sent back and keep 5 for puttin fear in the other nigga. I can't believe that your manz and

351

*'em would snake you like that, but then again, being
in this muthafucka all this time, nothin' don't
surprise me. Yo, I know you a real dude so I ain't
gotta worry about no cross on your end, but when
you finish reading this, memorize the info and get
rid of it!*

Knowledge
Knowledge
A Solider at War

P.S
My sis info:
Keema Benton
609 East 7th street
Plainfield NJ 07060

*when the paper drop
you'll hear about it.*

Malik was in a daze. He had carefully read word for
word on the note sent to him. Who had sent it was
not important and why was evident. What weighed
heavy on Malik's mind was a statement made
towards the end of the letter. His manz and 'em had
snaked him. That was all that stuck out to him. Who
was his manz and 'em the writer spoke about,
wondered Malik. A thousand possibilities cluttered
his mind. Who ever they were, there was no doubt
in Malik's mind that he would take advantage of the
opportunity presented before him. His life literally
depended on it. The fact that the writer mentioned

Justice's name was enough to convince Malik that the letter was on the up and up. With that in mind Malik knew what had to be done.

CHAPTER FORTY-FIVE

" JONES visit."

Malik was escorted to the visiting booth. Meesha stood there waiting. When he saw her he lit up like a Christmas tree. He had only been away from her for a few days but to him it felt like an eternity. He picked up the wall phone and placed his hand on the Plexiglas.

"Hey baby," he said as she placed her little hand on the glass up against his.

"Hey how you doin in there?" she asked not knowing what to say.

"I'm cool, it's nothin'," he replied wanting her to believe him.

"How are the girls?"

"Stressin', they miss you."

"Yeah, I know. I miss them too and you, you aight, you look like you ain't been sleepin'?"

Meesha hadn't realized it was that noticeable. The officer had told her she only had an half an hour visit so she wanted to get out what she had to say before she changed her mind.

"How can I Malik?"

"All I keep thinkin' about is how those people came in there and took you away from me, and the sad part about it is that I knew that this day would come but I refused to believe it. I never wanted to be a part of this in the first place. You know that. It was never about the money you ever gave me. I never spent a dime of it, because I knew this day would come and I'd be sitting here saying what I'm saying now. I put most of that money into a safe deposit box. Including that book bag full of money you had in the closet, and I put $5,000 in your account because I know you're going to need it, I will always love you no matter what and will see to it that you always have while your in here, but Malik I'm not built for this, and I refuse to try to pretend that I am. You will never see me again as long as you are behind these walls, I just can't do it. Your sisters agreed to stay with me until they are old enough to go out on their own. I will never turn my back on them or let my decision with you affect my relationship with them. I just need you to understand my position. Malik, I can't do this!" she said as she began to cry.

It was a lot for Malik to take in but he had always prepared himself for the worse. This wasn't his first time in jail; he wasn't new to this. Everything Meesha said, he understood. Although he didn't totally agree with her decision, he had no choice but to respect it. No other woman would have had the heart to give it to him the way she just had. Had she been a female of another caliber, she would have

bounced with the 200 grand the moment he was
taken out in handcuffs. There was no way he was
going to try to make Meesha change her mind about
what he knew she felt strongly about. Even if he
tried he knew that he wouldn't win, so instead he
only asked that she carry out one last thing for him.
"Baby, I'm not gonna sit here and front like I agree
with your decision. But, I respect you for being
woman enough to tell me to my face ahead of time
rather than string me along like you gonna ride it
out with me. Been there done that with Dawn. I
don't know the final outcome of this case but
honestly it doesn't look good. I'm feelin' how you
gonna be there for my sisters, and I know you
gonna keep your word on that. If I need some paper
I'll let you know but other than that just see to it
that they don't want for nothin'. It's a possibility
that little Chris and 'em gonna give you some more
paper for me. If they do, put that up for Mandy and
Jackie. If they don't, don't worry about it. I got
another 75 grand in a safe behind the house up
under the back porch. The combination is 15-38-28,
whatever you owe my lawyer pay him with that. I
need you to do me an important favor as soon as
you can. I need you to remember this name and
address Im'ma give you and get 15 grand to her.
Don't mail it and don't Western Union it, take it
straight to her and put it in her hands. I need you to
do that for me, can you take care of that for me?" he
asked staring into Meesha's eyes.
"Yeah. But to who?"

"Don't worry about that, just trust me on this one.
The less you know the better off you are."
"Okay."
"Good."
"Will all visitors hang up their phones and exit the
visit area, visits are now terminated," the officer
yelled.
"Malik I gotta go, I love you," ended Meesha
placing her hand back on the glass.
"Me too."

CHAPTER FORTY-SIX

fl week had gone by and Malik hadn't tried to
reach out to Meesha or anyone else for that matter.
His lawyer came to see him and explained to him
how there would be a preliminary hearing and they
would be using that to get a lot of information on
record for any future appeals. He informed Malik
that he was still working on trying to find out who
his co-defendants were and Malik hadn't had any
luck on his end either. The kid who sent the note
never mentioned his name or the names of the "Hot
Niggas" he referred to. Malik finally fell asleep
after listening to his cellie snoring for the past three
hours, shifting gears like he was an 18 wheeler;
each time Malik banged on the top bunk. In his
sleep, Malik thought he had heard some keys but
blamed it on his dream until he heard the cell door
crack.

"Jones! Jones!" the officer repeated.

"Huh?" Malik said wiping his eyes.

"Get dressed your being moved."

"Moved? Where?"

"Administrative custody per the Marshalls."

"For what?"

"We don't know Jones, we just doing what we were told," explained the black officer.
"Somethin' happened dawg," Malik's cellie said now awakened from his sleep.
"Smith be quiet. Let's go Jones."
Hearing what his cellmate had said, Malik had an idea why he was being moved, how it had been linked back to him was another story. Malik complied and the ten officers in their ninja turtle suits escorted him to another part of the facility. Malik had not been officially told what he had been moved for, but as he woke up for breakfast he heard two trustees talking outside his cell.
"I'm telling you, Master put that work in son. I was up when that shit first jumped off. We were getting ready to eat breakfast when he ran up in there. I seen that nigga with a banger in each hand with one of those kitchen mask on his face like he was some mu'fuckin' ninja or somethin'. I know them two niggas ain't hear 'em come in cause they asses sleep all day. They don't even get up for breakfast. When I seen that nigga creepin' I fell the fuck back just in case the nigga peeped me and wanted to add me to his hit list. You know the god crazy."
"Shit, I would be too if they hit me with all that damn time. That dude never going home off a 100 years.
"Word sun, but check, all I heard was them two birds screamin' like pigs up in that mu'fuckin cell. Sun had to be on their asses up in that piece. Before they locked the unit down I slid over there and

looked up in that joint. Yo that shit looked like mu'fuckin "Carrie" up in there. It was blood everywhere. Even on the ceiling.

"Word?"

"That's my word, the nigga went ballistic up in there sun," the trustee stated. "And yo, the brotha almost got away with it but that new white rookie pig heard a noise and walked down there, and saw Master coming out the room and hit the deuces. The nigga had blood all over his ass, looking like a human candy cane and shit. Them pigs got there in ten seconds flat, but when they saw who it was standing there with them things strapped to his wrists them pussies ain't make a move.

"You know them dudes only jump on the weak. They won't fuck with you if they think it's gonna be a problem. They probably thought that nigga Master crazy for real. But who was the niggas he banged up though?"

"You know them cats that was getting' it around the projects?"

"Who Cheddar and 'em?"

"Yeah. But not him, the other two dudes, Doub and Pete."

"Word?"

"Yeah, I heard they were tellin' on their manz Malik saying they was workin' for him and shit, crab ass muthafuckas. Them niggas got what they deserved. Sun wasn't even getting paper with them no more. He was fuckin' with the god Justice before he got slumped, and he was eatin' too, only been

home like six months. I heard they got him in the
building some where."
"What about the nigga Cheddar?"
"I heard the feds found 'em slumped in front of
some crib."
"Word?"
"Yeah."
"Yo that shit is crazy, but yo I'll holla at you I gotta
serve this food."
"Aight peace god."
"Peace."
Malik laid back down. Hearing the conversation in
front of his cell caused him to lose his appetite. He
had just had some major light shed on a dark
situation. Never would he have thought that Doub
and Pete were still alive. But that didn't disturb him
too much. What he had heard about them being the
ones who had brought him into their case and
putting all the weight on him was his major
concern. There was no telling what they had told the
Feds he thought. One thing Malik was sure of was
that whatever Doub and Pete had said were all lies
to help themselves. Whether they were lying or not
didn't matter when it came to the feds Malik was
beginning to learn and realize. He had heard how
hear say even from a crack fiend was like a
platinum credit card when it came down to
cooperating with the government. So he knew
whatever was said against him would most likely
stick. At this point trial was not an option for Malik.

J.M. Benjamin

"Jones, legal mail," the officer called out as he
banged on the cell door with his keys, breaking
Malik from a deep sleep.
"Sign, right there," he dryly instructed.
Malik signed as the officer opened the legal
envelope, shook both the letter and the envelope out
checking for contraband. He then handed the legal
mail to Malik through the cell door port hole.
When Malik unfolded the legal paper and began
reading the first words that struck him were the
words Superceding Indictment.
He and Darius Freeman, aka Master, were now co-
defendants. They had charged Malik with
conspiracy to commit murder against a federal
confidential informant and tampering with a federal
witness. As he continued on he noticed the numbers
848e right before he read the words C.C.E. Malik
remembered hearing the term Continuing Criminal
Enterprise and knew that he was being charged
under the King Pin statute. Malik knew that alone
carried a life sentence. Instantly he became light
headed. The next paragraph said he was facing
charges for the murder of Charles Spencer aka
Cheddar and Phillup Burris aka Phil.
The next day Malik's lawyer came to pay him a
visit. What he showed and explained to him only
confirmed Malik's thoughts. Malik could not
believe his eyes and ears. As he continued to flick
through the photo's his lawyer gave him. His
lawyer relayed to him what the District Attorney
had told him. The first few photo's he saw were

from the first night he had come home and Cheddar, Doub, and Pete had taken him on the elaborate shopping spree in New York, that night at Hugo's. The next few were of him, Pete, and Doub around Second Street projects when he went around his old hood to squash the beef between them and Justice. There were a few other photo's with he and Justice at the mall when they had ran into Pete and Doub. It was now obvious to Malik that when he came home he had walked right into a federal investigation. Based on what his attorney had told him, Cheddar, Doub, and Pete had been under surveillance and investigation for drug trafficking and racketeering for the past three years. When Malik arrived back on the scene instantly the Feds ran his picture and found out that before he'd gone to prison Cheddar, Doub, and Pete were his crime partners and immediately put him into the equation. Though he knew what he was being accused of and what the photo's may have showed was far from the truth. Malik knew that he was now up shit's creek without a paddle. He knew that based on his record and past association with his manz and 'em it would be almost impossible to convince a judge and jury that he was not guilty of the crimes he was being accused of. Life as he knew it was officially over for him he thought. In ten years he had only been on the streets six months. Throughout that time everyone and everything Malik had ever loved and possessed had been lost. He had lost his mother. His best friend and comrade. His sisters. His

relationship. His self respect. And even his faith.
Above all, the one thing he longed for while behind
the wall and tried to value the most, he had lost. His
freedom. Malik thought back to the chain of events
that's landed him back in a jail cell, wondering
when, where, and how he had gone wrong. Malik
cursed himself as he reflected back, knowing that he
had failed. Each time the answers had boiled down
to be the same. Maybe not directly, but because he
had come home and derailed from his initial plans,
Malik was now faced with a situation that could
possibly cost him the rest of his life in prison all
from dealing with his manz and 'em.
Malik sat on the edge of the cell's bed and placed
his head inside his hands. He was thankful that his
cell mate was out to court as his tears began to slip
through his fingers and stain the already filthy
room's floor. So many thoughts invaded Malik's
mind as he wept. "Damn," was all Malik was able
to utter.

Four months later…

"Mr. Jones please rise," ordered the judge. Both
Malik and his lawyer stood. For the past few
months Malik had been preparing himself for this
day and now it was here. He was ready to get what
he came for so he could officially start his time. His
lawyer tried to assure him that there was still a
chance the judge may show leniency during
sentencing but Malik was doubtful.
"Mr. Jones." The way the judge pronounced his
name only confirmed what Malik had already
known. "After hearing Counsel's argument,
reviewing all evidence against you, and based on
the facts presented before me, it is in the courts
decision under the federal guidelines to agree with
Counsel's recommendation and sentence you to a
term of and not to exceed 396 months."
396 was what Malik had embedded in his mind
when his lawyer first told him that's what the
District attorney was pushing for. 33 years.
"I'm sorry Mr. Jones," Malik's lawyer earnestly
stated. "You still have good grounds on appeal. I'll
be in touch. Malik nodded his head.
"We're ready Mr. Jones," the Marshalls informed
Malik.
As the federal Marshall's escorted him back to
Union county jail, Malik strained his eyes to peer
out of the van's tinted windows. The only thought
that crossed his mind was that if he survived, it

would be 33 years before he stepped foot outside
again as a free man...

Epilogue...

There are million's of Malik's spread throughout the world in ghetto's and hood's alike. In the world as we know it, everyday is a constant struggle regardless of gender or ethnic background. But it is a known fact that there is no progression without a struggle first, and Malik had failed that stage, like so many of us. Life is about choices and decisions. The ones that you make will dictate your future. As focused as Malik thought he was when he came home, mentally and emotionally he was not conditioned and prepared to make healthy and the right choices and decisions. Life is 10% of what happens to you and 90% how you react to it. Because Malik used emotions over intellect he made unhealthy and wrong choices and decisions. So many of us are faced with similar situations as Malik, growing up in poverty stricken environments, with minimal job and educational skills, and choose the same path. A path that only leads us into destruction. No one likes to struggle in life, but what Malik and many of us don't realize is that we must go through something and learn from it, to get to something and grow from it. Like so many who have gone through the system, in a sense, Malik used his past as a crutch to justify and dictate his present and intended future. He abandoned his plight to succeed, his family, his relationship, as well as his faith. And when it was all said and done, he resorted back to the same type of behavior that caused him ten years of his life and freedom. Malik simply gave up. Had he not returned back to the streets there would have been no room for his manz and' em to turn on him for a second time. How many of you know a Malik or are a Malik yourselves? Once upon a time, I was a Malik, which is why I can tell this story. Us as ex-offenders and individuals who have lived or are still living the street life, must change our game plan, find a new profession, and a new product. One that is constructive as a pose to destructive. If I were you, I wouldn't wait until you're in a position like Malik and have to count on ya manz and 'em...

My Manz and 'Em

COMING SOON
2007

HEAVEN &EARTH
By J.M. Benjamin

As Chill turned onto Walnut Avenue in his silver
2006 Dodge Magnum Wagon and parked, his eyes
immediately zeroed in and locked on Kwan. Hail
Mary's track off the classic "All Eyes On Me"
Tupac CD was cut short as Chill shut his vehicle off
and hopped out. Chill took a quick glance down at
his Rocawear hooded sweatshirt, making sure the
chrome 45 concealed underneath tucked in his
waistband was not bulging. Thinking that he had
noticed a slight detection of his weapons presence,
Chill smoothened out his hoodie before making a
bee-line over to where Kwan was standing.
   "Ayo K, lem'me holla at you for a minute kid,"
Chill called out walking up on Kwan.
Kwan was in the midst of puffing on a blunt of
goodness when Chill rolled up and instantly he
became agitated by Chill's sudden presence. He was
not surprise to see Chill having a good idea as to
why Chill wanted to speak to him, but he was not in
the mood and he intended to make it known.
"What'chu wanna holla at me about?" Kwan
retorted aggressively. "Can't you see I'm busy," he
added holding up the blunt to his mouth indicating
that Chill was disturbing his weed smoking session.
Chill disregarded Kwan's words. A grin appeared
across his face as he sighed. He knew confronting
Kwan was not going to be an easy task, but
nonetheless knew that it was long over due.

"Ayo Kwan, why you keep stepping on my lil' mans toes out here dawg?" Chill blurted out catching the attention of everyone within ear distance. "I know it's enough paper out here for everybody sun, you ain't gotta be on no cut throat shit," Chill continued.

After receiving the disturbing phone call that had interrupted him in the middle of something important, it was Chill's intention's to maintain his composure when he confronted Kwan, but as Chill spoke he could feel his adrenaline stirring up inside of himself. And Kwan's reaction did little to minimize it.

"Leek, you see this shit? This lil' bitch ass nigga gonna go run and call his daddy," Kwan chimed in disgusted, directing his words to one of his street colleagues by the name of Malik he had just been sharing the blunt of Purple Haze with. Malik made no reaction or gave no indication that he condoned or entertained Kwan's remarks. He was cool with both Chill and Kwan and remained neutral in the potential altercation, as he continued to puff on the blunt Kwan had passed him.

"Ain't nobody cut that lil' nigga throat B," Kwan barked in a DMX tone taking offense to Chill's accusation. "I told that ma'fucka that was one of my regulars," he continued in his defense, claiming the drug addict the dispute was over was a personal customer of his.

This was not the first time Chill and Kwan had exchanged words over a drug sale. And Chill was

not the only one whose workers had a problem with
Kwan's tactics in regards to how he hustled on the
block, known as Walnut Ave either. He was just the
only one who had stepped to Kwan about it.
Everyone else was either too afraid of the ending
result of a confrontation with Kwan or felt that his
antics were not affecting their pockets. But Chill did
not fall into either category. For him, it was merely
the principle of the matter. It was about respect.
Something he'd felt had diminished a long time ago
in the game, but because he was old school, he still
gave it, so in return he demanded it.
"Come on dawg. He told me how shit went down,"
Chill stated firmly, trying to hide his annoyance
with Kwan. He had believed all that was relayed to
him by one of his workers over the phone prior to
his arrival, despite the fact that he had known Kwan
longer. The only thing knowing Kwan longer than
his little man accounted for was the fact that Chill
knew how Kwan got down. He knew that Kwan
was as guilty as sin and had done exactly what he
was being accused of doing. "Yo he said that fiend
nigga didn't even know you son," Chill revealed
now getting fed up with all the word play between
he and Kwan.
Kwan's facial expression grew cold. "I don't give a
fuck what that lil bitch nigga told you," Kwan
quickly snapped back. "That was one of my
ma'fuckin cutty's and he wanted to cop from me
like I said," he added with emphasizes.
"Yeah aight" Chill replied dryly.

373

"I know it's aight nigga", Kwan said in attempts to chump off Chill.

Chill caught the sly remark but didn't feed into Kwan's attempt; instead he began to step off seeing that he was actually fighting a lost cause. That is until Kwan's next words caused him to pause in his tracks.

"What you need to do is find you some real ma'fuckas who can hold their own out here to hustle for you and get rid of them three pussies you got on your team," Kwan spit. Chill caught the combination of blatant and humor at his expense in Kwan's tone and it had instantly caught his vein. For the life of him he could not understand why his childhood friend was trying to provoke and force his hand. Chill had been in the game for a long time and had been through his share of trials and tribulations in the process and in his opinion had made it through just fine on his own.

No one had ever dictated or schooled him on how to move or conduct his business in the streets, or anywhere else for that matter, he simply learned and taught himself, which is why Kwan's words had bothered him so much. He did not take too kindly to someone trying to tell him how to run his operation or handle his B.I., especially someone who nothing about running or being a team player.

Chill spun back around. He was now an arm's length away from Kwan.

"Don't worry about who the fuck I got on my team
or what I'm doin", said Chill with emphasis, gritting
his teeth through clinched jaws.
"Well nigga then don't be worry about what the
fuck I'm doin then", Kwan spit back. "And back the
fuck up anyway unless you tryna see me fo'
somethin'," Kwan added.
"It's whatever yo," Chill replied with no intentions
of backing down.
"Yo both you niggas chill the fuck out", a next kid
named Troy intervened. "Niggas trynna eat, fuck all
that other shit, Kwan go 'head with that man."
If looks could kill Troy's family would all be
dressed in black sobbing over his casket the way
Kwan had shot him a rock stare.
"Mind ya ma'fuckin business, this don't have
nothing to do with you", Kwan ordered.
Troy started to respond but thought it best not to
comment on Kwan's remark. Not while he was
without the 40 cal. he normally kept on him. His
only intent was to try and defuse the arising
altercation between his two street colleagues, but he
knew that Chill was capable of handling himself in
any situation. Troy knew also that both men were
just alike and neither would back down, which is
why he was not surprised when Chill began to
speak.
"Yo, ever since you came home from Rahway you
think you run shit around here dawg, but yo, you
ain't Debo kid and this ain't Friday. You can't keep
tryna muscle niggas and think that shit gonna fly,"

Chill stated sternly. "Them days is over, this is '06 baby".

Chill's words only fueled Kwan's fire that had been slowly igniting inside him.

"You say that to say what dawg? You threatening me or something?" asked Kwan, with a distorted expression on his face, chest swelling up as his right hand grazed the butt of his gun. He could feel his own adrenaline beginning to kick into overdrive at the thought of what could possibly happen next. Despite him being aware of how everyone viewed him around his hood, Kwan knew that not everyone on his block feared him and Chill was one of the ones amongst that small percentage. And like himself, Kwan knew that Chill too had a reputation for being strapped at all times, not to mention a rep. for busting his gun when necessary.

As Kwan towered over Chills' 5 foot 5 inches, 150 pound frame there was no doubt in his mind that Chill was packing heat. There was no way that Chill would have ever rolled up on him. Not unless he was just plain stupid, had a death wish, or both, thought Kwan. No matter what the case, Kwan was growing tiresome of Chill's cockiness ready to put an end to the verbal sparing match. In the past he had put hot slugs in dudes for less, but Chill was an exception because they had a history. A good one. Before the drug game. But as the situation progressed Kwan was beginning to block all of that out. He was on a mission and Chill was trying to come in between he and his plight.

"Yo kid, I don't threaten. All I'm sayin is--."
"Fuck what you sayin nigga", Kwan interrupted in a
baritone voice cutting Chill's words short." I
helped pioneer this ma'fukin block and damn near
raised most of you niggas in the game out here.
You niggas got Drops and all types of trucks and
shit while I'm pushin' a old ass Beamer. Bottom
line, I'm doin what the fuck I wanna do out here
until I feel my paper right and if a bitch wanna test
me then that's their ma'fuckin' funeral, feel me,"
Kwan growled adjusting the burner in his
waistband.
Kwan's words drew attention in his direction.
Every hustler on the Ave had heard what he had just
said and felt some type of way about his statement,
but no one dared step up and voice their feelings on
the matter. But in their minds, each man plotted
and anticipated on the day they or someone caught
Kwan slipping. Troy was the only one who was
tempted to intervene for a second time but thought
better of it, seeing the visual daggers between Kwan
and Chill being thrown at each other.
Kwan's words tore into Chill like hot slugs. He
knew that this day would someday come. He had
tried his hardest to avoid him and his childhood
friend's clash. The fact that their was not a person
within ears distance that wasn't paying attention to
what Chill and Kwan were saying to each other
only heightened the situation because now
reputations were at stake. Most of the other hustlers
were glad that Chill had enough heart to say what

they had felt but kept to themselves, while others feared the worse. It was no secret that Kwan had come home from East Jersey State Prison, which was one of the roughest prisons in New Jersey six months ago, after serving six years and had been on a paper chase from day one home since then. Originally, he had only supposed to have served four years for the shooting case he went to prison for, but while doing his bid, he stabbed a kid from Camden in the neck in the mess hall over a verbal dispute about a basketball game. Luckily, for Kwan, the kid survived but the incident landed him in solitary confinement for two years and lost of 2 years good time, causing him to serve an additional 2 years. The word had spread throughout the entire Trenton how Kwan from "Walnut" put "work in" in the joint and those from his hood knew that when he came home he would be the same, If not worse, then before. And they were right. Coming home 6 inches taller an nearly 100lbs heavier, at 5'10, 240 lbs, Kwan tried to flex his muscles, literally, in attempts to intimidate other hustlers who he felt stood in his way of fattening his pockets. He even toted a snub-nosed 44 in his waist band in plain view to let everyone know that he stayed strapped at all times. That is why everyone knew that he would not let Chill's words ride. His rep depended on it. Judging by the situation at hand, Chill felt there was no way of getting around it today.

Feeling the tension and knowing both mans caliber, everyone began to fade into the background in attempts to stand clear of the potential harm and danger that existed. What started out as a minor confrontation was steadily erupting into something major. All eyes were locked on Kwan and Chill from a safe distance. Everyone was in fact so focused on the two that no one ever noticed the un-identified SUV parked a short distant up the street...

* * * * * * * * * * * * *

The navy blue stolen 2006 Cherokee pulled along side of the curb on Walnut Ave and parked.
"That's him right there", the backseat passenger of the Cherokee pointed out.
"Which one?" the driver asked.
"The big tall dark skinned one with the velour sweat suit on."
"It don't even matter which one he is", the front seat passenger interjected.
"It ain't like these niggas out here gonna just let us walk up on their man and do something to him, then just walk up outta here."
"I was thinking the same thing", said the driver.
"So what are we gonna do?" asked the backseat passenger.

379

"You ain't gonna do shit, you gonna stay ya ass in the truck while we handle this shit. If he see ya ass he gonna remember you."
"Look", the driver said to the front seat passenger. "Something's about to go down."
The front seat driver immediately drew attention to the commotion.
"Not without us it ain't," the front seat passenger said, snatching open door, just before pulling the black mask over their face.
"Get behind the wheel and be on point", the driver instructed the backseat passenger doing the same with their mask before exiting the SUV to back-up their partner.....

"Yo Kwan, you must think shit sweet dawg", said Chill, standing his ground. "Ain't nothing pussy about me kid so all that shit you poppin is extra. Ain't nobody tryna test you big homie. Niggas know how you get down, but just like I know you not gonna let a bitch carry you like a sucka you gots to know that neither am I. So, what are we gonna do? Huh? Shoot each other over a punk ass $100.00 sale, cause I got my strap on me too daddy," Chill informed Kwan lifting the Roca-wear hoodie up enough to reveal his 45 automatic. "And if you reach for ya joint that's exactly what's gonna

happen my nigga" Chill added giving fair warning.
Chill had hoped that Kwan used what little sense he
had given him the benefit of doubt for having and
saw the bigger picture causing Kwan to make the
right decision. The last thing Chill wanted was to
catch a body or get bodied over a petty drug
dispute. But he knew that in the streets people had
killed and died for less so he was prepared for
whatever.
Kwan grilled Chill intensively while pondering over
his words. Kwan knew him self all too well and
knew without a doubt in his mind that if he pulled
his gun he wouldn't hesitate to use it, but the two
things that weighed on his mental the most were 1.
Was he ready to go back to the one place he
despised the most and two, would he actually be
able to beat Chill to the draw? It was those two
reasons and them alone that caused Kwan to make
his decision to let sleeping dog's lie. For the
moment anyway, but made a mental note and a
promise to himself that he would finish what Chill
had started some other time.
"Fuck that $100.00", Kwan spit, reaching into his
pocket.
  A small load had been lifted off of Chill's
shoulders. At first, Chill thought Kwan was
reaching for his gun and was about to reach for his
own until he saw that was not the case. Instead,
Kwan pulled out a knot of cash. "Here take this
shit", Kwan then said tossing a hundred dollar bill
in Chill's direction.

Insulted by the gesture, Chill instantly replied,
"Man, I don't want ya money kid." In all honesty it
wasn't about the money at all with Chill but Kwan
did not get it. He now also felt insulted by Chill's
decline.

"Oh, my paper ain't good e---."

"Boc! Boc! Boc! Boc!,"

"Brrrgah! Brrrgah! Brrgah!"

"What the--- Boom! Boom! Boom!"

"Aaah!"

"Brrrgah! Brrgah!"

"Oh shit!"

"Boc! Boc! Boc! Boc!"

"Brraap! Brrraap!"

"Screeeech "Get In!"

"Boom! Boom! Boom! Click! Click!"

"Somebody call a ma'fuckin ambulance!" shouted
Troy.

The sound of Troy's voice caused Chill to end his
pursuit.

"Yo, who the fuck was that?" an out of breath Chill
asked making his way back to where shots had
moments ago erupted, with 45 still in hand. He had
just chased and unloaded his clip on the navy blue
Cherokee in the middle of his block the two masked
gunmen jumped in and sped off in. He watched as
the Cherokee's tail lights vanished up the street.

"I don't know, but Kwan's hit", yelled a bewildered
Troy.

By now, everyone had come out of their hiding
places and surrounded Kwan.

Kwan's body laid helplessly on the ground as blood spilled out of his mouth and seeped out of his bullet riddled body. Countless shots ripped into his flesh before he even had the chance to pull his own weapon.

Kwan could hear the voices surrounding him asking the questions amongst one another of "who" and "why," with no avail. The only one that was able to provide them with answers was Kwan himself but the blood that began to clog his throat passage prevented him from speaking out as he lay there fighting for his life. He made an attempt to speak but had only managed to grunt inaudibly. Kwan could not believe or rather, didn't want to believe that this was his final fate. During his time in prison, he had heard so many stories about other brothers getting out after serving years and years on lock down, going home in search of their ghetto 40 acres and a government mule only to have their lives cut short from making the mistake of underestimating a person capabilities. Now here it was Kwan was faced with the same type of statistical situation from making that same fatal error.

As his life began to flash before his very eyes, Kwan couldn't help but to think about how he had gone around the drug block the other day, smacking up and robbing the young pretty girl who had bruised his ego by rejecting him. He would have let the matter ride until the girl had added insult to injury by pulling more money out of her own pocket then Kwan had possessed in his own, after he'd tried to impress her with a baller demeanor. And now, it was because of his egotistical way of thinking that Kwan had gotten more than what he'd bargained for. And because he'd reacted first without thinking he had now felt the unfortunate wrath of Heaven & Earth.

That being his last thought on his mind, Kwan's eyes began to dilate in the back of his head as his body began to go into convulsion. Death had opened its door and embraced him before the ambulance arrived...

* * * * * * * * * * * * *

Chapter 2

"Le-Le, slow the fuck down", Earth commanded
from the backseat of the Cherokee pulling off her
mask. "You gonna get us knocked the fuck off."
Glancing at the speedometer, Le-Le did as she was
told. She hadn't realized she was doing 80 mph up
Walnut Avenue. Her only concern at that time was
getting her two girlfriends out of harms way after
the gun battle jumped off on Walnut and Chambers.
There was no way she would have been able to live
with herself if something was to have happened to
either of them. After all, it was because of her that
they had gone around the drug block in the first
place.
"Are ya'll alright?" Le-le asked looking back at
them through the rearview mirror
Yeah, we good", Heaven assured her. "But I can't
say the same for that nigga", she added.
"So ya'll got 'em then?"
"Fuck you mean did we get 'em? Of course we
did", Earth stated irritably.
"Cool out", Heaven said. She knew where her
friend's hostility was coming from and didn't blame
her, but now was not the time for either of them to
lose a level head. Still, Earth would not let it go.
"Nah, fuck that", Earth retorted. "We wouldn't even
be in this predicament if it weren't for this bitch. I
told ya dumb ass before about showing off for
mathafuckas", she spit directing her words at Le-le.

385

"I wasn't tryanna---."

"Just shut the fuck up and drive", Earth said cutting her off.

Heaven knew better than to intervene when Earth was reprimanding one of their workers. Not only were her and Earth partners in crime, but more so they had been friends even longer, so Heaven knew her girl all too well. There was no doubt in Heaven's mind that if she attempted to aid Le-le in any type of way, specifically trying to calm her road dawg, it would only add fuel to Earths fire. Earth had been that way for as long as Heaven could remember, extending back to their days when the two had first met at Edna Mahan Correctional Facility for women in Clinton, New Jersey. As Earth continued to scold and verbally chastise Le-le, Heaven could not help but to reflect on her and her partner's first encounter...

-Stay Tuned-